HOT DOG GIRL

HOT DOG GIRL

JENNIFER DUGAN

G. P. Putnam's Sons

G. P. PUTNAM'S SONS
an imprint of Penguin Random House LLC, New York

G. P. Putnam's Sons is a registered trademark of Penguin Random House LLC.

Visit us online at penguinrandomhouse.com

Library of Congress Cataloging-in-Publication Data
Names: Dugan, Jennifer, author.
Title: Hot dog girl / Jennifer Dugan.
Description: New York, NY: G. P. Putnam's Sons, [2019]
Summary: A lovesick teenager schemes to win the heart of her crush at her amusement
park summer job, all while dressed as a hot dog.
Identifiers: LCCN 2018019808 | ISBN 9780525516255 (hardcover)
| ISBN 9780525516262 (ebook)
Subjects: | CYAC: Dating (Social customs)—Fiction. | Love—Fiction. | Amusement parks—
Fiction. | Summer employment—Fiction. | Bisexuality—Fiction.
Classification: LCC PZ7.1.D8343 Ho 2019 | DDC [Fic]—dc23
LC record available at https://lccn.loc.gov/2018019808

Printed in the United States of America.
ISBN 9780525516255

1 3 5 7 9 10 8 6 4 2

Design by Marikka Tamura.
Text set in Aptifer Slab LT Pro.

For Brody and Olivia,
who make every day an adventure

CHAPTER 1

EVERYBODY SEEMS TO THINK THE SUMMER AFTER YOUR senior year is the stuff of legends. That it's two months of pure teenage bliss or something. It's almost as if there's this big conspiracy surrounding it, like, sure, kid, throw your cap in the air, cue up that hit pop song you will definitely hate by fall, and then you, too, will be guaranteed the most epic summer of your life. I mean, we all know that's not how it actually goes down, right?

Even though I won't kick off my own senior year for

another couple of months, I've already witnessed way more than my fair share of post-senior summers. It's a hazard of attending a tiny school—you can't really be picky about how old your friends are. But yeah, I think I can conclusively say that frantically searching Target for extra-long twin bedsheets while freaking out about what to major in does not an epic summer make.

So no, I don't buy into that whole post-senior-year magic thing. I think *pre*-senior year is where it's at, and for me, that starts right here in this tiny breakroom—with a stomach full of butterflies and a brain full of fireworks.

This is going to be my summer, no doubt about it.

I take a deep breath and slide my finger down the crisp page in front of me, searching for my name on the corkboard of destiny. Seriously. That's what we call stuff like this at Magic Castle Playland. It's not a bulletin board; it's a "corkboard of destiny." It's not a list of job assignments; it's a "character reveal chart." I swear to god everything here is about as whimsical as it is rusty.

I look lower, past the names of the ride operators and the food service people, over housekeeping and maintenance, until I get to the costume crew. I pause at the listing for princess. It's not my name. Okay, that's fine, disappointing but fine. I knew it was a long shot when I put in for it. My finger dips even lower, gliding past the prince, and the pirates, and all the furry park mascots, until it hits my name: Elouise May Parker. I drop my head against the board. No, no, no. Not again. I can't. This has to be a mistake.

My best friend, Seeley, nudges me out of the way. "What's it say?"

"I'm the hot dog."

Pity flashes in her hazel eyes. "It could be worse."

"Could it, See? Could it really?"

"Yeah! What if they put you in housekeeping and you were stuck in the bathroom by Swashbuckler Bay?" She shudders, cracking herself up.

"It's not funny." I pout, but technically, yes, that would be worse. I mean, the bathroom crew finishes every shift smelling like mildew and old diapers, so . . .

Seeley holds up her hands. "Hey, I'm just kidding, but it's going to be okay, Lou, promise."

She's right. I know she is. This is a minor speed bump. I mean, it's not like anybody died or there's a giant meteor about to strike Earth or anything. But still, there are so many things I have planned for these last few months before we're sucked up in the frenzy of senior year, and playing the hot dog isn't one of them.

I glance back at the list, letting out a little humph, and then look back at Seeley with an exaggerated frown. She bursts out laughing, shaking so hard her teal hair tips right into her sun-kissed face. Seeley's always got it a different color these days, almost like a mood ring. The happier she is, the brighter her hair gets.

Meanwhile I'm her slightly duller, significantly paler sidekick. My skin doesn't tan—it just burns—and my hair is this permanent mousy brown color because it doesn't hold dye. My dad calls it "caramel brown," which makes me think it's been way too long since he's actually seen any caramel.

Seeley grins and shoves her bangs out of her face as we start to walk toward the main stage for orientation. "Seriously, what are the odds that a vegetarian ends up in a hot dog suit two years in a row?"

"Shut up. What did you get?" I almost hope it's something awful like the Scrambler, where she's guaranteed to clean up tons of puke on the daily. It's only fair we both suffer.

"The carousel." She shrugs, her lips twisting into a smirk.

"I hate you."

"No you don't." She laughs. "Besides, would you honestly rather have Marcus or Brynn in charge of the carousel? They'd have Butters and Racer scratched all to hell from day one."

"I would kill them."

Seeley crosses her arms. "Exactly. So really, you should be thanking me for helping you avoid a lengthy prison sentence."

I snort, running my hand along the rock wall. This is the only time of year I even dare to touch it, the only time when it's still sort of semi-clean—well, as clean as the filthy old rock wall of a run-down amusement park can be, anyway. But tomorrow the gates will open, and everything will be sticky from the sweat and garbage of our less-than-stellar clientele.

I drop my hand, smiling at the familiar sight of co-workers finding seats and talking excitedly to everybody they haven't seen since the last time the cold broke in our unforgiving little mountain town. Most of them aren't townies like me; some of them live in neighboring areas, and some of them—the lifers, as I like to call them—follow the seasons. They spend their summers up here where it's a little bit cooler, and the winters down south where the weather is mild.

You don't realize how many people it takes to run an amusement park, even an old midsize one like ours, until you try to cram them all into the seats at Mr. Johnny's Magic Emporium. Even though our little rust bucket can't compete with the corporate giants, we have some cool stuff here—a couple roller coasters, some games, enough rides to pass an afternoon, and, of course, our namesake: a tiny pink castle smack-dab in the middle of the park—and it takes tons of people to keep it going each day.

Tons of people who are currently causing a human-shaped traffic jam right ahead of me. I take a sharp right and turn down the lower path to hit up the amphitheater's side entrance. Seeley follows close behind me, stepping hard on the back of my sneaker, so hard my heel pops out. I glare at her, grabbing onto her arm for support as I fix my shoe.

"Sorry." Her voice lilts up like this isn't an offense punishable by death.

"Hey, Seeley," a boy says, nodding at her as he walks by. It's Nick, because of course it would be Nick when I'm hunched over looking like I don't know how to operate a shoe. Seeley lifts her hand to wave and nearly sends me sprawling. Thanks for that, universe.

"Hey, Nick." I smile, jumping forward as I regain my balance.

"Hey, Elouise." He nods.

"Elle, Nick, call me Elle." I grit my teeth.

He clamps his hand on my shoulder, and I praise the gods that I decided to wear a tank top today. "If 'Elle' hasn't stuck by now, it's never going to. But I applaud your determination." He squeezes his fingers a little like he's giving me a massage and oh, okay, no big deal. I'll just be over here dying because Nick's skin is touching my skin and that's—

"Have you guys seen Jessa?" he asks.

Oh, right. Jessa. His super beautiful, so-nice-it-hurts girl-friend. How could I ever forget?

"Haven't seen her," I grumble, but then Seeley pokes me in the ribs and I force out a smile. "She might still be checking the list."

"Oh, yeah. How'd you two make out?" Nick shoves his hands into his pockets, and I try not to frown from the loss of contact.

"Carousel." Seeley grins, which Nick apparently thinks deserves a high five.

"I'm the hot dog. Again," I blurt out, which apparently Nick thinks doesn't. Not that I can blame him. My face burns and I huff out a breath so big my cheeks puff out.

Nick opens and shuts his mouth a few times, like he doesn't know where to start. "Another year in the bun? Tough break, Elouise." He shakes his head. "I'm so lucky I don't have to deal with random jobs."

He is lucky; I'm glad he realizes that. See, Nick's a diving pirate, which isn't exactly a job you can just walk into. He swam for his old school, I think, and he made the dive team at ours like two seconds after he moved here. He even got a partial scholarship to Presley University this fall, which I'm pretending doesn't exist. The last thing I want to think about is him leaving for college. But anyway, yeah, he doesn't have to worry about being a hot dog because he's too busy being the absolute best pirate on the planet. No way will Mr. P ever assign him anywhere else.

Nick brushes his hair out of his eyes. "All right, I'm gonna go look for Jessa and find the guys. I'll catch up with you later."

"Bye," I say, a little too eagerly, and I swear I see a tiny shake of his head as he walks away.

"Bye," Seeley repeats, stretching the word out with a little giggle. It's simultaneously her best and worst impression of me.

I wait until he disappears around the corner, then widen my eyes. "He totally just massaged my shoulder. You saw that, right? He was all in."

"All in on squeezing your shoulder?" If there's some kind of world record for highest eyebrow raise ever, I'm pretty sure Seeley just broke it.

"He massaged it. You witnessed it. It was glorious."

"Oh my god, Lou, it finally happened: you've lost your last remaining marble." I try to elbow her, but she grabs my arm, laughing.

"Hey, guys." Angie Martinez appears out of nowhere right then, giving Seeley a little nod as she skirts around us. Her black hair is pulled tight in a ponytail, which bounces against her light brown skin as she walks down the hill to the Emporium. Angie's a year ahead of us, like Nick, and she runs the Ferris wheel. I'm 93 percent sure she's got a thing for Seeley, but I'm also about 100 percent sure Seeley is oblivious.

Seeley tugs my arm, snapping my attention back to her. "Come on, Lou, let's go find a place to sit."

CHAPTER 2

WE FIND A SPOT IN THE MIDDLE OF THE THEATER, OUR butts sticking to the metal seats as we sit shoulder to shoulder with every co-worker we'll have for the next few months. Seb and Marcus plop down next to us, chattering away about their job assignments. Seb's in the rabbit costume again—now I'm wondering if Mr. Prendergast just copied the costume list from last year—and Marcus got the water park since he's already CPR certified.

This is Seeley's and my second year, but only the first one

that I'll be considered a full-fledged member of the team. Yet another hazard of having an August birthday: everybody else in my grade got their driver's licenses and upgraded working papers way before me. Luckily, my dad has been doing Mr. P's books since the dawn of time, so even though the official stance of the park is you have to be sixteen to work here, Dad fixed it so I could start last year when Seeley did. There were tons of rules about what I could and couldn't do, but at least I was with my best friend.

And okay, I definitely hoped for a cooler job assignment this year, literally and figuratively, but whatever. I can work with this. No matter what, I'm still determined to make this the absolute best, most carefree, oh-my-god-remember-the-time-I-can't-even-believe-you-did-that summer ever. But first, I gotta survive Magic Castle's orientation.

Seeley looks over to the side, and I follow her line of sight, scanning the crowd for familiar faces. Angie waves from across the way, and I wave back, even though she probably really only means it for Seeley. I notice Nick and Jessa off to the left, along with a group of the other pirate divers home from college. Jessa says something I can't make out and they all laugh, because of course they do; she's funny and perfect and gorgeous and will probably still be cast as the park princess even when she's 57,000 years old.

"You're staring," Seeley whispers, leaning into me. "Young loooove." She giggles, ducking her head. Good thing too, because I was about to flick it.

Feedback from the microphone screeches loudly across the audience, cutting me off before I can respond. I glance at

Seeley to let her know this isn't over, but she crosses her eyes and sticks out her tongue so I know that it is.

I turn my attention back to the stage, my eyes glued to Mr. P and the way the straps of his suspenders strain as he steps out and bows. He taps hard against the mic in his hand, which sends more thunder roaring across the crowd, followed by a jolt of screaming feedback.

"I guess this is on." He chuckles, his mustache twitching under his nose. "Welcome back for another great year." This is followed by an obligatory round of applause. Only some of us mean it. I, for one, definitely do.

"It's going to be a great year here at Magic Castle Playland. A great, great year," he snuffles. "And also, a very special year—"

Seeley gives me a look and I give her one right back. We heard this same speech last year, and we'll probably hear it a thousand times more before we're totally grown.

"—because this will also be our last year here at Magic Castle Playland."

Or maybe not.

I can't even hear what he's saying anymore, my focus narrowed to a tiny pinprick of screaming inside my head while I stare at Seeley. Places like Magic Castle Playland don't just close. That'd be like Disney shutting down its whole operation overnight, or rather a small, super run-down, beat-up, falling-apart, probably-wouldn't-pass-any-sort-of-official-inspection version of Disney. But still.

A bunch of voices clamor at once, everybody talking over each other and drowning one another out. Mr. P makes a downward gesture with his hands, urging us into silence. I look around wide-eyed at everybody else, confusion and disbelief twisting our faces into caricatures of ourselves.

I swallow hard. "This is a joke, right?"

Seeley shrugs.

"I'm sure you all have questions, and we'll get to those later. For now, we need to keep our focus on opening day," he says, as if he didn't just cause a nuclear explosion among his staff. He keeps talking, rambling on about team meetings and schedules like everything's fine, even though it definitely isn't, while I sit here trying to hold it together.

"Okay, guys, it's our last year here. Let's go out with a bang," he says finally, dabbing the sweat off his face with a rag. "Metaphorically speaking, naturally."

And then he's gone, and I'm stuck in place with my jaw hanging open trying to figure out what just happened.

"Wow." Seb stretches his arms up. "I can't believe he's closing Magic Castle."

I'd say something, but the panic alarms are still sounding in my head, and I can't form an actual thought . . . so instead I focus on Seb's forearm, and how the scar he got skateboarding last year—an unfortunate accident with a fence that he claims came out of nowhere—crisscrosses over his dark brown skin.

"He's old, and this place is falling apart," Marcus says. "It sucks, but it's not like it was going to be open forever anyway."

And okay, that snaps me out of it. "Of course it was supposed to be open forever!" I try to run my hands through my hair, but they get snagged up in the frizz. "Guys, come on. This isn't like when Arby's closed and we were all, 'Oh, that sucks, now we have to drive ten minutes away to the McDonald's.' This is our park! It's been the one constant in our whole, dumb, messed-up lives. We can't walk away from it."

"What choice do we have, Lou?" Seeley asks. Her words are quiet and soft, like if she says them too loud I might shatter.

I take a deep breath and stare down at all the little designs she's drawn on my Converse. "I don't know."

Seb tugs on my hair, and I flick my eyes to his. "Come on, Elouise. We gotta get down to the costume crew meeting. I'll walk with you."

"Okay." I swallow hard and nod, attempting to steel myself for the next meeting, the one where I'll have to sit next to Jessa and try not to rip her dress off like one of Cinderella's jealous stepsisters. I am Drizella on her worst day when it comes to her. I can't help it. She stole my prince, er, diving pirate or whatever.

"Try not to kill her," Seeley whispers as Jessa and Nick walk by. I raise my eyebrows but don't make a peep; it's freaky how well we know each other.

I mean, it's not that I hate Jessa or anything. You pretty much can't. She's perfect; totally, utterly, 100 percent perfect. She's sweet and kind, and disgustingly beautiful. She's the kind of person who would probably get out of her car to help a turtle cross the road, the kind of person whose teeth are straight even without braces. I literally have no rational reason to hate her. None. Zero. And Seeley tells me this on the daily.

Except Jessa's the princess, and I'm the hot dog. And she's

13

got Nick, and I've got a farmer's tan, a dog that ran away, and a best friend that everybody seems to like way more than me.

Jessa went to the private school one town over, and Nick went to mine, but they met at the park's orientation last summer. I guess that means they've been together for about a year, *if* you count all the times they broke up and got back together—which I personally don't, even though they still talked and hung out during their "breaks." I think the whole thing is weird. I think it's even weirder that breaking up was *always* her idea. Why would she ever do that?

And if you don't count the breaks, they've only been together for like six months tops and they weren't even consecutive. That's not that serious. I mean, yeah, my last relationship barely lasted six weeks, but we're not talking about me. We're talking about them.

People even have a name for them, a ridiculous combination of both their first names: Nissa. God, people are so annoying. Even more annoying because I've been trying to get everyone to call me Elle instead of Elouise for the better part of a decade, and all these two have to do is kiss and they're blessed with a nickname. It makes me want to scream. Except I can't because they are literally walking five feet in front of me, and that would be weird.

Seeley waves as she and Marcus cut left to go meet with the other ride operators and water park people, while Seb and I follow Nissa down the path. I don't even know why Nick's over here, to be honest. Okay, yes, his dive pool *is* right around the corner from the little castle where Jessa and I have to meet the rest of the costume crew—not that Jessa even really counts, since she'll spend most of her day in a beautiful gown riding around a cool fountain while the rest of us are busy trying not to die of heatstroke—but still.

Nick stops short when we get to the castle, pulling Jessa into a kiss right in front of us. I watch with a frown, trying really hard not to think about last summer, when it was just me and him and a broken-down car in the pouring rain. Come on, if that's not the epitome of a teenage dream, I don't know what is.

I mean, there I was, furiously pedaling my trusty Schwinn through the nastiest pop-up shower ever, cursing my luck that the storm clouds couldn't wait the ten minutes it takes to bike from my house to Seeley's before unleashing their fury on the world. I took a sharp turn onto Route 50, and boom, there was a *very* rain-soaked Nick Mulholland looking under the hood of his car like it was about to bite him.

For a half second, I thought about just pedaling on by— the whiteness of his teeth and the clinginess of his T-shirt triggering some kind of instinctual fight-or-flight response in my brain. But no, I was *not* about to give in to that. I know a little something about cars thanks to Seeley's dad, and if Nick needed a knight in shining armor to come fix his, then dammit, I was going to be that knight.

The more my bike slowed, though, the more my heart sped up, and just when I thought I was having an honest-to-god heart attack, Nick looked up and gave me that face—you know the one: Squinty-Eyed-Cute-Boy-Smirking-in-the-Rain™.

It was like the whole world went quiet right then, and he said, "Hey, Elouise, what's a pretty girl like you doing out in this mess?"

I didn't even know what to do with that. People don't really go around calling me pretty—I mean, I'm not a beast or anything, but when your best friend is Seeley Jendron it's kind of hard to compare—so anyway, I just sorta stared at him for a minute, and then I got off my bike and walked over to his car without saying a word. I am so smooth like that.

I started messing with the spark plug wires, just making sure everything was connected at first. Nick watched what I did, and then reached in and started doing it too. We worked shoulder to shoulder until we got it started again. Eventually I did talk to him—I'm not a total space cadet—and right before I left, he wiped a little grease off my face and gave me the biggest smile.

Now, if this were a movie, he *totally* would have kissed me right then, and it would have been AMAZING, and then we would have lived happily ever after and had lots of little floppy-haired, squinty-eyed babies or something. But that's not what happened because, hi, I'm Elouise. I'm the hot dog. So no. We didn't kiss. Instead he leaned forward a little and . . .

. . . started sneezing. Like uncontrollably. So no, no kiss, but still, total magic. He even offered me a ride home, but it had stopped raining by then and I didn't think my bike would fit in his car anyway.

I swear he looked disappointed when I said no, and right before I pedaled away, he said we should hang soon and to make sure I found him at orientation. I thought my head was gonna explode. I'd been swooning over him since he trans-ferred to my school a few months earlier, and now *he* was asking *me* to hang? Unbelievable.

So, the next day, I marched right up to him at orientation, totally prepared to say that he was sure to be my favorite diving pirate ever and yes, let's hang out in a way that doesn't involve rain and loose spark plug wires. But right as I got to him, Jessa fell in his lap.

Literally.

She literally fell in his lap.

She was trying to climb over the seats to get to her friend, but her flip-flop got stuck, and she went ass over elbows onto his legs. I'll never forget the expression on Nick's face when he looked down at her—it was the way he looked at me the night before times about a million.

I mean, it makes sense, I get it. I have eyes. But for one bright, shimmering second, the universe considered giving me everything I ever wanted. It was right there at my finger-tips, and it was *amazing*. I want it back. I want—

"Earth to Elouise." Karen, my team leader, snaps her fin-gers in my face, snagging my attention to her. "Come on," Karen continues in that stuck-up voice that only two semes-ters of college can give you. "We're all over here."

I don't know why it always seems to happen like this when people go away to school, but it does. Last year, Karen was awesome. We hung out the whole summer. But apparently, a couple semesters a few hours down the highway has turned her into little miss finger snapper. Whatever. I hop up on the ledge near Seb, but he's too busy talking to the girl next to

17

him to really notice. I watch him run his hands back and forth over his curly black hair, like he does whenever he's nervous. He's been growing it out for a while now, after a lifetime of having a close fade.

Karen stands in front of us, tapping her pen on the clipboard. There's a sticker on the back of it from her school, and I wonder if personalizing a clipboard is one of the perks of being a team leader. Also, I wonder where she got the sticker. Was she packing her bags, ready to head home, when suddenly she decided she just had to have a sticker for her shift leader clipboard? Or did she buy too many stickers and not have enough places to stick them? Is this the sad last sticker, the one without a home, without a purpose? I wonder if I'll get a sticker for my clipboard someday, but then I remember there won't be a clipboard because Mr. P is closing things down.

Wonderful.

Everything gets a little fuzzy and warm. I can't imagine not having this place. No matter what happened in life, no matter what changed or who left, this place was always here. Crap, I can't handle this right now.

Jessa plops down beside me, letting her legs kick and dangle excitedly beneath her. "Hi." She grins. "Did you have a good year? How was junior prom? Have you started thinking about colleges yet? Fill me in."

"It's good," I say, and drop my head back because she just asked me thirty-seven million questions and "It's good" answers exactly none of them. Okay, deep breath, start over. "School was good. Prom was fun—Seeley and I went alone together. And I'm pretending college is not a thing until my guidance counselor makes me."

Jessa looks at me with wide eyes. "Oh my god, my mother was already sending me for college visits sophomore year. You really should be thinking about this by now, Elouise."

"Noted." I sigh, wishing we could talk about anything else.

Jessa looks away, her perfectly curled hair swaying in the gentle breeze. A group of people walks by, and she waves. I don't recognize them, but that's not unusual; Jessa knows everybody. It's like she's part of the welcome packet or something: here's your uniform, here's your W-4, and here's a beautiful blond princess to highlight how absolutely inadequate you are.

Silence settles over us, and I realize this is my cue to say something great, something important and relevant and interesting.

"Did Nick take you to prom?" I ask, like I don't know, like I wasn't there with Craig, the boy who runs the water pistol game, even though I'm a year younger and go to a completely different school. We even all took a picture together and laughed about being the Magic Castle crew. My foot is so far down my throat, all I taste is sock.

Jessa opens her mouth to say something but snaps it shut when Karen comes back flipping through pages in front of her and underlining something with her pen. "Hey, Jessa," she says, like it's a relief just to say her name.

"Hey, Karen, how was school? When did you get back?"

"Last week," she says. "It's so weird being back home, living with my parents again." Karen shakes her head like she's some wise thirty-year-old and not some nineteen-year-old kid with the same exact posters on her wall that I helped her hang last year.

"I bet," Jessa says. "I can't wait for college orientation."

Karen smiles all patronizing-like. "Orientation is a very important part of the freshman experience. Where are you going again?"

"Vassar."

Of course she is.

"I can't believe this is going to be our last year here." Jessa's voice sounds a little sad, like she's upset about it too.

I glance up, gripping the edge of the retaining wall a little tighter and letting the busted concrete scratch against my palm. This is my place, not theirs, and I'm ill-equipped to share my grief today. These two have everything—the nice houses in the better town, the parents with fabulous marriages, the great relationships, the perfect colleges—the least they can do is leave me alone to wallow in this dirt pile of an amusement park that I call home.

Karen snaps her gum. "Mr. P must be really bad off to close it."

"He has a grandkid in Boca," I blurt out, thinking back to all the conversations I've overheard while my dad did his books. I mean, yeah, I'm mad he's trying to close the place, but the idea of someone else talking shit about him really pisses me off.

Karen narrows her eyes and does that half-laugh thing people do when they think they're better than you. "Okay, well, whatever," she says. "Anyway, Jessa, you're the princess again, and Ari is the prince. You'll need to get with him to plan your act." She turns back toward me, pointing the pen right in my face. "And you, you're the hot dog. Stay around the food service area. Got it?"

"Got it, boss." I salute, biting my lip to keep from laughing.

When Karen is far enough away to be out of earshot, Jessa bursts out giggling. "Oh my god, she's taking this whole team leader thing a little too seriously, don't you think? It's like, calm down, you're barely six months older than me."

"I know, right?" I nod, grinning back at her, because okay, maybe Jessa's not so bad at all.

But then Nick walks up, water still dripping from his dive shorts, and it all comes rushing back: the car, the almost-kiss, and Jessa's terrible chair-climbing skills.

Scratch that. Jessa is the literal worst.

CHAPTER 3

THERE ARE WORSE THINGS IN THE WORLD THAN BEING a hot dog, probably.

Like, yes, it's humiliating, but I'm pretty much left to my own devices, and I get a ton of breaks. It's the same for most of the other costumes too, except Cinderella and Prince Charming, which can stay on pretty much all day. Seb and Megan have it the hardest, though, in the fluffy rabbit and fuzzy cat costumes. They can only stay in their suits for about ten minutes at a time, on account of the big heavy heads. Seb tried to push it once but ended up passing out. Apparently, nothing terrorizes kids more than seeing their favorite park mascot passed out and twitching, except maybe when its head rolls off too. Yikes.

I have a little time to kill after my costume fitting before I have to meet Seeley for lunch, so I creep over to the gondolas to hide for a minute and process stuff. We're not actually supposed to be riding the rides today—today is just for test runs and inspections—but there's been such a weird vibe in the park ever since Mr. P's speech that I don't think anyone will actually care enough to stop me. Besides, if they do, I'll just point out that I have a finite amount of time left to ride the gondolas anyway, so it's practically their duty to let me on.

Marcus is on the landing talking to Sara when I get there, and they give me a little wave. I don't wave back, because Sara is the enemy. She broke Seeley's heart into about a million pieces when she dumped her for her next-door neighbor a few months ago. So, no, no waves for Sara.

They go back to talking, and I slide into one of the bright blue pods, pulling the safety bar down over me. The ride itself takes only eight minutes round trip—four minutes out over the swan boats, the castle, the dive pool, and the carousel, and then four minutes back. But it's definitely my happy place. I rest my head against the sun-warmed fiberglass and feel the hum of electricity against my cheek. It's so surreal, being up this high all alone.

The park drifts by beneath me: Jessa and Ari practicing their dance, Nick and the other divers goofing on the trampoline, and there's Seeley already at the carousel polishing the horses. I can't believe Mr. P is taking this all away from us. Maybe some people don't care, but Seeley and I practically grew up here, and my mom and I used to come here all the time before she—

Hot tears prick at my eyes and I wipe them away with the back of my hand. No. I'm not going there. I have to focus on what's right in front me. I have to find a way to save the park. There has to be something I can do.

Seeley's still buffing out the horses when I drop down onto the bench beside her. It's an old scratched-up thing, screwed down between our beloved carousel horses, Butters and Racer. Countless people have sat on this bench, but I like to pretend the history here is all ours, that every scratch came from our parents' belts and rings or from that one summer I spent on crutches.

"I'm getting your precious Butters all set for opening day," she says, scrubbing hard enough that all the muscles on her arms stand out.

"Is it weird being the one in charge?" I tilt my head. "There's gonna be all these little kids hopping on and off all day. That used to be us, you know?"

"I think it'll be kind of fun. Like a passing of the torch kind of thing."

I sigh. "It's kind of hard to pass the torch if the place is closing."

"Lou," she says, looking up at me.

There's a splash nearby, and I turn in time to see Nick in action, his bleached blond hair plastered to his head as he pushes himself out of the pool. He's not wearing the pirate suit, and I can't decide if that makes it better or worse.

"Nice view, eh?" Seeley says, the moment ruined as she flips the rag over her shoulder and leans against one of the horses.

My cheeks go pink and I roll my eyes, but yeah, it kind of is. "Pathetic," she snorts.

I try to ignore the way Nick steps to the edge of the platform behind us, staring up at the sky like he's praying. He does that before every dive. I wish I knew what he was saying. "Come on, See," I say, tearing my eyes away. "I'm starved."

"I can tell." She waggles her eyebrows. "All right, hot dog girl, let's go find some food." She links her pinkie with mine the way she has since we were little, and I follow her down the path with a smile.

Having a big catered meal together the first day back is kind of a Magic Castle tradition.

You'd think Mr. P would cheap out and get a bunch of burgers and hot dogs, but he doesn't. We have exactly one nice restaurant in this town, Bellini's, and he always orders from it. It's all Italian dishes: eggplant rollatini, lasagna, chicken parm, and these super awesome little cannoli that the pastry chef makes fresh every morning. They're my absolute favorite treat in the entire universe, but there are only two times a year I get them: opening day and my birthday. And it's not my birthday for a couple months, so . . .

I can't help but feel a little choked up again as I walk into the breakroom, the worn gray lockers that dot the canary yellow walls making me feel oddly sentimental. I used to dream of working here, and just when I finally have a place in this stupid breakroom, he takes it all away.

I sigh and shovel some of the eggplant rollatini onto my tray, grateful at least that Mr. P accommodates the non-carnivores among his staff, and then slide farther down, scooping up some spaghetti and letting it ooze across my plate. I reach the end, ready to grab some cannoli and be on my way . . . but there's a bowl of candy where my cannoli are supposed to be.

You have got to be kidding me.

"Where are the friggin' cannoli?"

This is Just. Too. Much. Maybe I could have come around on the whole "closing up shop" thing with a valid reason, but I definitely 100 percent cannot deal with not even getting some farewell cannoli out of it.

"Seriously?" I shout, turning back to look for Seeley. "He didn't even get us the cannoli?" Only it's not Seeley behind me, it's Mr. P, whose eyebrows about hit the ceiling. "Um, hi, Mr. P. Thanks for lunch, it's a really nice spread."

"Everything okay, Ms. Parker?" he asks, and the formality sounds so foreign. I mean, the man practically lives at my house during tax season.

"Yeah, everything's perfect. I was just saying how great the food is and not flipping out at all that you're closing us down and I don't even get cannoli." I gulp. "I'm gonna stop talking now."

He blinks hard, his lips a straight line, and if he's waiting for me to say something else, he's going to be waiting a long time.

"Always nice to see you." He steps around me and grabs some candy. "Tell your father I said hello."

"Will do." And man, I wish I could disappear right into the puddle of spaghetti on my plate. I scurry to sit at the nearest empty table and drop my head onto my arms. Worst first day ever.

The chair beside me scrapes back and I groan, glad that Seeley is finally finished getting her food. "I am literally the biggest asshole on the planet."

"Um," someone who is definitely not Seeley says.

I lift my head up, frowning at the sight of Nick in front of me. "What?" I snap. I meant *What is even happening right now?* but to him it probably sounded more like *What the hell do you want?*

"Sorry." He tightens the grip on his tray. "Do you want to be alone? I can go."

"Uh, no, sit." I hang my head and take a deep breath. "I just thought you were Seeley."

"It's okay." He crinkles his forehead. "I can sit outside, really."

"No, seriously, stay." I probably sound a little too eager, but I don't even care. "I made a huge fool of myself in front of Mr. P a minute ago—please don't also make me add 'was an ass to Nick' to the list."

He chuckles and shakes his head. "Wow, Elouise, great first day, huh?"

I stab my fork into the spaghetti and twirl it around. "Something like that."

"I can't believe this is our last summer here."

I sigh. "Don't remind me."

Nick leans back in his chair and looks around. "I'm even gonna miss this crappy breakroom. We all gotta hang more while we still have this place. Who knows where we'll end up next year."

"Oh, you mean like we did last summer?" And yeah, it was ballsy to say that, but I'm not gonna *not* call him out on his bullshit.

"Hey, I wanted to hang! You were the one—"

Seeley drops into the seat next to me. "What's up, loser?" I'm embarrassed for a split second, until I realize she's talking to Nick. And then I die a little inside because I'll never get to hear the rest of that sentence. I was the one that what? Didn't want to hang? WHAT WAS HE GOING TO SAY? I look over at him, but he's gone back to eating like nothing ever happened.

"Eh, not much. Just waiting to hear if I have to drive your ass to judo tonight or if you're skipping again."

I roll my eyes. Nick started taking the same judo class as Seeley when he moved here, and I've pretty much been seething with jealousy ever since. Lately, they've even been carpooling. If it wasn't so expensive, and they weren't both in the advanced class, believe me, I'd be right there karate chopping next to them—or whatever it is they do there. But there's no way I can even ask my dad for that.

"Remind me again when you leave for college?" Seeley laughs and flicks a chunk of her roll at him, which bounces off his tray and ricochets onto mine. Awesome.

Nick snorts, pushing his hair back and stretching. I notice he has barely any pit hair. I wonder if he trims it. Probably does. I can't decide if I like that. I can't decide if that's okay. I can't decide if this is an appropriate amount of time to stare at a boy's armpit in general. Probably not.

"You guys are lucky you have one more year," Nick says, attacking his food again. There's a little bit of sauce stuck on the corner of his lip, and my brain kinda short circuits when he flicks his tongue out to swipe it. "I feel like I just got here and now I have to leave, you know?"

"Um." I stare at him, because what are words even when you're looking at Nick Mulholland's tongue, but Seeley nudges me with her foot to snap me out of it. "Yeah, but you're only like two hours away. That's not bad. You can still come home all the time."

Please, please, please, let him come home all the time.

"Yeah," he says, "but Jessa's going to be about four hours away in the other direction."

I shove another forkful of food into my mouth and try to look thoughtful. I want to ask why he's worrying about that when she'll most likely just make them break up again, but it's probably best if I keep chewing instead.

"Where is Jessa, anyway?" Seeley asks.

"She was by the castle when I was on the gondola," I say. "I think she and Ari were just finishing up."

Nick hunches down over his plate and shovels more food into his mouth. "So." He lets out a small sigh. "What are you guys planning for this summer?"

And there it is, the tiniest hint of a lisp. It doesn't pop up often, usually only when he's all excited or worked up about something, but man, when it does, I just melt. It's like my favorite thing. I don't know if anyone else notices it. I don't even think he does.

"Working here and figuring out how to master sequential art so I can get into a good school next year," Seeley says.

"Sequential art?" he asks, and yes, please, keep talking while I melt into a puddle of goo beside you.

Seeley rolls her eyes. "Yeah, like comics and stuff."

Nick crinkles his eyebrows. "You can go to college for comics?" His phone buzzes before she gets a chance to answer, and he slides his chair back with a squeak. "Sorry, I gotta run." He picks up his tray. "I'll catch up with you later?"

"Sounds good." I smile, and okay, sure, the lisp disappeared again but it was there for a second, so . . .

Seeley at least waits for him to leave to shake her head at me. "Pull it together, Lou." She giggles, but the sound dies in her throat when she looks behind me.

I whip my head around, following her line of sight. "What?" But then I see it, or her, actually. It's Sara, walking into the breakroom and getting in line.

"Ignore her," I say.

Seeley huffs, angling her mouth so her breath makes her hair fly around. "That'd be like me telling you to ignore Nick. You can't help it. It defies rational thought."

"Yeah, but *she's* not worth it."

Seeley lowers her head and jabs at her chicken with a fork. "She is. Or was. I don't know, I think 'is' still applies."

"It's been three months," I say, like that matters, like time means anything when your heart's on the line. It doesn't, I know, but what else can I say?

Breakups suck, especially when you don't see them coming, and Seeley definitely didn't. Sara didn't even have the decency to give her a reason. She just said, "I would rather date Chelsea now." I mean, okay, I guess that's kind of a reason, but I think if Sara was like, "Oh, we fight a lot" or "I hate your parents" or "You chew with your mouth open," Seeley would have probably taken it a little bit better.

Because as it stands now, it's just like "You're not good enough" or "You're not Chelsea" or something. I've spent the last three months doing everything I can to convince Seeley that isn't true. Well, the "not good enough" part anyway, I can't help the "not Chelsea" part. But for real, Seeley is the best. She's funny, smart, she can draw, and, bonus, she has the cutest cluster of freckles on her left shoulder that I've ever seen in my entire life. In no universe should someone as awesome as Seeley ever be single, except for by choice. Sara is a total fool.

"Right, it's *only* been three months." Seeley sighs, glancing over to where Sara is sitting. I lean over and poke her in the side, right where she's most ticklish. She jumps and scowls at me, but at least it gets her attention off the girl behind us.

"None of that. We need to get you back out there." I flash my eyes.

"I don't like the way your face looks right now."

"That's very rude." I laugh. "I happen to have a very nice face."

31

She starts to crack a smile but looks away, pursing her lips to stave it off. "You have your scheming face on, Lou. Whatever you're thinking, no."

"What I'm thinking is: you're going on a date."

Seeley looks at me, rolling her eyes again. "With who?"

"Leave that part up to me." I grin. "But the fact that you said 'With who' instead of 'I'm not' tells me that this is definitely a good idea." I grab both of our plates and dump them in the trash, following her outside as the gears turn inside my head.

"I don't know, Lou."

"Trust me," I say, and she should, too, because if there's one thing I'm good at, it's finding people to fall in love with.

Seeley's barely out of sight before I start running through every option I can possibly think of . . . not that there's a lot in this small town, or at least not a lot that are out anyway. But it's not until later, when I'm walking back to my car, totally distracted while defining the parameters of the perfect-girl-for-Seeley rubric in my head, that it hits me. Or rather, I hit her.

"Oh crap, Angie. Sorry!" I say, grabbing onto her to regain my balance.

"Easy there, Jimmy Olsen."

I flash her a confused smile. "What?"

"You know, from Superman? The little reporter guy who's always lost in thought," she says.

"Right, totally."

Angie tilts her head. "You have no idea who I'm talking about, do you?"

I shrug, guilty as charged. "Seeley's really the one that's into comics. I just let her draw them on all my stuff."

Angie laughs. "I don't blame you. She's really good."

And *that* is the exact moment that I realize that Angie's really good too. Excellent, actually, in terms of being the most ideal girl for Seeley ever.

"Well, I'm gonna go," she says, drawing the last word out, and I realize that I've been staring at her for way too long without talking.

"Oh yeah, totally," I say, and I hope my smile doesn't give away how over-the-top excited I am right now. Because this, this is definitely going to work.

Angie gives me a strange look as she walks away, but honestly, I can't worry about that right now. Now that I've solved the mystery of Seeley's future soul mate, I've got bigger fish to fry.

CHAPTER 4

I MAKE IT HOME IN RECORD TIME AND DROP MY BAG at my father's feet. "Did you know Mr. P was closing Magic Castle?"

Dad is hunched over, running numbers as usual, with piles of paper crowding around the nook that houses his computer. He closed the office recently, opting to work from home to save money. Dad promised he wouldn't take over my space, not even when I leave for college next year, so he's holed up at a nice desk in the corner of the living room.

He shoves a pen behind his ear and leans back. "What's

that, hon?" There's a smudge of ink on his cheek, like a pen exploded earlier and he's been wiping at his face all day. I'm trying to stay mad at him, but he makes it so hard.

"Did you know that Mr. P was closing Magic Castle?"

"That's not really something I can discuss with you. You know that," he says, as if that's an acceptable answer.

"So, you knew, then?" I shake my head. "You knew and you didn't even bother to warn me?"

He looks at me, his brow furrowed beneath his shaggy hair. "Is everything okay?"

"No," I say. "Can't you talk to Mr. P? There has to be something you can do. I mean, you're his accountant! You can fix this."

"Businesses close every day, hon." My dad's words sound a little blunt, a little patronizing, but his voice doesn't at all. He sounds resigned—disappointed, even.

"Did you at least try to talk him out of it?"

"It's not my place to try to talk him out of it." A sad smile spreads across his face as he rubs at the scruff of his jaw, his lack of shaving a telltale sign it wasn't a client day.

"You mean you could have told him not to, but you didn't. Awesome." And here they come, those pointless, frustrating tears, welling up in my eyes like they do every time I get really mad.

I hate them.

My dad says I got this from my mother, that she was the exact same way. He said she used to tear up every time she yelled, like her heart was literally breaking from anger. I wish I was nothing like my mother. I wish I was stronger. I wish my anger was loud and wild, instead of wet and weepy. Stupid DNA.

Dad rolls his chair closer, tilting forward to meet my eyes. "Hey, where'd you go?"

I stare down at his toes, studying the dark brown hairs that tuft out over the tops of them. I hope I have a job that lets me work barefoot someday. Also, I hope I never get toe hair like that.

"Sorry," I say, "I was thinking about Mom."

His face falls, and I wish I'd swallowed those words. It's been years since she left, and it's still a sore spot for my father. "I see," he says, because there really isn't anything else.

I bite my lip and study the drawings on my shoes until I feel like I can speak again. "Sorry, the park closing is kind of messing with my head."

"I know this isn't easy, but sometimes you have to let things go." He sets his hand on my arm. "Unfortunately, this is one of those times."

Of all the things my brilliant, loving, amazing father could have chosen to say in this moment, that is absolutely the *worst*. The anger simmers in my belly and shoots right out of my mouth. "We've let enough things go, don't you think?"

"El—"

"I'm talking to Mr. P and I'll get him to change his mind, and that's it."

My dad shakes his head. "Please don't torture that old man. It was a hard enough decision for him as it was. Please, Lou, let it be."

"How am I supposed to do that? How?" I wipe my eyes with the back of my hand, huffing hard out through my nose. "It's not just some stupid park to me, and it shouldn't be for you either!"

I don't understand what's happening. I don't get how he's being so cool about this. That park is where he and my mom had their first date, and where he took me when she left. Not to mention every birthday I've ever had was spent there—except for the one time I went to one of those places where you make a stuffed animal, a choice I still regret, by the way—and I know it's silly, but I pictured my graduation party there too. And now it's going to be gone, just like everything else, and he doesn't even seem to care.

"I know it's not, Elouise, I know. But there's nothing you can do. You need to focus on the future, not on some falling-down park in a town you're already too big for." The pain in my dad's voice nearly knocks me off my feet. Maybe he's not as okay with this as he's trying to seem.

I shift from foot to foot and kind of half shrug. "I'm not too big for this town, Dad. I never will be."

He smiles. "Can I get that in writing?"

"Oh my god. Do you want it notarized too?"

"I happen to know a great notary, actually." He adjusts the certificate on his desk, a smug look crossing his face.

"You're such a dork." I sling my bag over my shoulder and dash up the stairs to my room. "I gotta go take a shower."

"Love you," he calls up, going back to his work.

"Love you too," I say, slumping against my bedroom door.

I take a deep breath and bounce my head against the door a few times before I shove myself back up. Enough wallowing. There's work to do: I have a park to save. And a best friend to set up. And also maybe my dad will make us waffles for dinner if I ask real nice.

CHAPTER 5

Me: What about Angela?

Seeley: ???

Me: To date, Seeley, to date. Keep up!

Seeley: She's obsessed with Superman.

Me: Perfect! You love Captain America!

Seeley: Exactly! She's DC!
I'm Marvel! It would never work.

Me: I'm sure you could find some indie comic to bond
over instead. Ooh! First date at the comic store?

Seeley: I don't know if I'm ready, Lou.

Me: . . . 🙂

Seeley: Why are you even up? It's 1 a.m.!

Me: Why are you??

Seeley: Because somebody texted
me and woke me up.

Me: What kind of jerk would do that? 😕

Seeley: It's fine. I needed to be up in . . . seven
hours anyway. Are you okay? I know this park
thing is messing with you.

Me: I think I miss my mom? Like, what? I
don't even know. It's dumb.

Seeley: Wanna FaceTime?

Me: No, you have to rest up if you're gonna woo
Angie tomorrow. ☺

Seeley: I didn't agree to that!

Me: Sssssssshhh. Sleep.

Seeley: Okayyyyy. Night!

Me: Night.

CHAPTER 6

MOM LEFT THE SUMMER I TURNED NINE.

It was a hot and sweaty process, but one that was way less dramatic than you would think. Mainly because Dad was at the store, and I didn't really understand the gravity of the situation. So, when she stood in the doorway with her suitcase and hugged me a little too tight, I was more worried about melting from the heat than I was about the fact that she was leaving. I mean, moms don't get up and leave forever . . . except apparently sometimes they do.

She was nice enough to leave a note for my dad, which he

read all stoic and resigned when he got back. Sometimes I can barely remember my mother's face, but I don't think I'll ever forget the way Dad looked while reading her letter. After he finished, he slid it back into its envelope, cleared his throat, and asked me if I wanted to go see the diving pirates. It was like, as long as we could go and laugh at goofy pirates, everything would be okay.

And it mostly has been.

Which is why I'm lying here with a brain full of bees trying to wrap my head around the fact that today is the last opening day ever.

"Wake up, kiddo." My dad pokes his head into my room with a big grin. "It's opening day."

"I'm up." I flash him a smile that I hope looks authentic.

It must not, because he comes into the room and sits on the edge of my bed, patting my arm the way he used to when I was little.

"I'm fine." I look him in the eye, hoping he believes me. "Really."

"I know this isn't what you want to happen." He pushes his glasses up higher on his nose. "But you'll get through it. In another year, you'll be off to college and you'll forget all about this old town anyway."

His voice is quiet then, and I can hear the unspoken words beneath it all. *Forget all about me*, he means. He's been making little comments like this ever since I got my driver's license a few months ago. Instead of being excited that he didn't have to drive me everywhere anymore, it seems like it almost made him sad.

"Never," I say, scooting forward to rest my head on his arm for a second. He scratches the back of my head, just the way I like, but I can tell by his sigh that he's not convinced. The alarm on my phone goes off, ending the little moment we were having. "I have to get ready."

He grins. "You're going to be the best darn hot dog on the planet."

"Well, that's something to aspire to if I ever heard it."

"Hey, the world needs good hot dogs, Elouise."

I can tell by his tone that it's supposed to mean something, that there's a secret double meaning to his words, but I don't really have time to figure that out right now. He keeps looking at me, like he's waiting for me to say something.

"I don't know that I agree with that," I say, "being a vegetarian and all."

"Tofu dogs, then." He chuckles, heading out the door. "The world needs good tofu dogs too."

And okay, maybe that's true. I mean, we can't all be princesses, right? But we can probably muster up enough dignity to be the very best tofu dogs the world has ever seen. Or something. I don't know. I'm pretty sure that's what he was getting at, and yeah, now that burning is back in my chest. But in a good way.

Seeley is sitting on her porch when I pull up outside. She's already got her uniform on, and it looks clean and pressed, like she was up all night getting it ready. Meanwhile my uniform is in a wrinkled pile in the backseat, where I tossed it after they handed them out. Awesome.

44

"You look nice," I say, because she looks good in everything. I swear, she's magic like that.

Seeley pops open the car door. "I look like a middle-aged man heading out for a golf match with his buddies."

"Okay, that too." I giggle. I can't help it.

Seeley slams the door shut with a laugh. "Thanks. How are you holding up?"

"Fine, because this isn't going to be the last opening day if I have anything to say about it."

"Oh good, we've reached the denial phase—now we just have anger, bargaining, and depression left before we get to acceptance."

"Ha-ha," I deadpan. "Except I'm serious about not letting it close."

"Lou—"

"So, Angie," I say, cutting her off when we hit the main road.

"I don't know."

"Come on, you gotta try."

Seeley slumps in her seat. "Why don't *you* date her, if you like her so much?"

"Because, first of all, I like Nick. And I know it's like a one percent chance, but maybe he likes me back. Don't look at me like that! How many times did he wait by my locker last year?"

"Your locker was right by the only vending machine students are allowed to use. Everybody waited by your locker, Lou!"

"Fine, moving on." I smirk. "Second of all, I don't have anything in common with Angie, plus she clearly likes *you*, not me. And third of all, she dated Malia right after I dated Malia. So, no way." I huff. "I can't wait to live in a place where there's not like one degree of separation between every queer girl in the entire area."

Seeley laughs and goes back to looking out the window. "What if she says no?"

"She won't, trust me. Did you see her at orientation? She was looking at you the way I look at Nick."

Seeley rolls her eyes. "No she wasn't."

I fiddle with the radio, stopping at one of Seeley's favorite songs. "Okay, maybe I oversold it a smidge. But she at least was looking at you the way *Jessa* looks at Nick."

"Oh great," Seeley says. "So, she'll dump me every five minutes for absolutely no reason? Perfect."

"Oh my god," I whine. "You're impossible."

Seeley shakes her head and proceeds to spend the rest of the ride staring out the window, but by the time I pull into our parking spot, I can't help but notice she's smiling—which means the plan is definitely still on.

"All right," I say, but I angle my body toward her too fast, and my seat belt snaps me back against my seat. Seeley bursts out laughing, and I glare at her. "Focus, Seeley, this is serious."

"Focusing!" she chokes out between giggles.

"You are so immature," I groan. "Anyway, here's how we're going to work this. I'm gonna go talk to her this morning, feel her out, and then you—"

But Nick pulls up in the car beside me before I can finish, throwing us a big wave. "Opening day!" he shouts, his voice snaking in through the open window. "You guys coming in or what?"

"Go." Seeley shoves my shoulder. "Walk with Nick; I'll be right behind you. Let me know what happens when you talk to Angie."

She doesn't have to tell me twice.

"Hey, Angie," I say.

Angela Martinez—Ferris wheel operator, comic book lover, and hopefully Seeley's future wife—is standing in the middle of the breakroom when I walk in. If that's not a sign, I don't know what is.

"Hey, Elle," she says. Because, yes, she is that awesome that she also totally respects my nickname request.

"So . . . " I say, and then everything goes kind of silent in my head because, crap, I didn't really think this plan through beyond "find Angie and say hi."

She sits down at one of the tables, kicking off her flip-flops and pulling on one of the park regulation sneakers. "Yeah?"

"You know, Seeley reads comics." Oh. My. God. Seeley reads comics? Seriously? That's what my brain decides to lead with? Awesome.

"I did know that, actually." She smiles.

"You guys should hang out at a comic store sometime."

Angie sets her foot down. "Okay?"

"I mean, it seems like you guys have a lot in common. You both operate rides, you both like comics, you both like . . . girls."

"Yeah," she says, only she drags it out into two syllables. "That's all pretty accurate, Elle."

My cheeks burn as I desperately try to right this ship. "I'm just saying, from the outside, for whatever it's worth. I feel like you guys should totally hang."

"Noted." She laughs as she pulls her long dark hair into a bun.

"She's single," I blurt out as Angie starts to walk away. And wow, okay, I am the least smooth thing of all the things in existence. It's like the world doesn't need sandpaper or rocky outcrops or tree bark anymore, because, hi, I exist to serve all of your unsmooth needs.

Angie hesitates, tilting her head toward me. "Wow, Elle, subtle."

"I am very bad at this." I totally face-palm. "Um, can you do me a favor? Don't tell Seeley any of this ever happened?"

"No promises there." Angie grabs her ID off the table and clips it onto her shirt. "Might be a good icebreaker for when we hang at the comic store."

"When you what?"

Angie grins. "Tell Seeley to stop by the Ferris wheel on her break, and we can figure it out."

"Really?"

Angie bites her lip and nods.

"Yes!" I jump up to wrap her in a hug but then catch myself.

Angie heads for the door. "I hope Seeley is as excited as you are."

"More, way more," I say, and as soon as she's gone, I pull out my phone.

Me: You have a date!

Seeley: Seriously??

Me: Yes! She wants you to stop by the Ferris
wheel to figure everything out.

Seeley: You didn't act all weird, did you?

Me: Nooooooo. Me? Never.

Seeley: . . . I don't believe you. But thanks. ♡

I shove my phone into my pocket and stare up at the
ceiling. Now that See's on her way to a happily ever after, I
should get back to work on mine . . . but first, it's hot dog time.

CHAPTER 7

I AM MELTING.

I am melting and dying.

I am melting and dying, and I hate this place. I don't know why I ever thought putting on a giant hot dog costume that smells vaguely of last year's throw up—sure, it only happened once, but yeah, it's that hard to get the smell out—and dancing around the food court surrounded by cranky children under the hot summer sun for barely above minimum wage was a good idea.

I hate this place. I. Hate. This. Place.

"Hot dog! Hot dog!" a little kid screams, tugging his mother over to me.

"Can I get a picture?" she asks, and I say *sure* in as chipper a voice as I can manage when it's eighty-five degrees out and I'm dying right here, right in front of her, and she's asking me for photographic evidence.

Oh my god, I hate this place.

"Looking good, Elouise." Nick grins as he walks by, his hair still dripping as he heads to the breakroom. He just finished his 12:30 show, not that I was obsessively checking on that or anything.

I hate this place and I'm glad it's closing.

And as soon as I think that, I wish I could take it back. Because no, that's not true, not at all. I love this place, and if I jinxed it to definitely-no-matter-what close now because of one day under the hot summer sun, then I'll never forgive myself. Because yeah, Mr. P says it's going to close, but I still don't totally believe him. Or at least I didn't, until now, when I cursed everything.

My stomach twists, bile lurching up my throat as I crouch down next to another child begging for a picture. I know it's a million degrees, but please don't lose it right now, Lou, please do not blow chunks all over this innocent little kid and his unsuspecting mother. Please, please, please, please, please.

"Are you okay, honey?" the woman asks. I nod frantically as I stand back up. "Maybe you should sit down. You look a little green." I can tell by the way she's looking at me that all her mom spidey-senses have been activated. Seeley's mom gets like that too, sometimes.

I shake my head fast, which makes my stomach hurt a little more, because this is too much. It's too much sitting here in the hot sun with a worried mom that's not my mom, never was my mom, never had a mom, in the place of all my best childhood memories, which is about to close down forever. Mostly probably because I wished it would.

I am an ungrateful little hot dog.

I smile at her and turn to leave, afraid to open my mouth in case I really do get sick. I rush down the path, down toward the breakroom and the air-conditioning, toward a quiet bathroom stall where I can hopefully recover in peace.

I start messing with the buttons and zippers on the suit when I'm halfway down the path, not caring if any little kids see me, because this is an emergency situation. I yank open the door, and the air-conditioning slams into my face. The change in temperature makes my stomach twitch again, and I swallow down the thick saliva. A few more steps and I'm safe. A few more steps and I'm good: fire the missiles, all systems go, mission accomplished.

The suit falls around my feet as I undo the last button, leaving me standing in the middle of the breakroom in only my tiny shorts and tank top. It's practically underwear, and I know it, but Marla—our resident costume manager—said it was the best option because I'd just sweat through everything else.

"Elouise?" Nick steps out of the boys' changing area, his eyes going huge. I must look half naked to him, standing here in a sweat-soaked glorified cami with the chills from the air-conditioning giving me the worst case of nip-ons I've ever had. Even my hair is all damp and matted down. Thanks, universe, this is swell.

"What are you doing?" he asks, and I can't tell if it's with disgust or concern.

I hold up a finger, the unmistakable sign of *Please stop talking*, as my body lurches all on its own. I turn toward the garbage next to me, puking up my breakfast from this morning and my dinner from last night, old popcorn kernels scraping their way up my throat along with everything else. Puking and heaving, in my sweat-soaked clothes, or lack thereof, in front of the boy of my dreams.

And oh my god, please, please kill me now. This is every nightmare I've ever had in my entire life. This is going to school naked times forgetting your own name times saying orgasm instead of organism in science class. This is bad. Oh god, this is bad. And surely this is as bad as it can get, right, surely this is the lowest of the low, nowhere to go but up? But as my stomach lurches again, I start to cry. Because of course I do. Fuck. Please. Please, kill me now.

"Elouise?" From the sound of his voice, I can tell he's moving closer. Closer to my sweat-soaked body that smells like puke. Awesome.

"Go away," I groan, bracing both my arms on the side of the giant gray garbage bin and pushing myself back upright. "Please."

"Are you okay?" he asks, and his hand is on my back. I've waited my whole life for a hot diving pirate to touch my back, and I can't believe it's happening now, when I'm sweaty, puking, and on the verge of passing out. I don't know what I did in a past life to deserve this. I really, really don't.

"Please don't." I roll my shoulders back where he's started to rub them. "I'm really gross."

"You're not really gross." He steps back, dropping his arms, and I give him a look. "Fine, you're *a little* gross. But honestly, you okay?"

"I guess." A fresh wave of goose bumps ghosts over my body, and I cross my arms over my chest with a sniffle.

"Hey, hey, don't start crying again." He perches his butt up on one of the tables behind us. "None of that."

"Sorry." I have no idea why I'm apologizing.

Nick arches his eyebrows. "Where are your clothes?"

"You can't really wear actual clothes in the suit. It gets too hot."

"Do you puke a lot?"

"Not usually," I say, "but I pushed it today. It's super hot out and I stayed in it way too long."

"Why would you do that?"

I shrug. "Opening day?"

Nick gets up and yanks his locker open, revealing one of the big, thick towels that the guys all wrap themselves in after their shows. "I admire your dedication to your craft." He tosses it toward me, and I grab it with a grateful smile.

"You want some water or something?" he asks. "I can go grab Seeley too."

"Don't bother Seeley. I'll be fine in a minute."

"Are you sure?"

"Positive." I pull his towel tighter around me. I wish it smelled like him, like his deodorant and hair gel and other good smells, but all it smells like is chlorine—because of course it does, the universe hates me.

Nick hops up from the table. "I have to go meet the guys to run through a new skit. Are you going to be okay in here alone?"

"I'm great, go," I say.

He walks over to a vending machine, shoving in a dollar and punching a few buttons. He turns back to me, holding out a bottle of Gatorade. "Drink this and hit the showers; you'll probably feel a lot better." He crinkles his nose. "And you'll definitely smell better."

"Thanks," I say, but what I'm really thinking is some weird combination of kill me now and wait, hold up, did he seriously just give me his towel AND buy me Gatorade??!!!??

He raises his eyebrows and kind of half shakes his head. "You're an interesting girl, Elouise," he says, right before the door slams shut behind him.

CHAPTER 8

SEELEY FLOPS INTO THE SEAT BESIDE ME. "I HEARD YOU christened the suit."

I'm still rehydrating, freshly showered and in my regular work uniform, and Seeley's joined me on her lunch break. I planned to walk the park for a little while, looking for lost kids or rowdy teenagers, since I have to take a break from the hot dog suit until my stomach settles down a little more.

"Who told you that?" I ask, even though I know. Of course I know.

"Your lover boy." She swoons. "He said you ran into the breakroom, pulled off almost all your clothes, and started crying and puking in the garbage can."

I slink lower in my seat because, wow, I was hoping his story wasn't going to be totally accurate, but yeah, it definitely was.

"He gave me his towel," I say, like that makes everything better or something.

"Are you going to fold it up over your headboard and make a shrine?"

"That was one time!" I raise my arms and drop them to my side with a *thunk*. "Seriously, See!"

Seeley dissolves into giggles. "You know what I mean."

And yeah, of course I know. She's talking about that time in eighth grade when my crush forgot his hoodie on the bus, and I may have taken it home with me. And then I may or may not have hung it up over my headboard, letting the scent of nice boy hoodie drift down over me every night while I slept. And okay, maybe I also slept in it a few times too. I only took it down a week later because Seeley threatened to tell if I didn't give it back. It didn't even smell like him anymore, so whatever.

I look at her, trying not to laugh. "It was one time—once—in the entire history of my life!"

"Once is one time too many." She smiles, pulling some fries from the puddle of ketchup and shoving them in my direction. "Can you eat?"

I shrug. Maybe I can. I guess we're going to find out one

way or the other. "I don't know. Nick was sweet, but then he also implied that I smelled." I take a bite, enjoying the familiar squish of fried potato goodness between my teeth.

"He said you smelled?" Seeley raises her eyebrows. "Seriously?"

"Not like in a bad way," I say.

"There's a not-bad way to tell someone they smell?"

I shake my head. "He also bought me this drink."

"As long as he bought you a drink." She laughs.

"Why are you being like that? I though you guys were best friends now that you have that whole judo carpool thing happening."

"He's cool, I guess, I don't know. He's a little doofy once you really start talking to him."

"He is not, he's . . . interesting," I say, stealing his word from earlier.

Seeley tilts her head as she turns back to me. "Books are *interesting*, Lou. The evolution of mankind is *interesting*. The way people utilize social media to subtly manipulate the reality of their lives is *interesting*. Nick Mulholland is not that interesting."

"You just don't understand him." I pull my hair back into a ponytail and check my watch. If I hurry, I can probably still catch the tail end of his diving show. I might even get there in time to see his high jump. "Shoot. See, I gotta go. I'm scheduled for rounds. I think I'm the only one that's supposed to be walking now too."

"Right." She laughs, making air quotes. "Rounds."

"I do have rounds." I scoot out of my chair. "Check the schedule yourself."

"You made your own schedule, so that proves nothing."

Okay, so maybe I timed my rounds to perfectly coincide with the dive show, but still, technically, I *do* have rounds.

"Tell Nick I said hi," Seeley calls out after me.

I turn back and pull a face, sticking my tongue out while walking backward . . .

. . . straight into Jessa. Princess Jessa to be exact, with Ari trailing just a few steps behind.

"Tell Nick what?" she asks. "Isn't he doing a show?"

"Uh, yeah," I say. "I think so. I wouldn't know, really. It's not like I memorized his schedule."

Smooth.

"Okay?" Jessa giggles.

I take a deep breath and look behind me, watching Seeley dissolve into a puddle of laughter as I jut out my chin and march off to do my duty. The park needs me, after all, and I need the dive show.

I take a deep breath as I dart across the food court, ignoring all the crying kids and full garbage cans. My stomach twists at the smell of all that fried food and spun sugar, but I swallow it down; no time to be queasy now. I'm a girl on a mission.

I get held up twice on my way by people asking for directions to the water park, but somehow still make it before Nick's high dive. I even find the perfect spot on the rock wall: no gum and an unobstructed view. I mean, what more could anybody want? The announcer drones on about the daring feats of all the pirates, and I mouth the words along with him, watching as Nick climbs the ladder for his finale. He is all lean lines and lithe angles: a dancer trapped in a diver wrapped up in a boy with a slightly pink nose from too much sun and not enough sunscreen. Meanwhile, I am sweat-soaked and graceless and . . . jealous.

Extremely jealous.

I'm sweaty where he is water-slick, pale where he is tan, soft where he is toned. We are opposites in every way and I'll never be—

"What are you doing?" Seeley bumps into my shoulder with a smile.

I look up startled to realize the dive pool's empty and most of the crowd has filtered away. Crap, how long have I been sitting here lost in my own head? Seeley scrunches up her eyebrows, clearly waiting for a response.

"Nothing. Rounds. Like I said." I grab a discarded soda cup off the floor and toss it into the garbage with great emphasis. "See, I'm making sure everything is on the up-and-up."

"Right. On the up-and-up."

I push my lips out into a sad little pout. "I am."

"Sure thing, whatever you say." Seeley glances back toward the pool, biting her lip as her eyes flick back to mine. "I have a date."

My eyes get huge. "Oh my god, seriously? When?"

"Next Saturday."

I squeal and wrap her in a hug. "I'm helping you get ready."

Seeley rolls her eyes, but I know she'll let me anyway.

"Tell me this is a good idea."

"It's a good idea," I say, fussing with her shirt collar a little.

"If you say so." She sighs, and then heads back toward the carousel to finish out her shift.

CHAPTER 9

SATURDAY NIGHT COMES FAST, AND WE FIND OURSELVES holed up in Seeley's room, where she's trying on about ten thousand outfits that, as usual, all look great. Downstairs, her mother is talking loudly on the phone, arguing with one of the doctors in charge of caring for Seeley's grandma. Grandma Bobby isn't doing well, and it's got the whole family worried and on edge. I'm doing everything I can right now to keep Seeley's mind off it.

"I don't know about this one." Seeley is looking at herself

in the mirror with a frown. She's tugging at the bottom of her shirt like she wants to hide behind it, which is hilarious because Seeley has the kind of body most girls would kill for.

"Stop, you look great." I hop off her bed and cross to where she's standing, making a face at her in the mirror as I grab some lipstick off her vanity. Lips are kind of my favorite thing.

"Not the red one," she says, turning to face me.

"Sorry." I throw it back on the table. I don't even know why she has it; Seeley can't stand red lipstick. It reminds her too much of Carrie from history class, whom Seeley has hated since the fifth grade, when Carrie told everybody that Seeley smelled like old cheese. It wasn't true, of course. Seeley always smells amazing, like strawberries and expensive shampoo, but Carrie is a total jerk. And, for some reason, when Carrie McCreedy tells the whole world that you smell like cheese, the whole world tends to listen. Well, at least the whole fifth-grade world, and really what world is there outside of the classroom at that age anyway?

But I digress.

No red lipstick, then, absolutely not.

I look over the options, grinning when I see the perfect choice. I slide it into the palm of my hand and hold it out to her like an offering. It's the extra-shiny handmade pink gloss from the shop in town. It makes anybody who wears it look totally kissable, which I figure is exactly what she needs tonight.

She nods, and I unscrew the cap, tilting her chin up and leaning in close to run it over her lips. Seeley shuts her eyes as I set to work, and my belly flutters a little. She looks so pretty tonight, Angie's not going to know what hit her. Her eyes open, and she breaks out in a huge grin as she admires my work. I set down the lip gloss and pass Seeley the mascara, raising my eyebrows when she hesitates.

"One more coat," I say, which is strange because, as good as I am with lips, eye makeup is totally her specialty. Seeley has the best eye makeup of anyone I've ever seen, in the entire history of ever. She must be super nervous to be this far off her game.

Seeley unscrews the wand, and her mouth pops open in a little O as she wiggles it up her lashes. "Do you really think this is a good idea?"

"Obviously." I cross my arms and lean against the wall, waiting for her to finish up. The second she does, I grab her by her shoulders and shake her until she laughs.

"Stop!" she says, but her eyes crinkle the way they only do when she's really happy. It barely lasts for a second, though, before she's back to that same freaked-out expression she's had all afternoon.

"Seeley, this isn't just a good idea, this is a great idea! Angie is literally perfect for you. Come on!"

"I just don't need another person to avoid at work if this doesn't work out. You know?"

"Okay." I take a deep breath. "No one is saying you have to make her your girlfriend, seriously. But you guys *do* have a lot in common, and I think blowing her off would be a mistake. Worst-case scenario, you go out, don't hit it off, and decide to just be friends; same as you are now. Best-case scenario, you end up getting married and living happily ever after. In which case, I should definitely get a cut of whatever money you collect at the wedding reception."

She smiles like she can't help it. "Such a schemer."

I shove my hands in my pockets and rock up on the balls of my feet. "It's what I do best."

"It's really not, Lou, but whatever you say."

"All right, maybe hoping for some joyful excitement is a bit of a stretch, but can we at least aim for cautiously optimistic tonight?" I hold up two perfume bottles and wait for her to pick.

She sighs, grabbing one out of my hand and looking back in the mirror. "Fine, cautiously optimistic," she says. "I can handle that."

"Yay," I squeak, snatching my phone off the bed to check the time. "Okay, you have to pick her up in like twenty minutes. You look amazing, she's gonna love you, ask her about Superman, draw her a picture on a napkin, smile a lot because you know you totally have resting bit—"

Seeley twists around fast and presses her finger to my lips. "Lou, please stop talking."

"Sorry," I mumble from beneath her hand.

She drops her arm. "I *have* done this before, you know?"

I pull out my hair tie and then shove my hair back into a fresh ponytail. "I know, I know, I just want it to go well."

"Why are you so worried about it?"

"Because a) you are way too amazing to be sitting around

moping over Sara, and b) at least one of us should be having the best time ever, and if it's not gonna be me—"

"Oh my god," Seeley snorts. "Do not get all mopey on me."

"I can be as mopey as I want. My summer is a mess," I say with an exaggerated sigh. "And, insult to injury, I didn't even get a cannoli out of it." I smirk when I say that, because I don't really want to bring her down or anything.

Seeley rolls her eyes and kind of shoves my face a little with her hand as she walks by. "You heading home now?"

I shrug. "I don't exactly have anything better to do. My hot date is probably on his own hot date with his actual girl-friend."

"We have got to get you over that boy. Anybody else catch your eye lately? Anybody at all?"

I shake my head, swiping some lip gloss on my own lips and admiring them in the mirror. I look pretty okay right now, actually. I mean, I'm definitely capable of cuteness—I can objectively recognize that my lips are fantastic and my nose isn't half bad either—but on a sliding scale where some-one like Seeley is a ten . . . well, you know.

"Lou?" she says, interrupting my train of thought.

"No way. Nobody. All the rest of the boys are doofy, and everybody else is either taken, straight, or in love with you." I make some kissy faces at her in the mirror and then spin back around to face her.

"That's not true."

I pinch my fingers together and squint my eyes. "It's a lit-tle bit true."

"You're such a dork."

"And you're almost late," I say, marching her to the front door. Her mother is mercifully off the phone and nowhere to be found. The last thing Seeley needs is to be worrying about her mom and Grandma Bobby on this date.

We pause when we get to our cars, and she raises her eyebrows like she's waiting for me to say something. "Go!" I laugh. "And don't forget to text me when you get back. I want all the details!"

"Fine." And yeah, maybe it comes out like a whine, but she's totally grinning and I'm glad. If anybody deserves whatever tiny drop of awesomeness this town can muster up, it's her.

My dad is in his room when I get home, which is nice because usually when we both end up home without Seeley I get stuck watching hours of *American Pickers* reruns with him. I yell a quick "Hey, Dad" on my way to my room but then bolt inside and shut my door before he can chase me down. It's not that I don't like hanging out with him, I do, but not tonight. Tonight's for plotting my next move to get this summer back on track.

Or rather, it was supposed to be. But then my dad knocks on my door a little while later, and all my plans and schemes fall to the wayside when I see his face. I can already guess what's coming.

"We got another postcard from your mom," he says, each word pronounced carefully, deliberately, controlled. He shifts slightly so he can look at me, and I swallow hard. Just because I guessed it doesn't mean it doesn't still feel like a sucker punch.

He pulls it out of his pocket and hands it to me. It's slightly curved and a little bit warm, and I wonder how long he's been walking around with it pressed against his thigh. I know how much he misses her, even if he thinks I don't. I stare down at the picture of the palm tree on the front, the words "Wish you were here!" scribbled across it in cheerful pink letters, scoffing before I can catch myself.

"Did you read it?" I ask.

Dad rubs his hand over the back of his neck and looks down, so that's a yes.

Mom sends us postcards every few months, pretending like she's on vacation or something. I don't know why, she just always has. She likes to ask questions in them too, like there's some way for us to respond, even though she never includes a return address. I hate that I still get excited when one shows up, even though I'm guaranteed to feel like shit after reading it.

"Do you want to talk about it?" he asks.

"It's fine," I say, mustering up a smile I hope doesn't look too fake. "It's another postcard. It's not a big deal."

"Elouise—"

"It's fine, Dad, I swear," I lie, pushing him back a little so I can shut my door.

"Okay. I'll be right downstairs if you need me."

"Go. Please. Watch TV or something. Relax," I say, widening

my eyes at him. "I'm not worried about it. I have a bunch of other stuff to do tonight." I don't, though. Well, I mean I do, but I know I won't go back to it.

Instead, I wait for my dad to go downstairs and then I turn on some loud music and settle onto the bed, flipping the card around in my hand and psyching myself up to read it. I set it down a little bit in front of me, smoothing it until the edges don't curl up as much anymore.

I'm not procrastinating really, just . . . taking my time.

She wrote in blue ink this time, remarkable only because her last four have been written in black. I wonder if this was a deliberate choice or if she just grabbed whatever pen was nearby. I wonder if she puts as much thought into writing them as I put into deciphering them.

I slide it closer, my eyes tracing over her handwriting, memorizing the way her letters curve and slant to make my name. I catalog exactly where she lifted the pen at the end of each word and note the small smudge of ink on the upper left-hand side. The postmark in the opposite corner says Miami, but the last one from six months ago was from Atlanta. Her writing slants upward in the usual way, her letters average instead of tiny or large, like she's not worried about filling extra space or fitting more in. I used to like the steadiness of that, but now it bothers me.

Okay.

Deep breath.

Read.

Dear Elouise,

I hope your summer is off to a great start. How did you do last year? I hope you are keeping your grades up. Only one year left of high school! How does it feel?

I saw a lovely shade of lipstick at the store today. It reminded me of that raincoat you used to wear when you were little. Do you remember the one? You never took it off! I bought three tubes of it and plan to wear it whenever I miss you.

Xoxoxo,

Mom

I set the postcard down on the bed and stare at myself in the mirror. Suddenly, I want it off, all of it. The lip gloss, the makeup. Every bit of it learned from Seeley and YouTube and other mothers because mine wasn't there to teach me. Mine was too busy buying her own lipstick in Miami and doing god knows what in Atlanta. I shove the postcard under my mattress and race to the bathroom, scrubbing my face until my skin turns pink.

When I open the bathroom door, my father is in the hallway, waiting. He gives me a sad little smile and wraps me in a hug. I burrow in without a word, nodding when he asks me if I want to watch some TV.

CHAPTER 10

Seeley: You awake?

Seeley: It was a disaster.

Me: Does this mean I don't get a cut of the wedding money?

Seeley: Hahahahaha. I'm going to kill you. I'm actually going to kill you.

Me: Why???? What happened?

Seeley: I don't even know where to start.
It was bad, Lou. Real bad.

Me: Okay, wait, back up. Start at the beginning.

Seeley: First, she ordered the lobster. On a first date.
You know what they say about that.

Me: Lobster? Where the hell did you take her?

Seeley: McDonald's in Plymouth.

Me: They have lobster at McDonald's?

Seeley: Yeah! Those roll things! It's seasonal.
I don't know.

Me: Wait, you took her to McDonald's on a date???

Seeley: Oh I'm sorry is that not classy enough for you?

Me: Brb, rolling my eyes forever.

Seeley: Then she said that all the Marvel
movies were formulaic!

Me: Can we back up for a minute? I don't think
a shitty lobster roll at McDonald's actually
counts as like first date lobster.

Seeley: It was like $8!!! And it didn't even come with fries!!!

Me: Are you serious right now?

Seeley: Also, the Marvel thing, tho.

Me: I am side-eyeing you so hard right now. What did you do after your romantic fast-food date?

Seeley: Mini golf.

Me: How was that?

Seeley: That was actually fun.

Me: OMFG HOW WAS THIS A DISASTER THEN???

Seeley: Because when I dropped her off she kissed me.

Me: And that's a problem because . . . ?

Seeley: Because I felt nothing. No sparks or anything. My toes didn't curl. Zero magic. It was like kissing my grandma.

Me: Gross. You kiss Grandma Bobby like you kiss your dates?

Seeley: Don't be an ass in my time of crisis.

Me: 🙁 I'm sorry, See, I was really rooting for you guys.

Seeley: Thanks. And now I'm freaking out because she wants to go out again next weekend.

Me: What are you going to do?

Seeley: Look into witness protection and never show my face again?

Me: I don't think you can join witness protection to avoid a second date.

Seeley: That's bullshit. My taxes pay for that program! I think? I don't know. My mom's always saying that about things . . .

Me: We pay like zero taxes, Seeley. Butttt I'm falling asleep here. Sorry. 🙁 Hang tomorrow?

Seeley: Obviously! I need your little scheming brain to find me a way out of this.

Me: I have a very big scheming brain, thank you very much.

Seeley: 🙂

CHAPTER 11

I WAKE UP PLANNING TO HEAD STRAIGHT OVER TO Seeley's for a complete and total post-date-with-Angie debriefing, but unfortunately Dad has other plans for me. Since we both have the day off, he wants to spend it together, which is fine, but he wants to spend it shopping for office supplies to fix up his spot in the living room. I'm dying to get to Seeley's house, but I can't tell Dad that when he's looking at me with puppy dog eyes and asking if I want to drive to the Target two towns over.

"Should I go with the black one or the teal one?" We are

standing in the middle of a brightly lit aisle, and Dad is holding up two plastic crates.

"What are you even going to use it for?"

"I don't know, anything? Trust me, you're going to want a few of these around yourself when you head to college next year."

"Why?"

Dad looks at me like I stabbed him in the heart or something. "Everybody had milk crates when I went to college. You use them for everything. You can sit on them, you can put stuff in them. We used to have to steal them from—"

"Why are they called milk crates? Wait, did you just say you had to steal boxes to sit on? Did your college not have chairs?"

"They're called milk crates because that's what they are." Dad pinches the bridge of his nose. "Yes, we had chairs, but it was a different time and sometimes we had to improvise. We didn't have superstores, you know, and Amazon wasn't invented yet."

"Sounds tragic."

Dad gives me a little shove with his shoulder and drops the teal one into our cart before gesturing back to the shelves behind us. "Look, if people weren't still using these, they wouldn't be all over the store."

"Touché."

"What's next on the list?" he asks.

"Nothing—milk crate was the last thing you wrote."

He looks a little sad then, and as much as I want to rush off to Seeley's, I also kind of don't. "Do you want to get food somewhere?"

The way his face lights up tells me it was definitely the right call.

I know that in the real world, like when you live someplace where you don't have to drive forty minutes to get to Target, Applebee's isn't considered a super nice restaurant or anything. But even so, when I walk in with my dad and we slide into a big booth by the window, it still *feels* special. We don't come here much; it's too far away to go to on a whim, but it's perfect when you want to celebrate something special but not like cannoli-from-Bellini's-level special. It's our in-between place, and it's just for me and him. I've never been here with anyone else, not even Seeley.

Dad makes a big show of flipping through the whole menu and making comments, but I know he's going to end up getting a burger, and I'm going to end up with a house salad (hold the bacon) and fries. It's what we always, always get. Sometimes, when we really want to live on the edge, we'll start with chips and salsa too.

"Hey." My dad nudges my foot under the booth. "Everything okay?"

I look up from the menu and sigh. "Yeah."

"You're a terrible liar," he says just as our waitress comes to take our order. He waits until she's out of earshot to go back to the conversation at hand. "What's wrong?"

"Nothing," I say, because that seems easier.

"Elouise," he says, and takes a sip of his soda.

"It just feels like everything is changing all at once, in a bad way."

"Oh, Lou." He says it with so much love, but somehow it makes me feel worse. "Is this about the park?"

"It's about the park, yeah, and you keep talking about me leaving in a year, and that new postcard was messed up." I groan, and wipe at my eyes. "I don't know."

Dad sighs, and I swear I just caught him rolling his eyes. "I'm sorry, hon. Your mother—"

"I don't want to talk about it. There's no point. What I do want to know is why you won't at least help me try to figure out a way to save Magic Castle."

"Honey, you can't save the park. It's not—"

"Don't say that. That place is all we have left."

"That is not true, Elouise. You have a lot more in your life than just that. We'll always have each other," he says, squeezing my hand again, and I squeeze back because I want to believe it. "And you have a lot of good friends who'll always be there for you—"

"Yeah, well, historically 'always' hasn't ever come through for me. People leave. It's what they do. But places—"

"That's not fair."

"No, but it's true. Think about it. When you married Mom, did you ever think she would take off? I mean, even our dog ran away. Nothing sticks around in our family, nothing! It's like we're cursed!"

The waitress arrives right then, dropping our food in front of us. I watch the cars whiz by through the window until she leaves, embarrassed by my outburst.

"We're not cursed," he says. "And by the way, I'm still not

entirely convinced that thing you brought home was a dog and not a coyote with a dye job."

I cross my arms. "Buster wasn't that bad."

"Bad doesn't even begin to cover it, Lou. He ate through a wall! How does a dog even do that?"

And okay, he has a point. Buster was not . . . ideal. Maybe someday I'll tell my dad the truth—although he probably already suspects—that Buster wasn't actually a lovable stray that followed me home like I said, but was in fact a half-feral dog that Seeley and I came across in the woods one day. It took nearly two months of bribing him with food before I could get him to follow me to my house—against Seeley's better advice, naturally. She just didn't get it, you know; she has two cats and tons of people that love her unconditionally. I have my dad, her, and for a minute, a dog from the woods.

Buster only ended up living with us for a grand total of about three weeks anyway, most of which he spent hiding under my bed and/or peeing on my clothes, which, okay. One day, we came home to find out that he had chewed through the kitchen wall and escaped through the garage. Dad was furious but eventually went through the motions of helping me look and posting flyers. We never saw Buster again, though.

I take a deep breath. "Sorry, today was supposed to be fun, and I'm being all cranky and dramatic."

"You? Never." He smiles, giving me one last squeeze before letting go. "But, Elouise, if you feel—"

"I don't want to talk about this anymore." I wince. "Okay?

I'm sorry. But can we just talk about something else. Something better?"

Dad takes a bite of his burger, staring at me like he's appraising the situation. Please, let him drop it. I don't even know why I decided to stir all of this up.

"Sure, Lou," he says. He takes another bite and swallows it with a smile. "What do you think we should put in our milk crate?"

I ball up my napkin and throw it at him—I can't help it—and then we're both laughing and talking, and it feels amazing.

But then my phone is buzzing, and we're both staring down at it.

"Who's that?"

I slide my finger across and flick open the message. "It's Seeley. I guess Mr. P is letting us swim later. Everybody's meeting there tonight."

My dad nods. Mr. P does that sometimes, especially on really hot nights. He says those are the nights kids usually find ways to get themselves into trouble, and he'd rather have us all swimming at the park, safe. Sometimes he even keeps the popcorn poppers on for us. It's pretty awesome, actually.

"Who's everybody?" Dad asks.

"I don't know. Seeley, me, the dive crew, probably Seb—"

"Which one is Seb again?"

"The rabbit costume one." Dad gives me a blank look. "Sebastian Porter—he helped me out with French homework last year," I grumble.

Because yeah, I'd definitely like to forget all about my little foray into advanced French. I only took it so I could sit next to Malia Berkus and figure out how to woo her. Joke's on me, though—Malia ended up being the worst girlfriend ever, and then I had to spend the rest of the year dodging her while trying not to fail out of a class I was in no way qualified for.

"Sharon Porter's kid?"

"Yeah." I roll my eyes. Sometimes it's weird living in a town so small that you can say a kid's name and your dad can immediately name their parent and probably their parent's whole life story.

"I didn't know you hung out with him much outside of school."

I shrug. "He's always around. He's friends with everybody and we both work at the park."

My dad makes a little humming sound and drags a chip through some salsa. "Do you like him?"

"He's okay. Why?"

"Just making conversation," he says, but I swear his cheeks get a little pink.

"What am I missing here?"

"You're not missing anything, Lou, don't worry about it." But the sheepish way he bites into his burger tells me otherwise. "But tell Sharon I said hello if you happen to ever see her."

"Okay." I chuckle, stabbing my salad with my fork, and then it hits me. "Wait, do you . . . do you have a thing for Seb's mom?" It sounds impossible, but I have to ask.

I don't have a problem with it if he does, don't get me wrong. Seb's mom is pretty cool, and she's been divorced nearly as long as my parents have. Seb's lucky, though—his dad stuck around and both his parents get along.

But anyway, yeah, I'd love for my dad to find his happily ever after, but the closest I've ever seen him get to a date is drinking beer and reading through mom's old postcards. The idea that he might have a crush on someone, a crush I didn't even know about, seems slightly bananas.

"What? No, of course not."

I narrow my eyes. "Then why are you suddenly being so weird?"

"Sharon is an old friend, that's all," Dad says, wiping his face with a napkin. "I ran into her in the grocery store the other day, nothing more scandalous than that. Scout's honor. Now, what should we do with that milk crate?"

"Anything, apparently. I hear they're very versatile." I laugh and take another bite of my salad. It's not that I don't notice he's changing the subject, it's just that I decide to go with it. I mean, I don't really want to talk to him about my crush either.

Seeley's hair is dyed dark, dark purple when I pull up to get her. This isn't good. It hasn't been this dark since Sara dumped her. I frown when she climbs into my car and starts to buckle without even saying hi.

"Are you okay?"

"I'm great." She plugs her phone into my car and turns on one of her favorite songs. It's loud and angry and a little bit annoying; basically, the exact opposite of how I want this night to go.

"Wait, are you mad?"

"A little." She huffs.

I flick my eyes over to her as I drive. "Not at me, right?"

Seeley drops her head back against the seat and groans. "No, Lou, I'm not pissed at you. I'm pissed at me. I shouldn't have gone along with this whole dating thing. I wasn't ready."

"I think the fact that you agreed to go meant you actually were ready, honestly."

Seeley snaps her head up. "Doubtful. I kissed one of the coolest girls I know last night, and it felt like nothing. Nothing! I think I'm broken, Lou. Sara ruined me for all other girls."

"Oh my god, now who's the dramatic one?"

"It's true. What if for the rest of my life, whenever I kiss my girlfriend, I compare it to kissing someone else?"

"You won't." I ruffle her hair with my hand, amazed by how soft it is despite how much she dyes it. "But even if you do that for a little while, someone will come along to blow any kiss you ever had with Sara right out of the water."

"You can't possibly know that."

"I know you're wrong."

Seeley rolls her eyes and goes back to looking out the window.

It turns out Seeley texting that "everyone" was going tonight was kind of a misrepresentation. It's pretty much just me and Seeley, a few of the pirate guys that I don't really know, plus Nick and then Marcus. The guys have been practicing their flips on the trampoline next to the pool most of the night—they said they wanted to work up a sweat before they swam—so we've just been sitting on the edge of the platform, dangling our feet into the cool water below.

I tried to get Seeley's mind off her so-called disaster date a few times by talking about how we absolutely positively cannot let the park close, but that just seemed to somehow annoy her even more. So it's kind of a relief when Nick comes charging up behind us, fresh from the trampoline, all sweaty and out of breath.

"Hey." Nick drops a pile of towels beside us. "Why do you guys look so bummed?"

"Because I can't stop thinking about how this is our last summer to swim here," I blurt out, because apparently the filter on my mouth has completely stopped working. Nick shrugs and peels off his T-shirt. I try not to stare.

"I get that. It blows. But it's still here now." He tosses his shirt behind him and reties the little strings on his board shorts. "What's the point of sitting here being sad about the future when we could be enjoying what we have while we have it?"

I open my mouth and then snap it shut because he sort of has a point.

Nick grins, nudging me with his knee as he steps to the edge of the pool. "Last one in's a rotten egg." He gives me a little smile and then dives in, the water swallowing him whole and leaving tiny little ripples in his wake.

"You heard the man," Seeley says, standing up to kick off her clothes. My eyes slide up her body, marveling at how put-together she always manages to look. She's wearing her favorite white bikini underneath it all, which stands in stark contrast to the sleek purple hair on top of her head. "Come on." She laughs.

Seeley jumps into the pool, a giant cannonball that sends a wave splashing up all over my legs. A couple of the pirate guys follow suit, whooping and hollering as they backflip into the pool. I stand on the side, watching them having fun and trying not to feel self-conscious about the fact that they all have athletes' bodies and I . . . don't.

"You coming in?" Marcus asks. I forgot he was here.

I could say no. I could go back to sitting at the edge of the pool, beg off for some excuse or another, and just let my insecurities swallow me whole. But everyone is laughing and having fun, and even Marcus, who never swims because he hates to get his hair wet, looks like he's about to jump in too.

I yank my shirt over my head and add it to the pile, kicking off my flip-flops and tugging down my shorts. A bead of sweat trails down my spine, dipping beneath the top of my tankini only to get sucked up in the waistband of my bottoms. I slide my thumbs under the elastic, tugging it back into place, and do my best not to compare my curves and sliding lines to everyone else's hard edges.

I turn around just in time for Marcus to yank me into the pool after him. It was meant to be playful and fun, but he caught me off guard and I'm left choking and sputtering in the water, chlorine burning my nose as the panic sets in.

Two big arms wrap around me and tug me back toward the side, holding me up until I can stop coughing long enough to grab on myself. I assume it's Marcus, and open my mouth to apologize for being such a colossal doof, but it's not. It's Nick swimming in front of me, looking worried.

"You good?" he asks, and his eyebrows crinkle together a little while he waits for my answer.

"Yeah, perfect. I mean, nobody's ever actually died from embarrassment, right? So, I think I'm pretty safe."

Nick laughs and splashes a little water at me. "You have nothing to be embarrassed about."

"I literally almost drowned trying to get into a pool." Saying that triggers another coughing fit, and I bury my face against my arms with a groan. "Please swim away now."

"What if I don't want to?" he asks, and I lift my head to look at him—which is the exact moment Seeley swims up in a panic trying to make sure I'm not dead.

She thwaps me hard on the back and spins me around to face her. "Oh thank god. If Marcus drowned my best friend, I would have had to kill him."

"Hold that thought," I say, and look back at Nick, but he's gone off to the other side of the pool and seems to be having a very intense conversation with the other guys.

Seeley hoists herself up onto the platform and holds her hand out, which I take, slipping twice and scraping my thigh in the process. Awesome. Seeley tosses me a towel and we wrap ourselves up, walking over to the trampoline to sit where it's dry.

"I'm glad you're not dead," Seeley says, bumping her shoulder against mine.

"Me too." I glance back at Nick once more. "I can't believe he saved me," I say, my voice barely above a whisper.

"Yeah, well, he's CPR certified, so doesn't he have to?"

"Marcus is too, and he was closer."

"Well, then Marcus is a jerk, and you should be pissed."

"But Nick saved me," I squeak, biting my lip.

"You should aim higher than someone helping you not die," Seeley says. "That's sort of setting the bar pretty low, you know? Most people would try to help someone not die, if they had the chance."

I scrunch up my shoulders. "I think you really overestimate mankind."

"Well, I think you really underestimate your self-worth."

"Whatever," I laugh.

"No, not whatever," she says, and she looks kind of serious. "Stop selling yourself short. There are people who would die for a chance with you, and you're too busy mooning over a guy with a girlfriend."

I frown. "Nobody is dying to get with me, trust me. I'm the weird girl who always says the wrong thing and ends up puking in the breakroom on opening day. But this isn't about me, this is about you. Can we just move on to phase two of getting you a girlfriend?" I wrap the towel tighter around me and huddle in. "So, okay, Angie didn't work out. Who else do we have to consider?"

"Oh my god, Lou. Why won't you let this go? Why do you get to be all woe-is-me about dating, and I don't?"

"Because you're the one that actually has a chance!"

"Lou," she says, but I hold up my hand.

"Whatever you're gonna say, just don't. Just let me do this. Let me make this the best summer of *your* life, while I'm still figuring out how to make it the best one of mine too. Please?"

Seeley looks away, but I can tell by the way her lip quirks up that I've won her over. "Well, when you put it like that—"

"Perfect." I grin. "Now, all we have to do is find a girl that's willing to say 'I love you, Seeley. You're the most important person in the universe to me. And also I am single and would like to date you exclusively. For all times. But most importantly, I love you and you are my everything.'"

"Awww, Elouise." Seeley laughs all dramatic and fake-breathless-like. "I love you too."

"Oh," Nick says, and I didn't even know he was there. "Wow."

I turn around, getting ten shades of red because of course he would walk up when we were being such total dorks. "Hey, Nick."

"I thought you were hooking up with Angie now," he says, narrowing his eyes at Seeley before looking back to me.

"It didn't work out between them," I say.

"Oh," he says again, and then he looks down for a second.

I bite the edge of my thumbnail. "You win some, you lose some, right?" And yeah, okay, if I could maybe just be a little less awkward, that would be swell.

Nick scrunches up his face; he looks sort of sad. "I guess."

Wait, what? I look at Seeley but she just shrugs.

"I didn't know you guys were a thing all of a sudden," he says, and his tone seems a little off. "Seems really fast to me."

And okay, is it me or does he sound a little jealous? I can

really, definitely, maybe build on this, I think. I mean, what would happen if—

"We—" Seeley says, but I cover her mouth with my hand.

"Haven't been together long," I say, at the exact moment she bites me and I jerk my hand away.

Nick's eyes flash just enough to let me know I might be onto something here.

He looks away and scratches the back of his neck, but when he looks back, he has his usual smile plastered on his face. "I'm happy for you guys, really, you just caught me off guard. We should all go out sometime. Jessa loves double dates. But, good for you guys, seriously."

"We're not—" Seeley says, but I shoot her a look.

"—telling a lot of people yet," I finish, and now it's Seeley's turn to look at me like I'm losing it.

"Oh, gotcha. Yeah, people can be real assholes about stuff like that." He rubs a towel all over his head, which makes his hair stand up in a thousand different adorable directions. "I actually have to go pick up Jessa soon, so I gotta run." He pauses for a second, biting the inside of his lip. "She mentioned wanting to hit up the movies tomorrow night. You guys wanna come?"

"Uhhhh," Seeley says.

I hold back a smirk, but inside I'm grinning down to my toes. "Yeah, definitely."

"Cool." He grabs his clothes and starts walking barefoot toward the parking lot. "I'll shoot you guys a text with the time and stuff."

"Sounds good." I smile, watching him walk off.

Seeley waits until he is totally, definitely, 100 percent out of sight to turn back toward me. "What the hell." She grits her teeth.

"What?" I ask, trying to buy myself time.

"You told him we were together! What are you doing?"

"It's not like I had time to think."

"Right, of course not." She pushes off the trampoline and picks her clothes up off the ground.

"Wait." I chase after her, tugging on her wrist to keep her from walking away. "Are you seriously mad?"

"It depends: are you seriously asking me to do this?"

"What?"

"It doesn't even make any sense, Lou. How is this going to help you guys end up together? He doesn't seem like the kind of Neanderthal that would see two girls dating and suddenly have to have one of them."

"Eww, gross. If he was like that, I wouldn't want to be with him."

"If you're not doing it to get his attention, then why *are* you doing it?"

"You saw him. Didn't he seem jealous to you? This could be my chance to figure out what's really going on between us, all incognito-like."

Seeley sighs. "I don't know whether to be relieved that you're not actually some tired stereotype or if I should just be worried that you are *this* delusional about Nick being in secret love with you."

She gets a little shouty at the end there, and I take a step back. "Please," I beg. "People have thought we were together before and you didn't care. Like half the park assumes we're dating at any given moment."

"Yeah, but we always correct them." She pulls her clothes on and looks at me. "Remember how annoyed you were last time? You said, and I quote, 'Just because Seeley always dates girls and I mostly date girls doesn't mean that we're dating each other.'"

"That was because it was Gordo, and he was a being a perv about it."

"Gordo is always a perv about everything."

"That's beside the point." I sigh. "Come on, let's just see what happens."

"This is completely messed up. You get that, right? Maybe he is jealous and you're right, but maybe he's totally happy with Jessa and this is all in your head." She hangs her head back and groans at the sky. "You're just gonna end up hurting yourself, the way you always do whenever one of these schemes goes bad."

I cross my arms. "I can take care of myself."

Seeley raises her eyebrows. She doesn't even have to say it; I know what she's thinking.

"Okay, fine, I acknowledge there's a certain degree of risk here, and historically my ideas don't always work out the way I want them to. But sometimes they do!"

Seeley crosses her arms. "This is different."

"I'm begging you here."

Seeley shakes her head again. "I don't know."

"You know you wanna say yes."

"I'll think about it." Seeley rubs her hands over her face. "I should go home. I'm gonna see if I can catch a ride with Marcus."

"Come on, I can give you a ride. Don't be like that."

"No," she says. "He's practically my neighbor anyway. It makes more sense. Just text me later or whatever."

"Okay," I say. "If you're sure."

"I am," she says, jogging away to catch up to him. And I wave as she disappears around the corner, because, hey, at least that wasn't a no.

CHAPTER 12

Me: How hot do you want your girlfriend to be tonight????

WE'VE BARELY TALKED ALL DAY, BUT I TOLD MYSELF it's probably because she was busy helping her mom make new living arrangements for Grandma Bobby, and not because she's still mad about our fake date. Apparently, her mom wasn't happy with the old place, so they're moving her grandma to a newer, more expensive facility nearby. Seeley said she's giving part of her paycheck to her mom now to help pay for judo, which is why I offered to cover the movie tonight . . . but then she got weird about it, so I dropped it. Until now.

I wrench open my closet and flop onto my bed to stare at my clothes. What does one wear when heading to the movies for a faux date with a faux girlfriend? I don't even know. I grab my phone again and stare, like if I look hard enough she'll write faster.

The little dots that tell me that she's writing back appear on the screen, but then they disappear. They reappear a few more times, sometimes for long stretches. I bite at the skin on the side of my nail and wait. When I absolutely, positively cannot stand it for another second, I fire off another text.

Me: YOU KNOW I CAN SEE THAT YOU'RE WRITING, RIGHT?

Seeley: I'm not going.

She writes it all plain like that, like she didn't just crap all over my hopes and dreams. I mean, I get it, sort of, but also *come on*. I really, really, really need this.

Me: I'm begging you. Please.

Seeley: I don't think it's a good idea.

I close out of the message and call. When she sends me to voicemail on the second ring, I know it's time for more drastic action. I throw on the cutest clothes I have and trot downstairs, shouting a quick goodbye to my dad. There's only an hour before the movie, which is hopefully, probably, most likely, barely enough time to get Seeley to change her mind.

My heart sinks when I pull up to her house because every single light is off, and crap, what if she took off to avoid me? But then there's a sudden flicker of light coming from her room, a television maybe? And where there's a television on, there's usually a Seeley sketching in front of it.

I start toward her front door but stop myself. I have a key, it's on my key chain right next to my own house key . . . but where's the fun in that? I take a deep breath and cross around to the back of her house instead.

Twelve perfect little chunks of wood are hammered into the tree and lead perfectly up to the roof. Her parents put them up when I said having a key made sneaking over less fun. I mean, walking up the front steps and unlocking the door doesn't have anywhere near the same magic as scaling a tree, even if the tree has cheater steps nailed to its side now.

I reach up, dragging myself by my fingertips as my feet cling to the boards beneath me. My shirt catches a little on one of the branch stubs, and I freeze, praying it won't rip. I'm trying to be careful, so careful. It's not usually this hard.

Usually, I swing up all carefree and whatnot, but also usually I'm not about to go on a double date with Nick. On a normal day, if I fell on my ass and needed stitches, no one would really care. Well, maybe my dad and Seeley's parents, but still, that doesn't exactly count.

I can't believe I'm doing this right now.

No, more like I can't believe she's making me do this right now.

I climb onto her roof and catch my breath, running my thumbnail underneath one of my other nails and groaning at the sight of all the tree bark gunk underneath. I chipped one too, not the nail polish—I'm not wearing any—but an actual nail. Now it's a jagged mess, a line once perfectly filed, worn raw and ragged beneath the weight of things. Swell. There's a metaphor here somewhere, I'm sure.

I walk over to the window and try to psych myself up; I don't know if I should barge in or knock on the glass first. The last time I tried to crawl in her window when she was mad, she chased me right back out. Okay, that means I should probably knock, but I'm not going to. I mean, making poor life choices is kind of my specialty, and as my best friend, she should pretty much expect this already.

I reach my hands under the window, my heart thumping in my chest, and for the first time it occurs to me that maybe I'll find it locked. If it is, that's it, really. There'd be no coming back from something like that. We don't lock each other out, like ever. We scream, we fight, we chase each other out, but we don't ever flick the lock and say, "This is it. I'm done. No entry."

The tension runs from my head to my heart to my fingers, making them twitch before I'm ready to face the obvious: that I could have ruined everything in thirty seconds with one foolish idea. Maybe I should go. Maybe I should ditch the movie and head home instead—wash all this junk off my face, crawl into my coziest pajamas, and hide under the covers until my dad comes to tuck me in.

But who am I kidding?

On nights like this, when my head is whizzing around in about five million directions, I'm way more likely to barricade myself behind my door and pull out the postcards. I can't help it. It's almost like—

The window flies up before I can finish that thought. I yelp in surprise, and Seeley reaches forward at the last second, grabbing my shirt before I fall off her roof. We tumble through her window together and land in a heap on her floor. She's pinned beneath me, squirming and elbowing me to get off.

I roll to the side, flopping onto my back and panting as I stare up at the ceiling. "Nice save," I say when the adrenaline starts to fade and I feel human again.

Seeley turns her head to look at me, smiling a little before she catches herself. "Thanks." I glance around the room again. She's watching *Doctor Who*, an episode with Ten and Rose— the one she only watches when she's really upset. I can tell from the smudges on her hands she's been sketching it too.

I frown. "What are you doing?"

Seeley rubs her eyes, dropping her arm across her face so I can't see her anymore. "I *was* wondering how long you were going to stand outside my window and freak out, but now I'm only wondering what you're doing here."

"You knew I was out there?"

"Grace and dexterity aren't exactly your strong points, Elouise. I could hear you coming before you were even half-way up the tree."

I push her arm gently, sitting up beside her. "If you knew I was out there, why'd you make me wait?"

"I wanted to see how long it would take you," she says, like that even makes sense, like playing games is something we do instead of something we complain about.

I tug at one of the strings on her hoodie, making them uneven. It's always so cold in here. "I was going to leave."

She draws her knees up to her chest, watching me. "Why would you leave?"

"I don't know." I bite at the rough edges on my thumbnail. "I didn't want to know how mad you were, like if you locked the window or something."

"I would never lock the window."

"You sent me to voicemail."

"I was in the bathroom."

"Oh. Well, still," I say. "But seriously, come on, what's the big deal?"

Her eyebrows shoot toward the ceiling. "Are you kidding, Lou? What you're asking is off-the-wall for so many reasons."

"Look, if they're so happy, then why did they keep breaking up and getting back together?"

"Who knows? Maybe 'cause her mom is super strict. Remember last summer she made Jessa leave the staff barbecue because her shorts were supposedly too short?"

"Yeah, and they were like practically capris," I snort.

"Exactly." Seeley nods. "What if her mom demanded she break up with Nick, but true love or whatever, so they keep finding ways to be together?"

Then why does he keep flirting with me, I want to add, but I know she'll never believe me. I don't even know if I completely believe me.

Seeley sighs. "I feel like—morals aside—there's a really good chance this is going to all blow up in your face. And then what?"

"I'll be fine. I'm always fine."

"Lou, you're not thinking straight. You've already built this summer up in your head so much that there's less than a five percent chance it could ever meet your expectations. You need to take a step back. You're making really bad decisions, even for you."

"Even for me?"

She frowns, straightening out the strings of her hoodie. "That came out wrong. I just mean that you've had some random ideas over the years, and I've always stood by you, always. God, I even helped you figure out how to get into that stupid French class so you could try to get with Malia, and look how well that worked out! But come on, this one is *way* out there. Let's say Nick was actually jealous for some reason. What happens after tonight when he thinks you're super gay and has no idea that you're really just a creeptacular stalker?"

"Okay, a) I'm not creepy, and b) even though the whole thing with Malia didn't exactly work out, I learned a lot of French, and c) the whole bisexual thing isn't exactly news to anyone!"

"Oh really? Not anyone?" she asks, and I know what she's getting at.

"Okay, can we not do this right now?"

Because she's talking about my dad not knowing. Again. It comes up a lot. She can't stand that I'm not out to him. But it's not like that. I mean, I don't hide anything, I just haven't said the words. Not because he'd care, just because it's super icky to talk to my dad about things like sex and dating and whatnot. Like, he's a guy, you know? He doesn't always get it.

Sometimes I imagine what it would be like to have a mom to go to for this type of stuff. Seeley swears it's just as bad, but I guarantee you she didn't have to sit there while her dad read the instructions on the tampon box when she got her period for the first time. Like, I'm sure her mom has that kind of thing down, you know?

That's sorta why Seeley and I ended up coming out to each other so quickly when we were younger. I definitely didn't want to ask my dad about it, so I asked her instead. I still remember her face when I asked, "Do you ever think about kissing girls?" I was so nervous that she was going to freak out, but then her eyes got so big and she was just like, "Uh, that's actually all I think about kissing."

It was pretty much the most perfect conversation ever— so easy, so simple—and after that, there was no more hiding, really. If anybody at school had a problem with it, screw them. Because who cared what other people thought, when Seeley had my back and I had hers.

That's how it's *always* been with us . . . until now, maybe.

Seeley crosses her arms. "I need you to admit that pretending to be with *me* to go on a double date with *someone else* is basically the definition of creeptacular. Like, you have to see that that's messed up."

"Okay," I snap, but I swear I don't mean to. "Can I think for a second?"

"Fine, think away." She sighs. She waves her hand like I'm dismissed, and goes back to watching *Doctor Who* and sketching Rose and Ten burning up a sun to say goodbye. It's literally the saddest part of the saddest episode, which, you know, isn't really the tone I wanted to set for tonight, but whatever.

I bet Nick would burn up a sun to say goodbye too. He seems like that kind of guy. I mean he's already the kind of guy who goes out of his way to save someone from drowning even when he's on the opposite side of the pool. Burning up a sun for someone he loves isn't too much of a stretch, probably. All the more reason to win him over.

"All right," I say.

Seeley pries her eyes away from the screen. "That was quick."

I sit up a little straighter. "How about this: We go on a date or two and hang out with Nick. It lets me get to know him better without Jessa being sketched out. Then I can figure out for sure if he has any feelings for me and what's up with his relationship with Jessa, and we'll go from there."

Seeley throws her hands up. "Why do you think you have the right to meddle in their relationship?"

"If I can break them up, then obviously their relationship isn't that great. I'd practically be doing them a favor."

Seeley sets down her pencil. "You. Are. Bonkers."

I cross my arms. "It could be good for you too."

She rolls her eyes. "How?"

"You'd be off the market as far as anyone knows. That would solve the Angie situation."

"I see, this is for my benefit, then?" Seeley laughs and then takes a deep breath, staring down at her sketch. "Yeah, okay, you get me out of a second date with Angie, but now she'll think I was leading her on the whole time. What about that?"

"I'll talk to her."

"You'll talk to her?" And I can tell by the way she drops her chin and looks at me that she thinks that's a terrible idea.

"I don't know, okay? We'll figure that out tomorrow. But, please, we're gonna be late tonight."

Seeley looks up at me, tilting her head. "Hypothetically, *if* I was going to agree to do this, what would the plan be?"

"I don't know. I was thinking like once Nick and I got closer, you and I could fake problems so he becomes my shoulder to cry on or whatever. Then we break up, and boom, Nick comes running and you and I are back to being platonic best buddies."

"Just like that?" I can tell by her tone she doesn't quite believe me.

"Just like that." I beam, hoping I can force out enough confidence for the both of us. "I'll seriously owe you for this. I'll do whatever you want, I swear, but I need your help. Please. I can't do it without you."

"This seems like a terrible idea."

"Just come tonight, please. We'll figure it out, I promise." I check the time on my phone. "They're probably already waiting for us."

"I don't know," she says, but then I realize that she's packed up all her art supplies while we were talking.

I grab a pillow and throw it at her head, missing horribly. "You were gonna come this whole time?"

She cackles, feigning innocence. "I have no idea what you're talking about."

"Come on, then." I grab her hand and drag her to the window. "We're gonna be late."

"Stairs, Elouise." She groans, but follows me anyway.

"Nah." I step to the edge of the roof and grin. "Not this summer, Seeley. This summer it's windows only." And I can tell when my foot hits the first step that everything is coming together. This summer is going to be awesome, perfect; everything I dreamed of and more. Unfortunately, I can also tell when my foot hits the second step that it's totally rotted. The step, I mean, not the summer.

I careen down the rest of the tree, having just enough time to curse my luck before I land with a thud onto the ground below. I'm scraped and bloody, and oh god my butt hurts so bad, but I'm still laughing. Seeley is on the roof, screaming down, asking if I'm okay, but I can't stop laughing long enough to catch my breath and answer.

She disappears into the house and reappears a second later, flying out the front door. I don't know if it's the fall or all the tension that's been coiled up in my belly since Seeley got mad, but I'm still laughing so hard I can't breathe. It's not until she wraps her arms around me and tells me I'm okay that I finally stop, that I can finally believe it.

CHAPTER 13

"I CAN'T GO LIKE THIS." I AM SITTING ON THE EDGE OF the toilet in Seeley's upstairs bathroom, chin tilted up, as she dabs at my face with gauze and antiseptic.

She leans back to admire her work. "It's not even that bad, now that all the blood is off."

"Great."

She smooths my hair a little, tucking some of it behind my ear. "Besides, we'll be in the dark anyway. It's not like he'll even notice."

"Perfect, just what I wanted, to not be noticed at all," I grumble.

"Fine." She smirks. "Maybe he'll notice and be really worried about you. Maybe he'll dote on you and kiss your boo-boo and whisk you off to urgent care in a panic."

"You think?" I tilt my head enough to see her through the corner of my eye.

"No." She pulls a face at me, and I know it well. It's the same face she's given me every time I've said something ridiculous for the past ten years.

"Thanks for the vote of confidence." I stand up, wincing at the motion. Apparently, my butt is just as bruised as my ego.

"It's not that." Seeley laughs and pulls a few stray bits of grass out of my hair. "Nick is going to be there with his girlfriend, and you're supposed to be there with yours. He's not gonna want to cross a line or anything. Besides, if you were Jessa, would you want your boyfriend fawning over another girl?"

"I'm in a committed relationship, remember? But as far as I'm concerned, Nick should be able to hang out with as many girls as he wants. *Especially* those in committed relationships."

"You're a wolf in sheep's clothing," Seeley says. "It's freaking me out."

"You said you'd go."

Seeley sighs. "I know, but that doesn't make me feel any less crappy about it."

"It's just for a few dates, promise. Then we'll break up, like I said, and it'll be fine."

"Oh really? It'll be fine?" She tosses the bloody gauze into the wastepaper basket with a frown. "What happens after we break up?"

"We won't pretend anymore. No more fake dates for us. You're free to run off with wild abandon, chasing every hot girl that crosses your path," I say.

"Right, because that's me: girl chaser extraordinaire."

I drop back against the wall. "You know what I mean. Things will go back to normal."

"Right, except the whole park thinks we were together."

I raise my arms in frustration. "Half the park already thinks we are."

"And now they all get to watch me get dumped again." Seeley rests her head on her knee. "It was bad enough last time."

I scrunch my eyes shut. Shit. I didn't think about all the dust this might be kicking up in her head about Sara. "I—" I start, but then it hits me. This could actually be good. This could be really good. A smile stretches across my face.

Seeley furrows her eyebrows. "Do I want to know what's going through your head right now?"

"You can dump me."

"What?"

"You can dump me. It'd be like therapeutic or whatever. Dumping me will totally help you work out all the crap from when Sara—"

"Stop," Seeley says, and it sounds like she really means it.

"Okay." I huff, scowling at my scraped-up chin in the mirror while I fluff out my frizzy hair. "Sorry, forget I said it, then. Bad idea."

"I'm not mad," Seeley says, but then she doesn't say anything else, so it doesn't really make me feel any better. "Tell me one thing, though: Why Nick? Why are you wasting all your time on a guy with a girlfriend?"

I take a deep breath and turn to face her. "I feel like he sees me, really sees me. Most people don't."

"I see you."

"Besides you, I mean," I say, smoothing down my hair as best as I can without a mirror. "To everybody else, I'm just background noise, like a water fountain or a slamming locker or something."

Seeley frowns. "That's not true."

"It is. The only time people notice me is when I mess up or do something weird or say the wrong thing. But then Nick transferred in, and even though he's a year older *and* popular, he always sought me out and said hi. Even if it was just two-second conversations here and there as we rushed to the next classroom, it felt good."

"Lou—"

"Are we going?" I ask. "Because if we are, we gotta leave now. The movie starts in a half an hour."

"It's five minutes down the road."

"I know, but I want popcorn and good seats and stuff."

"And time with Nick before the lights go down?"

I grab my bag off the floor. "Maybe a little bit of something like that."

"Come on, then." Seeley slips her feet back into her flats. "Let's go."

CHAPTER 14

MY NERVES GET THE BEST OF ME DURING THE WALK TO
the car, so I'm grateful when Seeley offers to drive. She keeps
the radio off the whole ride over, and her slow, steady breaths
keep me grounded no matter how many times my head starts
to spin out.

Current status: excited, nervous, nauseous, hungry,
happy, and scared.

Basically, I'm a little bit of everything that I possibly can
be, and things I never thought of too, a bundle of nerves so
twisted up I can barely think. I love it. Or maybe I hate it. I

can't even tell the difference anymore. Is there a difference, really?

"It's only a movie," Seeley says, her voice soft and delicate.

"I know." I cross my arms tighter over my chest. I've never felt like such a fraud, such an invisible fraud, as I do sitting next to my best friend in the whole world, pretending to pout when really I want to cry. She's making this impossible. I mean, yeah, maybe she's right, maybe this will all blow up in my face but, still . . .

It's not supposed to be like this.

This is supposed to be fun, something we'll giggle about when we're old and boring. The first of the never-gonna-die, live-forever moments to kick off our impossible summer.

Seeley looks over at the next red light, her lips a flat line to match the irritation in her voice. "Don't do this."

I sigh and go back to looking out the window. "You said you would. We're almost there."

She pulls into an empty parking space and turns off the car. "It's your funeral."

I take a deep breath and stare up at the looming theater in front of us. The Grand Marquis is the only movie place we have here. I love it, even if it is kind of a dump. The big nice theater with the new movies is almost an hour down the highway, a trek reserved for only the most special of shows. Here we only get second- and third-run stuff, months after they've left other theaters. But hey, when you live in the mountains, you take what you can get.

I pop open my door and slam my feet onto the pavement. Seeley's parked nearly on the line, a huge pet peeve of mine. I can't help but wonder if she's done this on purpose. She slams her own door and turns toward me, waiting. I can see it in her eyes. Nothing to wonder about, then; definitely intentional.

I open my mouth but snap it shut, smiling instead and refusing to take the bait. "Ready, darling?"

"Absolutely, *sugar*," she says, but the word rolls off her tongue like venom.

Seeley trails behind me as we make our way around the front of the building, mumbling something I can't make out. It's probably better that way.

I yank open the front door, the air-conditioning a welcome reprieve as I make my way to the concession stand. The popcorn here is always stale. God knows how long it's been sitting under the warming lights, waiting for someone desperate enough to come in and start snacking. I order it anyway, like I do every time, along with a Sprite, because I'm too cool to ask for Diet Coke even though that's what I want. Diet Coke is for parents or librarians or senior citizens. It's not something a cool kid drinks on a fake double date with her long-suffering best friend and the pirate of her dreams. Except, on second thought, maybe I should double check with Seeley to be sure.

"Sprite?" I ask, because we always, always share. But I can tell when she looks at me that something is off, like somehow the whole world shifted a bit when I wasn't looking.

"No." She smirks. "Let's have Fanta tonight."

I try to cover up my groan, clearing my throat as I turn back to the cashier. "Fanta it is," I say, despite the fact it's literally the only soda I can't stand.

"Hey, lovebirds," a booming voice shouts from behind me. "What's good?"

"What's good?" Seeley raises her eyebrows. "Really, Nick? No. You can't pull that off. Please don't ever say that again."

"Seeley," I shriek, because he hasn't even been here a full minute and she's already ruining everything.

"Nah, it's cool." Nick shoves his bleached hair out of his eyes. "I appreciate the honesty. If there's one thing I know I can count on with Seeley, it's that."

Seeley kinda sighs and glares at me, and okay, okay, I get it. "Where's Jessa?" I ask sweet as can be, all the while hoping she suddenly found herself coming down with a bout of the plague or something.

"She's running late," he says, looking down. "Had to do a last-minute rehearsal with Ari."

I peek at my phone. "Still? It's like nine o'clock at night."

"It happens."

I take my popcorn from the counter and walk over to the saltshaker. "That's a little weird."

"It's fine," he grumbles, but I can tell I've struck a nerve.

"Hmm," I say, with tiny butterflies forming in my stomach, because this is something I can work with. This could be the hint of gold at the end of my very long treasure hunt. I look at Seeley, but she rolls her eyes and looks away.

"You guys are adorable," Nick says, simultaneously mocking us and misinterpreting everything.

I grab a wad of napkins and shove them in my pocket. "Should we find our seats?"

Nick's mouth twists up in a half smile. "I should probably wait for Jessa. She'll be here in about ten minutes."

"Can't she text you when she gets here?" I ask. "I mean it's not like this place is huge. She doesn't need you to guide her inside or anything."

Seeley snickers behind me, and I stomp her foot to shut her up.

"I guess," he says, only it sounds more like a question than an answer.

"Great." I smile. "Let's go, then."

The floor in theater two is sticky, but then again it always is. I'm pretty sure the last time anybody cleaned the floors here was sometime around 1955. Maybe. And probably just the once. The seats are hard, the fabric faded to various shades of red and pink, lighter on some than others, and you can sometimes even feel the coils inside them when you sit down.

I don't care. I love this place, warts and all.

Seeley leads us to her favorite seat, just slightly left of center in the eleventh row. It's the seat she's been sitting in since we were kids. It's where we saw *Captain America* for the first time, where we sit for *The Rocky Horror Picture Show* every Halloween, and where we've watched every movie in between. This is where the magic always happens for us, and hopefully where it will happen again.

She takes her seat first and I drop down beside her, which leaves Nick kind of awkwardly standing in the middle of the aisle. He glances back at the door, a faint frown pulling at his lips before he sits next to me.

I shove my popcorn in his face and accidentally spill some in his lap. "Popcorn?"

"Uh, no, I'm good." He pushes the bag away. "I hate popcorn."

Seeley leans across my lap and pulls the bag from my hand, shoving handfuls of popcorn into her mouth and chewing loudly. I look at her and sigh, wishing I could drag her outside and freak out on her in a not-so-obvious way. I twist back toward Nick, pointedly ignoring her and her ridiculousness.

"What's it like diving on the school team? Is that really different from doing it at Magic Castle?" And I feel ridiculous, because oh my god yes, Elouise, I'm sure diving competitively is a little bit different than dressing like a pirate and jumping into a pool.

He scratches the side of his nose. "Pretty different."

"I figured," I say, trying to backtrack.

"What'd you do to your chin?" he asks, gesturing to my face.

"I fell out of a tree."

He squints his eyes. "You fell out of a tree?"

"It's a really long story. Can we not?" I'm already bright red and embarrassed and we're barely five minutes in. This is going so *swell*.

"She was trying to be all Romeo and Juliet and scale a tree to my window. It was super romantic," Seeley says. I kind of sit there stunned because she's being nice again, and I did not see that coming at all.

"That is fucking adorable." Nick laughs and looks down at his phone. "Oh shit, Jessa texted me a few minutes ago that

113

she was parking, I gotta go grab her." He shoots out of his seat and doesn't look back. He reappears a few minutes later, his beloved princess in tow.

They slide up the aisle in unison, with their own popcorn and soda now, and it's like she's the planet and he's her moon. Gross. Jessa plops into the seat next to me, all full of eager greetings and too-tight hugs. I can't help but be disappointed; so much for leaning my arm against his when the lights go down.

Jessa offers him popcorn, and I smirk. How do I know something she doesn't? Nick grimaces but takes it, dutifully shoving a bunch in his mouth. Wait, what?

"I thought you hated popcorn?" I ask, the words tumbling out of me before I can swallow them.

Jessa cranes her neck, looking quickly from his face to mine. "Nick doesn't hate popcorn." She laughs. "He'll eat anything. Which is perfect, because if my mom finds out I even ordered this, she'll kill me." She scrunches up her face. "Two handfuls for me, and the rest is his."

I look back at Seeley like *Did you just hear this?* but she's leaning back in her seat with her eyes shut. I can't tell if she's sleeping or just trying to meditate her way out of here. Either way, I'm not messing with it.

"How was your rehearsal with Ari?" I ask, but then Nick kind of stares at his shoe, biting his lip, and I feel guilty.

"Oh, it was the best. He learned this kind of old-timey waltz, and he couldn't wait to show it to me. We're going to waltz through the park a few times a day now. It'll be so much fun."

"Awww, that sounds great." Which is true, it kind of does, but mostly I just want to encourage her to continue flirting with Ari as much as humanly possible. I mean, I don't know for sure that she's actually flirting with Ari or anything, but Nick seems to think she is, which is close enough.

"Ari is the best! He takes this very seriously." She grins. "I couldn't ask for a better partner, really."

Nick clears his throat, choking on a popcorn kernel until his face goes all red and watery.

"Arms above your head." Seeley cracks her eyes open wide enough to peek at him. "Can't go dying on us. It'd be the worst double date ever."

Jessa turns toward him, whapping him on the back, but he brushes her off. "I'm fine," he rasps when he catches his breath.

"Did it go down the wrong pipe?" I ask and instantly regret it.

Nick raises his eyebrows. "Yeah, Grandma, it went down the wrong pipe."

Jessa looks back at him with a confused look, and then turns back to me, mouthing the word "Cranky."

I shrug and smile at her, because keep your friends close and enemies closer and all. I'm just following protocol.

"What animal are you again?" Jessa turns back toward me. "Are you the bunny this year?"

"No." Nick grabs another handful of popcorn. "Elouise is the hot dog."

"Yep." I sigh. "I don't know why Mr. P keeps doing this to me."

"Well, bright side, I guess you won't be the hot dog next year," Jessa says. I can tell from her voice that she truly means it, that she really thinks there is a bright side to the park closing.

I scowl. "I'd rather be the hot dog forever than have the place close."

"Oh," she says, probably trying to figure out exactly where she went wrong. "It was a joke, sorry. A bad one, clearly."

Her apology sounds so sincere that I sort of feel like I should apologize back now, but she's being so polite tonight that it would probably kick off this never-ending cycle of "No, I'm sorry" until we both run out of air. No thanks.

I give her a half smile. "Magic Castle means a lot to me and Seeley. I've been trying to think of a way to get Mr. P to keep it open, but so far I got nothing."

"Yeah, I think it's a done deal," Jessa says. "It's been on the news and everything."

"It was?"

She nods and reaches for a single kernel of popcorn. "Yeah, they were doing all these man on the street interviews about it."

"What were people saying?" I lean forward in my seat, hope blooming in my chest. Maybe someone has an idea how to keep the park open.

Jessa shrugs. "It was mostly people sharing memories from the park, nothing major."

I roll my eyes. Leave it to the adults to waste time reminiscing instead of taking action. I guess this is going to be up to me to fix after all.

Jessa rests her chin on the palm of her hand. "Hey, how long have you and Seeley been together, anyway? I always thought you guys were just friends." Thankfully, before I can embarrass myself any further or answer with another lie, the previews kick on.

"A little while," I whisper. I mean, it's not a lie. It has been a little while. An extremely tiny little while. Like a twenty-two-very-fake-minutes kind of little while.

I slouch back in my seat, flicking my eyes over in time to see Nick drape his arm around Jessa and give her a kiss. They didn't even make it to the second trailer. This is going to be one long-ass movie. Seeley slides over next to me, dropping her head on my shoulder. It's heavy and warm, and keeps me from totally flipping out.

When the movie is over and we're shut back safely in my car, halfway back to her house, I thank her for being so cool about everything. She hesitates before answering, fumbling with the dials on my old radio until she finds a song she likes.

"You're welcome," she says, but her voice comes out a little quiet.

"We're good, right?" I ask. We're parked outside her house, her fingers already tapping on the door handle of my car.

"Yeah, Lou," she says, letting the door bang shut behind her. "We're fine."

CHAPTER 15

ONE OF THE COOLEST PARTS OF MY JOB IS REUNITING lost kids with their parents. It doesn't happen too often or anything, but when it does, I feel like a superhero—which is why I'm not totally annoyed to be crouched down beside this very concerned little kid, doing little dances and wiggles to make him laugh while park security finds his parent.

"Why are you a hot dog?" he asks, when he stops crying long enough to catch his breath. And I don't know how to answer that. I want to say something wise and clever, like "Some people choose hot dogs, but some have hot dogs thrust upon them," but all I get out is "Um" before his dad comes rushing up to us and wraps the boy in a big hug.

I start to walk away—I've seen this half mushy/half you're-in-big-trouble thing play out dozens of times before—but I barely make it ten steps before the little boy is wrapped around my legs with a big smile.

"Thanks, hot dog," he says, running back to his dad. I give them both a little wave and walk back to the breakroom grinning. Not a bad way to start the day.

I don't see Seeley until lunchtime. It's not really a big deal, it's just that she had a dentist appointment this morning, so she came in late with her mom's car. But still, things feel a little weird between us, even though she says they aren't, and I hate it.

She slides into the seat next to me, her tray overflowing with fries. "Hey."

"Hey, yourself." I snatch up a fry before she can stop me and shove it into my mouth.

"Did I miss anything this morning?"

"Only the sight of me dressed like a giant hot dog." I sigh.

"I do love that sight." She laughs, and I can't help but smirk as I grab another fry.

Wait. Hang on.

Seeley is a ketchup douser. She literally smothers her fries in it and waits for them to get all cold and soggy before she eats them—like to the point where she says she's marinating them if anybody teases her about it. But these are different. These are warm and crisp and greasy, and have a tiny cup of

119

ketchup sitting beside them, not even touching. These aren't for her—these are for me.

"Thanks." I pop another fry in my mouth, smiling so wide my cheeks hurt.

"Sorry I've been kind of a jerk lately."

"It's fine. Last night was kind of weird all around."

"Agreed." She grabs the little cup of ketchup off her tray and completely upends it over the fry in her hand. "So we're good?" she asks, echoing my words from yesterday.

"Yeah, we're great."

She nods, and takes another bite.

I tap my fingers on the table. "So, I was thinking—"

Seeley sighs. "Maybe you could take a couple days off from scheming. Consider it a mini break to rest your brain."

"Ha-ha, you're so funny," I say. "This isn't about us. This is about the park."

"Oh god." Seeley drops her head back. "What now?"

"I think we should come up with a plan to save it. There has to be a way to convince Mr. P to keep it open."

"You can't guilt the poor guy into staying open, Elouise. That's not how it works."

"It works on my dad sometimes." I shrug and lean back in my seat.

"It works on your dad for little stuff. It wouldn't work on your dad if you were asking him to keep an entire amusement park open for your benefit."

"It's not just for my benefit, though. Think about all the people who work here. Think about us! Where are we even supposed to find new jobs around here?"

"Okay, that's actually a good point," Seeley says.

I tap my thumb against the table. "What if we got everybody involved. Like started a movement or something."

"A movement?"

"Yeah, a movement, like a community movement, like save our parks or whatever. Jessa did say they were talking about it on the news."

"I think that slogan only relates to wildlife parks and stuff, Lou. I don't think it'd work for getting people to rally around an eyesore like Magic Castle."

"Don't talk about our baby like that." I frown. "But listen, we'll make a big announcement, get people to rally, and then Mr. P will have no choice but to stay open."

Seeley raises an eyebrow as she bites into her oversized burger. "Do you really think anybody will care?"

"I'm positive." I take another bite of my fries, pausing for effect. "We'll start a petition, get one of those online fund-raisers, host a gala."

"A gala?" Seeley snorts.

"My dad gets invited to galas like every few months to support whatever random charity he's doing the books for. I bet they raise a ton of money."

"We're in no way equipped to put on a gala, Lou. Are you even listening to yourself?"

I sigh. "Okay, fine. Just the petition, then, and some fund-raisers."

"How are we even going to do that much by ourselves?"

"We'll get people to help us."

Seeley narrows her eyes. "People like who?"

"I don't know, the people from the news. And like, Nick, maybe."

Seeley groans.

"Hey, he loves the park too."

"Right." Seeley shakes her head. "I'm so sure that's why you want him to help."

"Maybe other reasons."

"Hopeless," she says, grabbing another fry. "You are hopeless."

CHAPTER 16

I'M CURLED UP IN THE CHAIR AT MY DESK, BASKING IN the glow of my laptop. My notebook rests beneath my hand, and I scribble little doodles of hearts and spirals with my pen while I google the crap out of "ways to save amusement parks" and "how to influence people." I figure one or the other should lead me to a solution for this conundrum, but they don't really.

All I get is more articles talking about how people are going to miss it when it's gone, and a few articles talking about the businesses already vying for the land. Which, come on, at least wait for the body to cool, you know?

I stare down at my list and frown at the ratio of doodles to actual ideas. The doodles are winning by a landslide. So far I have: *set up a GoFundMe, go to the news, get a petition going,* and *???.* Of course, I have literally zero idea how to bring any of those to fruition. Thus, the frantic googling.

My dad knocks on the door and pushes it open, frowning slightly as he looks around. "No Seeley tonight?" His eyes linger on the pile of laundry in the corner, like if he stares long enough, she might pop out of it and say hello or something.

"Nah, she had some family stuff to do. Grandma Bobby isn't doing well."

"Aww," he says. "Bobby's having a rough go of things lately. I hope she pulls through." He sounds almost as sad about it as I am.

"Yeah," I say, clicking through the pages of results in front of me.

Dad steps closer to my laptop and squints. I wonder where his glasses are. I wonder if he lost them again.

"What are you working on, sweetie?" I still love it when he calls me that. It's like a concentrated dose of love shot straight into my brain.

I sigh. No use trying to hide. "I was looking for ideas to save the park."

"The park?" He rubs the back of his neck and frowns. "The amusement park? Elouise, honey, you have to let it go. That's not going to happen."

"Why not?"

"Because Will Prendergast doesn't want it to," he says—gentle, gentle, gentle—like the words might break coming out of his mouth. Or like they might break me.

"I don't care." Maybe I sound like a child to him, maybe he still thinks I am one, but I'm not. I'm a woman. I'm fierce, and I'm strong, and I can save this park if—

Dad sighs. "Please let this go."

"The town needs this park."

"The businesses that this could bring in would do more for this town than that little park ever could. This is a good thing, hon, even if it doesn't seem like it right now."

"It's not a good thing. Stop saying that." I drop my pen down on my desk. "This is *our* park. It's mine, and yours, and it used to be Mom's too. I don't care about whatever crappy, boring businesses want to tear it down. I can't believe you're willing to let it close like it doesn't even matter."

"Elouise—"

The tears well up now, kicking my anger up ten notches to an unmanageable level. "So you're just going to let Mr. P walk away from everything? Really?" I slam my notebook shut. "I don't even know why I'm surprised. That's kind of your MO anyway, isn't it? Look at what happened with Mom, I mean—"

"That's not fair, Elouise. Your mother left *us*. I didn't—"

"Like I said, nothing ever sticks in this family!" I stomp over to my bed and rip her postcards out from under the mattress, flinging them in his direction. "Look at these. These are all I get because the two of you couldn't figure it out. I don't know why I'm surprised you're telling me not to fight for the park—you wouldn't even fight to keep our family together."

125

His face gets all pinched and crumpled as he bends down to scoop them up, and all the fight drains out of me. Here is my dad, the man who has been there for me since day one, hunched over and picking up the scraps my mother left behind. The scraps that I threw in his face like little paper swords for him to impale himself on. Shit.

My heart swells up into my throat and I feel like if I really cry now I'll never ever stop. "Dad, I didn't mean—"

He waves me off, standing up with the last of the postcards in his hand. His eyes look a little bit glassy, and his jaw is clenched so tight I can see it even from across the room.

"I shouldn't have said that," I mumble. "It just came out. I know it's not true. I know you didn't—"

He gives me a sad smile. "It's okay."

"I have to go meet Seeley," I say, because it's the one thing I know he'll believe without question, the one place he'll always let me run off to. And I need to run right now, I do, because if I have to spend one more second looking at my dad like this, I'm going to break into a million tiny pieces.

"Elouise," he calls as I run down the stairs and out the front door. But if he says anything else, I don't hear it over the din of the car engine screeching to life.

I don't know where I'm going until I get there, pulling into the empty lot and throwing the car into park beneath the shadow of what I used to think was the biggest roller coaster in the world. It's not, of course it isn't, but when you're little and it's big, and you've never left this tiny town, that roller coaster feels like the whole world. Like an achievement. Like something sure and steady and so much bigger than all of us.

People might come and go, but giant roller coasters are forever. Or at least they're supposed to be. Tears well up in my eyes as I stare at the rickety ride looming above me, all peeling paint and rusted tracks. When did it get so old? Was it always like this?

I don't know how long I've been sitting here when suddenly my passenger side door opens. I jump, hitting my head on the roof of my car as a body slides in beside me. I claw for my pepper spray in a panic, and oh god, oh god, is this how I die?

"Hey." Seeley reaches for my hand and pushes it away, grabbing the spray from my cup holder before I regain my senses. "It's just me."

"How?"

"Your dad called to make sure you made it over okay. He said you were upset."

"Shit." I drop my head back against the seat, wishing it hurt more. I can't believe what I said to him tonight.

Seeley grabs my chin, turning my face toward hers with a smile. "Relax, I told my mom you texted me to meet you at the diner instead of our house. She let me take her car and everything since she was so worried." She lets go of my face, nudging my wrist with her hand. "I was worried too."

"How'd you find me?"

She drops her arm and rolls her eyes. "Seriously, Lou? I think I know you pretty well. You weren't that hard to find."

"But I was a little bit hard to find?" I shouldn't care, but I do. I don't want to be that predictable.

"Oh my god, Elouise, yes, fine, you were a little bit hard to find. I had to go to two whole spots to find you."

"The lake?" I ask.

"The lake."

I look up at the roller coaster again. It kind of feels like I'm on it right now, like I'm at the very top about to fall. "Everything is so screwed up." I go back to looking out the window, afraid of what will come out if I keep talking.

She cranks up the air-conditioning full blast and reclines her seat all the way back. "Yeah, it's a mess. I don't want to say I told you so, but—"

I glance over at her, and my eyes catch on the way her hair kind of curls up into little flips around one side of her chin, frizzy from the humidity and still damp from a shower. She's not even wearing any makeup—she must have rushed right over.

I twist the key in the ignition, shifting my car into reverse as Seeley locks her seat belt into place. She doesn't sit up, not really, but I can see her peeking at me. I wonder if she knows where we're going. Probably. Like she said, I'm pretty predictable.

She smiles when the gravel crunches beneath the tires of my dad's old Chevy. There's a click and a grind as she tries to snap her seat up, laughter shaking her body as it jerks too far forward and catapults her more than upright.

"Swimming out your problems like we used to?" She pops open the car door and lets the hot air swirl around us.

"You wanna try?" I can't help but grin when I look at the lake. It's not really a lake; we just all call it that. It's more of a kind of enormous manmade pond. It's probably a mile wide and a few miles long, if we even measure lakes like that. Wait, what's the nautical equivalent, I wonder, grabbing my phone so I can google. I kinda want to find out and measure it now, like oh my god our lake is six nautical miles long, which are totally different from road miles because—

Seeley shoves my shoulder with the palm of her hand. "What are you thinking about right now?" Her eyebrows are way, way scrunched up on her forehead.

"I have no idea really." I laugh. "Nautical miles, I guess."

"What?" She shakes her head. "Come on, the water's waiting!"

She runs down the bank and onto the beach, tearing off her shirt and nearly falling over as she scoots out of her shorts mid-stride. I open my car door and trail after, watching the water break apart and glide together as she disappears beneath its inky black surface.

I pick up her shirt and shake the sand out of it, doing the same with her shorts as I carry them over to one of the ten million picnic tables that dot the beach. We shouldn't be here. The place closes at dusk and the cops patrol the area, especially on hot summer nights like this, but—

"You coming or what?" She laughs. She splashes some water in my direction, like it could fly all the way up to where I'm standing, feeling awkward and about as sixteen as they come. I pull off my shorts, but on second thought, keep on my tank top.

"Yeah, yeah." I shift the clothes on the bench, buying time to steel my nerves, and then walk down to meet her. The water laps at my toes; it's unexpectedly cold. I step back with a giggle, and Seeley swims forward until she can stand, walking toward me with her hands on her hips.

"You are such a baby." She grabs me with cold wet hands and tugs me after her. I let her move me a little and then stop. "What now?" she asks.

"I just thought this summer was going to be amazing, like I would die of happiness or something. But instead it feels like, I don't know, like an ending or something." We are hip-deep in the water, and I'm shivering so hard now my teeth clatter.

Seeley tucks my hair back behind my ear and lets her hand linger on the back of my neck. "It's not, Lou, promise. We have another whole year before we even have to worry about stuff like that."

"And what happens after that?"

"Hopefully we find bigger lakes to stand in?" She splashes me again and disappears under the water, reemerging farther out, down by the ropes the lifeguards use to keep everybody corralled. "Come on!" she shouts, but I just shrug. "Suit yourself," I hear her say as she ducks under the rope and heads out to the deeper water. Even when we were little, Seeley always begged to go deeper; me . . . not so much.

I wriggle my toes in the sand and let my fingers ghost over the top of the water, content to watch Seeley swim under the bright moonlight. It's quiet out here, only the occasional cricket or car interrupting the stillness of the night. I wish I could freeze this moment, just bottle it up and live in it forever, instead of hurtling toward this future where college is a thing and Magic Castle doesn't exist. I look up at the stars, trying not to cry.

Seeley comes back a little while later, kicking her legs dramatically and sending waves crashing all around me. "Hello," she says when she pops onto her own two legs. "Whatcha doing?"

"Just thinking," I say, trying to sound happy about it, but the tears are still there, just barely beneath the surface.

Seeley grabs my hand. "Lou."

"Everything's changing so fast. I hate it."

"Change can be good."

I roll my eyes, wiping at them with the palm of my hand. "Says the person with two parents, and a billion friends, who's basically guaranteed to be super popular when they inevitably get into an amazing art school next year."

Seeley pulls her hand back. "What's that supposed to mean?"

"It means like maybe you don't really know. Maybe you shouldn't be telling me that change is good, since in my experience it's always been awful."

Seeley crosses her arms. "Wow, Elouise. Sorry, but after spending the night with my dying grandmother, I'm not really up for a competition about which one of us has suffered the most." Her voice is bitter as she stomps off toward the beach.

"Seeley, wait—" I chase after her, grabbing her hand to stop her, but I only succeed in making her lose her balance. We both go sprawling in the sand, adding insult to injury.

"Dammit, Lou." She pushes herself up, doing her best to wipe off her legs as she walks back toward the car.

"Seeley," I say again, grabbing as many of our clothes as I can find before chasing after her.

Another set of headlights pulls into the parking lot, and I pick up my pace, wishing I could just disappear into the darkness around me. Maybe I can dive into my car before whoever else is here now can see me. Odds are, it's gonna be somebody awful like Gordo or one of the other jerks we go to high school with, who think because they live in a small town they have to act like it all the time.

The other car shuts off, and Nick steps out of the driver's side door. "Elouise? Seeley?"

Fuck my life.

"Hey, Nick." I try to sound normal, but I kind of want to scream.

He crinkles his forehead. "You guys leaving?"

I can see Jessa in the passenger seat, and she smiles and waves at Seeley like we aren't standing here, half naked, dripping wet and covered in sand. I hesitate before I answer. I want to stay but . . .

Seeley pushes past me and gets in the car. "Yeah, we're leaving."

I drop my head. "Yeah," I echo, and then get in my own side. Nick stares after us, a confused look on his face, as I slam the car into reverse.

It's not until we're back on the road, blasting the heater for the first time since winter and feeling cold in places that nobody should, that I realize Seeley's trembling.

"See—"

"Just drive, Lou."

I don't argue with her for once, just do as I'm told, my hair soaking into the car seat and sticking to my skin in uncomfortable ways.

We don't say a word the whole ride back, not even when I pull up beside her mom's car and shut off my own. She looks at me and shakes her head, rolling her eyes back the way she does when she's trying not to cry.

I squeeze her knee and give her a sad smile. "Please don't cry. I'm sorry your grandma's sick again."

She laughs, short and bitter, and wipes at her eyes. "I'm not crying about my grandma."

"Then what?"

"Nothing, Elouise." She gets out, shaking out her clothes and tossing her shorts onto her trunk. "Great, where's my shirt?"

My car door creaks open and I come around to stand in front of her. "We could go back?" She glares at me and hops up onto the back of her car. "Or not. Right. Probably not a great idea. Um, can I sit?"

She hesitates, but then scoots over a little, making room for me beside her. "If you scratch my mom's car with those shoes, she'll kill you."

I nod and kick off my flip-flops, climbing up beside her and lying back. I can see the stars, warm and glowing in the sky. I kinda wish I was up there with them. It's weird how some things can make shining seem so simple.

I rub my hands over my face and stretch out for a better look. "They're so pretty."

"What, the stars?" Seeley scoffs.

"Yeah."

"You know they're already dead, right? You're basically romanticizing the beauty of something that died a trillion years ago."

"It doesn't make them any less beautiful. I mean, people still have Marilyn Monroe posters everywhere, and she died a trillion years ago too."

Seeley laughs, and it's small and quiet, but I'll take it. I nudge her with my elbow and turn my head to look at her. "What," we both say at the same time.

"I feel like everything is my fault," I say.

"Probably because it mostly is all your fault." She scrunches up her nose the way she does when she's being extra sarcastic.

"I just wanted us to go to the lake and forget about all the ridiculous drama, but I guess that sort of backfired."

"Uh, it's not your fault because you drove us to the lake and we got in a fight." She raises her eyebrows. "It's your fault because you're forcing me to go along with another one of your schemes, and you're making me mess with people that I consider friends to do it."

I sigh and shut my eyes because she's right, but there's nothing I can do about that now. "I'm sorry," I say, because what else is there?

"I hope you mean that." She hops down off the car and shimmies into her shorts. "Up and at 'em, girlie. I told my mom I'd have the car back by ten."

"I could follow you and we could go to the diner?"

"Nah, I want to wash the lake off me and head to bed." She smiles, but it doesn't quite reach her eyes.

"Okay, but we're good?"

"Yeah, Lou." She sighs. "We're fine."

The light is on under my dad's bedroom door when I get home. I shuffle down the hallway and stand outside it, my hand poised to knock, but I can hear him in there, snuffling and sighing, the unmistakable sound of a man trying to hold it all together—and I caused that, me—and I just can't. I drop my arm and then crawl into bed, pulling the covers so tight over me I can barely breathe.

CHAPTER 17

IT'S SO HOT THAT I'M ONLY DOING FIFTEEN MINUTES AT a time in the hot dog suit, and all the parents are grumping by with their hands clenched too tight in frustration. The entire park smells like sweat, and even Mr. P was in a bad mood this morning. I hate days like this.

I'm tired too, which doesn't help. I couldn't sleep last night, pressed tight between crisp sheets in the cold air-conditioning, replaying the day over and over in my head until I couldn't stand it for another second.

But still, the show must go on.

"Dance, dance!" the little kid shouts at me, and oh my god, it's fifteen million degrees, doesn't he realize that? I mean, I know he looks maybe three, but still, if he's hot, I'm hot. It's not rocket science.

"Oh no, you don't have to," the little boy's father says as I start to shimmy, but then Karen walks by with her perfect little clipboard and glares at me.

"Actually, she does," Karen says. "Right, Elouise? You don't want to disappoint your fans."

"*Frankly*"—I force out a grin—"I always *relish* the opportunity to make people happy."

The dad laughs at my terrible puns, but Karen just nods and walks away, her perfect ponytail bobbing behind her. If my gloves had any degree of dexterity, the garbage-eating crows that flock to the park wouldn't be the only birds she saw today.

"Dance, dance!" the boy shouts again, so I do.

Nick walks into the breakroom, stretching up his arms as he yawns. "Hey, Elouise."

I'm furiously pounding Gatorade after my latest walk-about in the hot dog suit and I nod back, trying to squash down the butterflies. I'm too tired for this crap today; too tired for butterflies, and lies, and kindhearted sort-of-doofy hot guys that—

"About last night." He bites his lip all sheepish-like, and I don't want to find it adorable, I'm way too cranky for that, but I do.

I twirl the Gatorade bottle in my hands and chip away at the label. "What about it?"

He looks down, and a little of his hair, still damp from his last show, sticks to his face. "Is everything okay?"

"Everything's fine," I say, because apparently lying is just something I do now. "Why?"

"No reason, I guess. Anyway, I found this on one of the picnic tables." He opens his locker and pulls out Seeley's shirt.

"Thanks." I swallow hard and snatch it up. "I gotta run, I gotta go do rounds."

I don't catch the rest of what he says as I rush out the door and up the path, the sudden shift in temperature giving me an instant headache. I clutch her shirt a little tighter. Seeley's got another hour or so left before her lunch break, but I don't even care.

"Hi," she says when I step into her booth. "What's up? Nick doesn't have another show for an hour and a half." She looks all confused, and it kind of hurts that she thinks that's all I came up here for.

"No, I know. I came to see you."

"Oh." Her eyes scan the carousel as it slows to a stop. "Hang on a sec?"

I lean back across the wall, folding and refolding her shirt from last night as she opens the gate and helps a few little kids with their seat belts. I remember when it was us up on the carousel; everything seemed so simple then. I wish I could find a way back to that.

When the last little kid rushes off to meet his mother, Seeley locks the gate and walks over to me. There's nobody in line, unsurprising since the majority of the park has emptied out in this ungodly heat. Most of the people left are too busy trying not to drown in the kiddie pool to worry about hitting up the rides.

Seeley tilts her head. "What's up, Lou?"

"I got this back for you." I hold out the T-shirt.

"Thanks." She tosses it on the shelf beneath the controls, like it burned her.

"You okay?"

She looks away, and I pull her into a hug so hard she almost tips over. "I hate fighting with you."

"Yeah," she mumbles into my shoulder. She steps back, grabbing a dustrag and some polish and walking back toward the carousel horses. "Did you and your dad make up yet?"

"Not yet." I shift from foot to foot. "I've kind of been avoiding him."

"You know how he is, Lou. He'll probably say it wasn't your fault and then make you waffles or something. Don't get all worked up about it."

I frown. I don't even know if I deserve that after what I said to him. "Maybe." I sigh. "Maybe he will."

Oh god, I hope she's right.

CHAPTER 18

I SPEND THE NEXT WEEK WITH MY HEAD DOWN, DOING my best not to disturb the little bit of peace that has set-tled between me and Seeley. We're good, but not great, and if I spend too long thinking about that, it feels like I can't breathe. Meanwhile, my dad and I are still tiptoeing around each other, neither of us bringing up that night in my room. Which is why I'm currently chasing Mr. P down—because if the rest of my life is going to be one giant mess, then dammit, this park can't be one too.

"Mr. Prendergast," I call out. He's making his way down to the front gates, probably to grab the cash drawers since we close in like fifteen minutes. Normally this would be the park manager's job, but Mr. P gave him two weeks off paid because his wife had a baby. Mr. P is super big on family like that. Even if it means more work for him.

And today, it definitely does. Mr. P looks flushed and tired, sweat streaming down his face. He pulls a little rag out of his pocket and greets me with a smile. "What can I do for you, Elouise?"

"Um," I say, losing my nerve a little. "Can I talk to you for a second?"

He looks a little bit surprised. "Of course. Is everything okay with your father?"

"Oh yeah, no, he's great. This is about something else."

"In that case, how about we meet back in my office in about five minutes? I have to get the cash drawers from the girls up front and then get out of this heat."

"Perfect." Now I have to just not lose my nerve for the next four minutes and fifty-nine seconds.

I dip into the first ladies' room I pass, trying to ignore my reflection as I shove my head under the faucet and let the water run over me. I know I don't have the face of a woman who walks into an office and demands answers—I have the face of a girl trying to be too many things at once.

But maybe that's okay.

I wet my hands and dry them off on my pants, straightening up my back and squaring my shoulders. I could be her, maybe, that confident girl whose hair probably never escapes her ponytail, or who doesn't care if it does. The kind of girl who Mr. Prendergast would have to listen to. Maybe I *could* be Elle, the real Elle, instead of mousy Elouise, or little Lou. I smooth my hair back a little more and paste on a smile, but it slides off my face into a frown. I look too much like my mother when I stand like this, confident and taking up too much space, so I slouch a little, just to spite her.

"I can't do this." I shove my hands in my pockets and walk out the door, fully intending to ditch Mr. P and slink away . . . except he's there at the end of the path, smiling.

"Hello again," he says. "Shall we?"

"Actually." I glance back at the mirror once more. I can still sort of see her, that confident girl who maybe looks a little like her mother, waiting in the reflection where I left her. Screw it, what do I have to lose? "Actually, yeah, that'd be great."

"What's on your mind, dear?" He's got his sweat rag out again, dotting it over his face with a casualness I'm not sure I'm on board with.

"So, basically, I was thinking about how you're closing the park and I feel like I don't want you to do that." Oh. Awesome, Elouise. What a super compelling mature argument you just made. I'm sure he'll definitely take you seriously now. Ten out of ten would recommend this approach. I sigh.

"I see." He clears his throat. "And is this what you were coming to discuss with me?"

"Sort of?" I scrunch up my shoulders in a way that says I totally get how messed up this conversation is, but also that it's way too late for me to back out now.

"I know this is a special place for you kids, I do, and I appreciate your input, but—"

"Hey, Mr. P," Marcus says, cutting off our conversation. He's changing one of the garbage cans outside the office, something we all take turns doing at the end of our shifts. "Thanks again for letting me use your car. I seriously owe you one."

"You're welcome." Mr. P smiles, pulling open the door. "Thanks for all your hard work today."

I follow him inside and drop into the seat across from him. "You let Marcus borrow your car?"

"His wouldn't start, and he had to get his brother from summer school," Mr. P says, like it's no big deal. Like loaning out cars to kids they employ is something bosses do every day.

"See, that's the thing," I say, leaning my elbows on his desk. "You're always doing stuff to help us out, and I was thinking maybe we could return the favor." I pull out my notebook. "Look, I've already been working on ideas. If it's about money, we could do a GoFundMe or—"

"Elouise." He smiles at me in that strained way adults do when they really, really want me to stop talking. "It means a lot that you would come to me with this, but I'm afraid it is what it is. Magic Castle Playland will be closing after this season."

"You can't really mean that," I say. "I mean, that can't be it."

He sighs, rubbing his hands over his face. "I appreciate how important this place is to you, Elouise, I truly do. But you have to understand that things change; circumstances, people, everything changes. Instead of fighting against the tide, what you really need to do is learn to swim in it."

"What if I don't want to?" And I wish that didn't sound as petulant as it definitely just did.

"Welcome to adulthood." He smiles, but it's not a mean smile, more like a pity smile, and I think I hate that even worse.

CHAPTER 19

MY DAD ISN'T HOME WHEN I WAKE UP THE NEXT MORNING.

This is a rare occurrence; rarer than, say, witnessing a cluster of migrating monarch butterflies, but not as rare as like seeing a Sumatran rhino up close or whatever. I mean, he goes to the grocery store and runs errands and stuff, but usually only when I'm at school or work. He has this thing about "always being present."

It started after my mom left; I think he's working through some guilt or something. I don't know, it's kind of cool, but also a little annoying. I never actually had that desperate need for his attention that he thought I did, but I felt as if he needed it, so I've always gone along with it. Or maybe I do have that need, but my needs have always been met. Huh. Anyway, I'll have to unpack that later, because right now, with him gone, it's the perfect time to snoop.

His workspace is totally covered with papers and files, disheveled in a way that only could ever make sense to him. I shift them around carefully, like an archaeologist on a quest. Somewhere there is a file labeled *Prendergast*, and I. Will. Find. It.

It's not on his desk or in the file holder hanging over his desk or underneath it all in the stack beside his chair. I migrate to the file cabinet next—a place where files go to die—and I'm not expecting much. It's rare that they ever make it back where they belong, all cozied up and alphabetical, without me helping him put them that way.

The garage door goes up, which, crap, means I have maybe one minute and thirty-seven seconds before Dad parks and is standing two feet away from me, asking me what the hell I'm doing going through his work stuff. I yank the drawer out, and there it is—filed right where it belongs between *Pet Connection* and *Putt Putt Pavilion*—*Prendergast, W.* I snag the file and pull it out, shoving it under my arm and then opening the drawer labeled *M* to hunt down the one labeled *Magic Castle*. I nearly rip that file yanking it out of the cabinet, which, man, that would have blown my cover for sure.

My heartbeat pounds in my ears as I race up the stairs to my room, and I barely get them stashed under my mattress before I hear him calling my name. I take a deep breath and grab a hair tie, wrapping it around as much of the mess on top of my head as I can while I walk into the kitchen.

He gives me a quick one-armed hug, wrestling with some bags as he does. "You're up early." He pulls a jug of maple syrup out of a bag; he must have been at the farmers market. "You want some food? I could use a few waffles myself."

I guess this makes day nine of us pretending the fight never happened, then. I swallow hard and try to ignore the way the guilt twists up inside me. He's being so nice, and I'm just standing here not apologizing for anything AND stealing his files to boot. Wow.

He tilts his head. "You okay?"

Not really, Dad, I'm kind of drowning in guilt over here, but . . .

"Yeah," I say, snapping out of it. "Waffles sound great. I'm gonna grab a quick shower, okay?"

"Okay, kiddo," he says. "Are we thinking Star Wars, Avengers, or plain today?"

"Avengers, definitely." I smile, hamming it up as much as possible as I glide back up the stairs and race to my room. I kick the door shut behind me and pull out the files. Worst daughter ever, probably, but I'll worry about that later.

See, I can't stop turning over in my head how Mr. P said, "Magic Castle Playland *will* be closing" and not "I *want* it to be closing." What if all of this is happening because he's too proud to ask for help, even though he needs it? That makes it practically my duty to get to the bottom of this, and hopefully the stuff I took from my dad's office will help.

My dad has always said Mr. P is one of his "high-maintenance" clients, which means Dad handles not only his business stuff, but every last bit of his private stuff too. I used to think that was super weird—like why would you want someone to know that much about you—but now, flipping through the files, I'm grateful for the info.

Granted, most of the papers in the files are boring junk, but there are a couple things that catch my eye. For one, Mr. P really has been making a ton of withdrawals, and his personal account balances have been looking pretty low lately. I flip over to the business file and page through, looking at the tax returns and the total income minus expenses and stuff. Dad taught me how to read profit and loss statements in the fourth grade, so this is all pretty standard stuff.

Magic Castle Playland brought in a nice income last year, sure, but it costs a lot more to run than I expected. So, yeah, he's doing well, not like billionaire well, but well enough. Which makes it all the more weird that those numbers aren't being reflected in his personal bank account.

I can use this, maybe. I mean, if it's not the park itself that's failing, maybe it's just whatever those withdrawals are for that's making him have to close up shop. All the little gears start twisting around my head, conjuring up ideas of fund-raisers and charity races and stuff. If I can replace some of that money . . .

I flip to the next page and see a proposal, well, an offer, really. I read a little slower, my eyes glazing over a little from all the legalese, but I can understand enough to get the gist of it. It's from a land developer, and they don't seem to care about the park at all, just the ground it sits on, and something about a chip manufacturing plant or something. A factory. A factory on top of Magic Castle? Nope. So much nope. I slide the files back under my mattress and hit the shower, more determined than ever to keep this place alive. At least now I know what I'm dealing with.

I spend my entire shower plotting and planning different ways to save the park, but as I walk back down the stairs and see my dad pouring over the waffle maker, I'm hit with a fresh wave of guilt.

"Hey, Lou." He grabs a plate out of the cabinet and tosses a waffle on it. "You're right on time."

I try to smile, but it comes out as more of a grimace as I take my plate and make my way back to the table. He turns back around to tend to the next waffle, and I sit down and douse mine in syrup. And okay, I can't take this anymore.

"Just so you know, I'm really sorry about the other night. I had no right to say the things I did about you and Mom." I say it fast, all in one breath. "Sometimes I get so mad about it. I want to just scream at someone, and I can't scream at her because she's never here."

My dad freezes, like he knows it's so much easier for me to say this with him facing away.

"I don't blame you or anything," I say, cutting my waffle straight in half with my fork. "I know it wasn't your fault. Like, I realize how much you guys used to fight and stuff. I know she left all on her own and I know she's the one who stays gone. I just . . . it sucks sometimes, you know? And with everything else going on lately, it's just been *so much*. I'm sorry that I say stupid shit to you when I can't handle my life.

And I hope that you don't feel crappy because of me. That's all." I shove a forkful into my mouth before I mess things up even more, and hope that he hears what I'm trying to say and that somehow it helps.

He opens the waffle maker and slides his food onto the plate, carrying it over to sit across from me. It takes me a minute before I can look him in the eyes, but when I do, they're all watery again. He swallows hard, and I slide the syrup toward him. We eat without saying another word.

When I get up to clear my plate, he stops me and gives me the biggest hug, and it feels like maybe, somehow, everything is going to be okay.

CHAPTER 20

"OKAY, SO HERE'S THE THING: I DIDN'T WANT TO JUST
hang out tonight," I say, shifting in my seat. I texted everyone
to meet me at Dylan's Diner under the guise of taking advan-
tage of the stack of "20 percent off your entrée" coupons my
dad got while doing their books—but, unbeknownst to them,
this is really a strategy meeting.

"What now," Seeley groans, which makes Nick raise his
eyebrows in confusion and Jessa scrunch hers up.

I pull a few files out of my bag. "I also wanted to talk to
you guys about this."

"Schoolwork?" Nick frowns, but Seeley grabs a file and flips through it.

She looks up at me. "Did you steal these from your dad?"

"Borrowed." I pull the papers back in front of me. "But that's not important."

"Okay, what's going on?" Jessa crinkles up her nose a little, which reminds me of this little baby rabbit I saw once. It's disgustingly cute, and she probably doesn't even know she's doing it.

I roll my eyes. "As you guys know, Mr. Prendergast is going to close down Magic Castle Playland." I pause for effect. "Unless we do something to stop it."

"You're ridiculous," Seeley says.

I grit my teeth. "Just hear me out, okay?"

"I'm listening," Jessa says, and it sounds like she means it. Which, okay, great, but I didn't even ask her to come, Nick just assumed she was invited and brought her. Effing perfect.

"So, I was going through Mr. Prendergast's financials and stuff—"

"Oh my god, Elouise." Seeley sighs, crossing her arms, but I ignore her.

"Anyway, he's been making some super big withdrawals lately, and his accounts are getting low. I don't know what he's up to, but I bet it's a factor in his decision to close. Further complicating things is that he appears to already have an offer on the land from somebody who wants to tear down the park and put a factory on it. From the notes in the file, it looks like he wants my dad to crunch some numbers and see if it's a fair offer. I was thinking, if we could raise enough money, maybe Mr. P wouldn't have to sell it to the developer."

Nick leans forward. "You want to buy Magic Castle Playland?"

"No, I want to donate enough money that Mr. P doesn't have to sell it at all."

"What's the offer?" Jessa asks.

I slam the file shut. "It doesn't matter."

"What's the offer?" Seeley drops her hands onto the file, pinning it before I can pull it away.

I swallow hard and stare down at the table. "One point eight million dollars."

"Wow, Elouise." Nick shakes his head. "We can't compete with that."

"I set up a GoFundMe account. It even has one donation already. We just have to spread the word, and host some fund-raisers, and—"

Seeley looks me straight in the eye. "Did you seriously donate to your own GoFundMe account?"

I wince and look down at that file. "That's irrelevant."

Nick laughs and I kind of want to disappear.

"Wait," Jessa says, looking at Nick. "Hear her out. I don't really want to see an ugly factory sitting on the place where we met, do you?"

Nick blushes. "Guess not, no."

Ugh, gross. I'm scowling so hard my face hurts.

Jessa lifts her chin. "I say we help."

He turns toward me and shrugs. "What's the plan, then, Elouise?"

I flick a smile back on my lips and tap my fingers on the table. "That's the thing," I say. "I haven't quite worked that out yet. I set up the fund-raising site, and we can plaster it all over social media, but we need to do more than that. We need to be out in the community, spreading the word. Obviously, I don't think we can raise two million dollars all in one summer. But maybe if we raised some of that, like enough to replace what he's been withdrawing, it would give him enough breathing room that we could convince him not to take the offer."

"You know Mr. P, he loves that place as much as we do," Seeley says. "I don't think it's about the money, I really don't."

Nick slumps back against the booth. "Maybe he's sick of dealing with kids crying and rides breaking down all day."

"Then why all the sudden withdrawals from his bank account?" I ask. "I mean, something has to be going on there, right? Face it, he needs us."

"Maybe he's doing home renovations or paying back taxes. Or, I don't know, a thousand other things," Seeley says.

"Oh, shoot." Jessa checks the time on her phone. "I have to go. I promised my mom I'd be back by seven thirty. She flips if I'm even a minute late."

Nick starts to slide out of the booth after her, but then Seeley stands up and drops a few dollars on the table.

"I can give you a ride home," Seeley says. "I have to get going anyway." She looks at me when she says that, and I can't tell if she's mad again or not.

"Oh no, that's okay." Jessa smiles.

"But if I give you a ride, Nick can stay and get all the details from Elouise," Seeley says, and I kind of want to hug her. "He can tell you all about it later."

"Yeah," I say. "That'd be perfect!"

"You did want us to help out," Nick says with a little smile. He's still kind of half in and half out of the booth, caught in the middle of this awkward exchange right along with us.

Jessa narrows her eyes a little, looking from him to me, and I drop my gaze down to the notebook in front of me. "Yeah, that's fine," she says, but it comes out all slow and stuff, like she doesn't quite mean it. "Just don't let my mom see you, Seeley. She's weird about me riding with people she doesn't know."

"Deal," Seeley says, twirling her keys around her finger.

"Text me later?" I ask, testing the waters to see how annoyed she still is.

"Obviously." She makes a goofy face at me, and I feel a million times better.

And then it's just me and Nick sitting here, and he's looking at me all expectantly and it's making me kind of nervous, a little panicky, a little I-can't-breathe-with-him-looking-at-me-like-this.

I shove my notebook in front of him as I head to the ladies' room. "I'll be right back. If you think of any ideas, write them down or whatever."

I flick the lock the second the door shuts, leaning against the cold tile wall. Okay, I have to think this through. I have to break it down: Nick is sitting out there waiting for me and we need to come up with a plan to save the park. This is a good thing. This is the best thing actually. This is—

—taking way too long to figure out.

Because Nick is sitting out there, alone, waiting for me, and all he knows is that I'm in the bathroom. Oh my god, it's been like minutes. What if he thinks I'm still going to the bathroom in here or something? Oh my god, oh my god, oh my god. Why did I even come in here? I groan and thunk my head against the wall a few times.

"Okay, Elle," I whisper to myself. "You got this. You may not have any idea what *this* is, but you have got it." I nod again, like nodding will somehow make that statement true, and I push the door open . . . straight into Nick, who has his hand raised in front of him.

"Oh sorry," I yelp, barely sidestepping him in time. "Wait. Were you about to knock on the ladies' room door?"

He shifts his weight from foot to foot. "You've been in there a long time."

"That's a weird thing to do, Nick."

"Okaaaay," he says, drawing the word out. "I was just trying to be nice."

"How is it nice to knock on the bathroom door when you already know someone's in there?"

"What if you were sick or something?"

And oh god, that makes everything so much more awkward. We both slide back into our respective seats, and he pushes the notebook back in front of me. I notice the word "bake sale" scribbled across the page in barbed wire chicken scratch.

"Bake sale?"

He snatches the pen off the table and scratches it out. "It's a bad idea."

Wait, is his lisp back a little? Cute.

I grab the pen from him and write BAKE SALE down again, this time in all caps. "No, it's a good idea." I mean, it's not and we both know it, but it was his idea, and he seems so self-conscious and adorable about it that I kind of want to find a way to make it work now.

"They did it a lot at my old school whenever they needed to raise money. It's all I could think of. It's stupid."

"No, a bake sale sounds great," I say, hoping I sound even somewhat convincing, because in my head I'm still sort of half screaming at the ridiculousness of it. Great idea, Nick, one two-million-dollar bake sale, coming up.

"You don't have to." His cheeks turn pink as he fiddles with the pen in front of him. "I don't really, people don't really come to me for ideas about things."

I reach out to still his hand. He lifts his head a little, looking at me through his eyelashes, and I smile. "I like it. We should definitely do it. We can use it to spread the word about the GoFundMe too, like we'll hand out a flyer with every cupcake or something asking people to donate more. It's the best idea ever." But I must sound a little too excited because he pulls a face and chuckles.

"Glad you think so." His eyes crinkle when he smiles,

and he tilts his head. "Hey, is everything cool with you and Seeley?"

"What do you mean?"

"She seemed kind of annoyed, especially about the park stuff. When Jessa gets like that, it's usually because she's really mad at me for something else. Let me know if you want me to try to check in with her or anything."

I take a sip of water and look up at him. "She's just mad I took the files from my dad."

"If you say so." He leans back in the booth, tucking his hands behind his head. "I know Seeley really loves you, if that helps any. You guys are lucky."

I snort, I can't help it, and go back to doodling in the notebook.

"I'm not kidding, Elle. Whenever we talk about you, it's obvious. I know she's stressing about her grandma and stuff, but you guys'll figure it out. Don't let Seeley push you away just because she's overwhelmed by everything else. Jessa did that with me last year and it sucked."

Wait, who is this boy giving me high-quality relationship advice, this boy whose first idea for a fund-raiser wasn't a bikini car wash but a bake sale? Also, what could Princess Jessa possibly have to be stressed about? And did he just call me Elle?

Nick swipes at his hair and looks down at his hands. "Ignore me, I don't know what I'm talking about." He flips his phone around in his hand a few times. "Are we all set? I gotta go meet the guys soon."

"Yeah, we're all set." I nod as he hops up and heads for the door.

I stare down at my notebook, flipping to a blank page to scribble some more notes, smiling at the idea that Nick is maybe even sweeter than he seems.

CHAPTER 21

"HOW DID IT GO WITH YOU AND NICK?"

Seeley and I are sitting at the way-back breakroom table, trying to inhale our lunches before break is over. I shrug. "He wants to have a bake sale."

"A bake sale? A bake sale to raise two million dollars?"

"Hey, don't make fun of him." I feel a little protective now, like I saw a side of him most people don't, a peek behind the curtain or whatever. It's kind of making me feel a little weird about this whole scheme now, to be honest.

Seeley frowns and takes another bite of her fries. I got the salad today, I don't know why, I really wanted pizza. I stab a bit of lettuce with my fork and swirl it around in the dressing until it's smothered.

"Noted." She sighs. "I won't tease your little lover boy anymore."

"He's not." I blush hard when the word "lover" sends my thoughts spinning in fuzzy directions.

"Not yet anyway," she says, like it's a forgone conclusion. I appreciate the vote of confidence.

"He said you guys talk about me." I take another bite, studying her face.

"I have to sell it," she says. "You want it to seem legit, right? Believable?"

"What do you say?"

"I dunno." She scratches the back of her neck and looks back at me. "Just stuff."

"What kind of stuff?"

"I don't know." She widens her eyes, craning her neck the way she does whenever someone really gets on her nerves. "We just talk about school and stuff, and sometimes you come up."

"He thinks you really love me."

Seeley laughs. "You're basically my sister, Lou—of course I love you."

"Right, obviously," I say, and I don't know why I feel a little disappointed, but I do. It's not that I want her to love-me-love-me or anything, that would be weird, but it's more like the idea of someone as incredible as Seeley being in love with me is kind of nice or whatever. I don't know.

"If you're upset that I talk to Nick about you, I'll stop. We never really talked about boundaries or anything, so I've been winging it."

"No, it's okay," I say, leaning into her so our shoulders bump. "How was your ride with his other half?"

"It was—"

Angie chooses that exact second to come walking up, standing in front of our table with her hand on her hip. "Is it true?"

Seeley looks at me like she wants to disappear, and I raise my shoulders a little and shake my head. "Hi, Angie. What's up?" I say, right as Seeley kicks me under the table.

"What's up?" She seethes. "What's up? How about what's up with you setting me up on a date with the girl you're seeing?"

Oh shit. "I didn't, we weren't—"

"This is really new," Seeley says, jumping in. "I was going to tell you, I swear. I was trying to figure out the best way."

"The best way? The best way would have been to be honest." Angie turns to look at her, her face furious. "You used your sick grandmother as an excuse all week, when really you were blowing me off because you already had a girlfriend. That's disgusting." She narrows her eyes. "And I had to hear it from Jessa of all people. Do you know how stupid I felt? I'm sitting there gushing about you, and she's confused because apparently you're now dating the very same person that you swore to me was just a friend."

"Angie," Seeley says. "I didn't mean to hurt you. You're—"

162

"Don't," she says, whipping around to stomp out the door. "Lose my number, both of you."

Everything goes quiet then, and the whole breakroom is kind of staring at us waiting to see what we'll do next. Seeley drops her head to the table, leaving me to fend off the stares. I sit up a little straighter and stab another piece of lettuce.

"This is a disaster," Seeley grumbles. At least I think that's what she grumbles. It's hard to hear when she's got a face full of folding table.

I notice Jessa near the door, arms crossed with a little smirk on her face. Okay, what's that about? Only I don't have time to worry about that now, because Seeley is on the verge of melting down beside me. "It's not a total disaster," I say, squeezing her arm, but she just grunts.

She pulls her food back in front of her, sitting up in her seat. "Yeah, Lou, it actually is."

"It's more like a tiny disaster, really, in the grand scheme of disasters. You weren't going out with her again anyway, right?"

"I'm a horrible person," Seeley groans.

"You are not." I stab my cherry tomato with a fork and drop it onto her plate. She loves those things, and it's the closest thing to a French fry apology I've got. "Come on, try not to dwell on it. It wasn't going to work out anyway, right? And we have a bake sale to run."

Seeley pops the cherry tomato into her mouth and nods. She looks like she's just humoring me, but I'll take it.

"Okay, planning session, my place, seven o'clock." I smirk. "Mr. P won't know what hit him."

• • •

"I was thinking about the bake sale." It's 7:01 p.m. and Seeley is already flopped across my bed, her notebook and scented purple marker spread out in front of her. "There're a few problems we need to figure out. One, where do we have it? Two, where do we get stuff for it? And three, how do we to explain to Mr. P why we're trying to raise money that we aren't even sure he wants? On the flip side, a bake sale is super easy, people do like to eat, and I can make a mean cupcake. We can use it to spread the word about the GoFundMe account—which I looked at, by the way. Ten dollars, Lou? How very generous of you. But I was thinking we could also combine it with your idea for starting a petition to keep the place open. As much as I think this is a ridiculous idea, I'm sure you're not the only one who feels like this. Probably not, anyway."

"Okay." I nod, trying to get my brain to catch up because she's barely been here two minutes and she's already getting down to business. "Nick and I didn't get into the details much, but it's his idea, so I know he'll be down to help. We can definitely bake everything ourselves here. And maybe we could have the bake sale at Magic Castle, or in front of it, or like in the parking lot or something? Someplace where there will be lots of people."

"Oooh, the parking lot is a great idea. People are always leaving to go eat lunch out of the backs of their cars and stuff. I bet we'd make a killing. I'd definitely pitch in for a few boxes of cake mix or brownies or whatever you want. I'm sure other people would too."

"Okay, so parking lot."

I watch her write it down next to the word *Where?* I notice she's drawn a little doodle of our carousel in the corner of the page. "Do you think he'll let us?" she asks, not even looking up from the page.

"He doesn't have to know."

"How are we going to have a 'Save the Park' bake sale in his parking lot without him finding out?"

"I didn't get that far yet," I say. "Maybe we can just say it's for a local family in need and leave it at that?"

"That's lying, Lou. You gotta quit that. Plus, people will get really pissed when they find out, which they will almost immediately, because you want to hand out flyers about the fund-raiser."

"It's not a total lie." I pout. "I mean he is a local family, sort of? He lives in town. But I see your point, I guess. What if we just labeled it 'for a good cause' and left it at that?"

"Would you donate money to a 'good cause' with no information on what that good cause actually was?" Seeley laughs, pushing herself upright and setting the notebook on her crisscrossed legs.

"If it came with a cupcake, I probably would." I twirl around in my chair. "Do you really think most people will even notice?"

Seeley raises her eyebrows. "I don't think you're going to make two million dollars in one summer without anyone noticing."

"Okay, point taken. Do you think I should talk to Mr. P again, then? Try to get him on board?"

"I have no idea, Lou. This whole thing seems super out-there to me, but—" She shrugs.

I tap my pencil against my thigh. "But what?"

"But I know how much this place means to you. If I have to raise two million dollars fifty cents at a time by secretly selling cupcakes from the back of my car for a mysterious good cause, then I'm in. Even if it absolutely annoys the shit out of me."

I drop my pencil, sort of floored by how cool of her that is.

She scoots forward, dangling off the foot of the bed to grab it for me. "Are you okay?"

"Yeah, no, that's just ridiculously nice," I say, and it hits me right then, for the first time, exactly how awesome she's been about everything.

"That's me, you know, ridiculously nice." She fakes a scowl and growls.

"You are," I say, before I can stop myself.

"Well, don't go saying that in public." She looks back down at her notebook, and everything goes quiet for a moment. I shift my gaze down, studying my toes until the moment passes. It seems safer that way.

Seeley clears her throat, drawing my eyes back up to hers. "I need to talk to you about something actually important."

"Saving the park is important," I remind her.

"Right, of course." She smiles. "But something equally important we need to talk about is you blowing your date with Nick."

"A) I didn't blow it, and b) it wasn't a real date anyway."

"I left you guys alone at the diner," she groans. "I literally

166

whisked his girlfriend away so you guys could hang out, and you seriously, honestly spent the whole time planning a bake sale?"

"Yeah. He's been so lovey-dovey with Jessa anyway. Plus, he got super insecure about the bake sale idea. I almost feel icky messing with him now."

"What does that mean? The diving pirate of your dreams, the last few months the universe is going to force you together, and you're gonna walk away now and let him live happily ever after with his fake fairy princess? After everything?"

"I think she's Cinderella, actually," I say. "She has a blue dress and a prince and stuff."

"What does she need a diving pirate for, then? Cinderella didn't end up with a diving pirate."

"Neither does the hot dog."

"How do you know?"

"I just do," I say, thinking about how he looks at her like she hangs the moon. "Besides, you've been totally against breaking them up this whole time—how come suddenly you're all 'Down with Cinderella, I only ship hot dogs and pirates'?"

"Probably because helping you win him over has screwed up my life, so I at least need it to be worth something."

"It did not."

"Lou, everybody thinks we're together. Angie is pissed at me. I don't even know what Sara thinks. And now you're telling me that maybe it was all for nothing. And I . . ." She rolls onto her back and stares at the ceiling, letting her words trail off.

"You what?" I ask.

Seeley drops her hands over her eyes. "Just, seriously, make up your mind already."

I fiddle with some pens on my desk. "I'm just saying, the more I get to know him, the less I want to ruin his life."

"Dating you wouldn't ruin his life!" she says, her voice kicking back up a notch.

"Come on, Jessa's perfect; she's beautiful, she's nice, she's loaded. Why would anyone want to give that up?"

"She's only loaded because of her stepfather. Underneath it all she's a townie just like us. She's not any more perfect than you or anyone else." Seeley bolts upright and glares. "You're so frustrating!"

"I'm not trying to be. I'm just saying I recognize my limits. This is me accepting that."

"That's such bullshit." Seeley shakes her head. "You're pretending to be all noble about not wanting to break them up, but what you're really saying is 'I could never have him anyway.'"

"Why are you getting so upset?"

"Because you never give yourself any credit! You're the most passionate person I have ever met. Not everybody's like that!"

I roll my eyes. "Like what? Weird? Obsessive?"

"No, not weird. Amazing. Lou, listen to me." She leans forward, her eyes searching mine. "You go out there and you make stuff happen, for better or for worse. And that's just . . ." She looks down, shaking her head. "It just really pisses me off when you talk shit about yourself. You say you want to be noticed, and you say Nick does that, but so do a lot of other

168

people. The only one who doesn't seem to notice how awe-some you are is you."

"Seeley—" I start, my brain flooding with a thousand emotions.

"Besides, Jessa's not all that perfect anyway." She sighs and cracks her neck. "I'm pretty sure she's been screwing Ari on the side since last summer."

And that, right there, stops my brain right in its tracks, because what?

"No way," I say. "I don't buy that for a second."

Seeley rolls her eyes. "Why not?"

"Because Jessa is ridiculously nice. And, I don't know, if even people like Nick can get cheated on, what hope does that leave for people like me?"

"Jesus, Elouise," Seeley groans. "You're ridiculous." Her phone buzzes with a new text, and she grimaces as she reads it. "It's Nick."

"What's he want?"

A tiny divot appears between her eyebrows, the way it does whenever she's concentrating too hard. "He wants us to come over."

"When? Right now? Why?"

"He wants us to come over and bake cupcakes." She sighs. "Which, I'll admit, is a little bit cute."

"More than a little," I say, a smile spreading across my face.

"He's really into bake sales, huh?"

"I think he's just really into somebody being into his idea." I bite my lip. "You can go alone if you want."

"I'm not going if you're not," she says.

"He texted you. He didn't text me."

"It says both of us." She shoves her phone in my face so I can read it. "Besides, it's the perfect way for you to get more time with him." Her phone buzzes again in her hand and she snatches it back, flicking open the message and laughing. "Oh my god, Lou, look!"

She holds it up, and I can't help but smile at the picture he just sent. It's him giving a thumbs up with a giant bowl of cupcake batter in his hand. He's even in a "Kiss the Cook" apron and everything. A pathetic little "aww" rips out of me before I can catch it.

Her fingers fly over the screen again, and a tight smirk tugs up one side of her mouth as she presses send and shoves her phone into the pocket of her ridiculously tight jeans. I wonder how she can even fit her phone in that pocket. Honestly, I can't believe the pockets are even real.

I sigh. "What did you do?"

"Told him you couldn't wait." She laughs, dangling her mom's keys in front of me with a grin.

CHAPTER 22

NICK'S HOUSE IS BIG—WELL, BIG FOR OUR TOWN, AND even big for the nicer, newer part his family moved to when they came here. It's a huge two-story, with too many windows to count and landscaping that looks like it's from a magazine. Nick's dad is a doctor and his mom is a lawyer. They somehow managed to never get divorced, and it seems to have paid off.

Seeley doesn't hesitate at all when she parks. In fact, she bounds up the steps to his porch, rapping twice on his door and then twisting the handle. I wonder how many times exactly she's been over here, because she's clearly comfortable. That feels weird.

"Helllooooo," she calls out, sticking her head inside.

"Come on in," he shouts from somewhere, and I follow Seeley through the rooms.

We walk past the formal living room and the beautiful staircase leading up to the second floor. The house is cold, really cold, and the mix of dark hardwood floors and icy marble doesn't help to make it any more inviting. Seeley weaves through the rooms, leading us to the back of the house.

Nick is in the kitchen. It's a huge bright space, all open windows and great lighting that somehow seems to force out even the darkening night sky. Everything is pale wood and peach granite; not just peach, but peach with little flecks of gold in it. This is exactly the kind of place that a guy who dates a girl like Jessa would live in. My brain can't help wandering back to the laminate countertop running the length of my own kitchen. No matter what Seeley thinks, who dates a laminate girl when you're a golden peach granite guy?

Nick smiles when he sees us, all-out grins really. It's literally impossible not to smile back when a boy in an apron looks at you like you just made his whole night. "Taste this." He shoves a still-warm cupcake into my hand. "Tell me what you think."

I take a bite; it's buttery, light, and absolutely perfect, even though it doesn't have any frosting on it at all. "This is so good," I blurt out. I at least have the decency to look embarrassed when a few crumbs drop from my mouth and land on the counter. Seeley brushes them off with a glare.

"Be cute," she whispers through her teeth, and I would die right now except I'm still holding Nick's half-eaten cupcake and that would be rude.

"Do you really like it?" he asks. "Or are you just saying that?"

"What mix is this?" I ask, after I've wiped my mouth and set the cupcake down on a napkin that Seeley dug up from somewhere.

"I made it from scratch." He smiles so wide that I can't help but smile back. "I googled it."

"You googled it?"

When he turns back around to grab his iPad, Seeley gives me a little shove. I lose my balance, catching myself on the counter beside him. He grins and leans into me, flipping the screen around to show me the recipe.

"It has the highest rating," he says.

And yeah, he really did do it from scratch, and even has the mess to prove it. I feel a little warm, a little giggly, thinking about him taking the time to do all this; to research it and make it and then to be too excited to wait until tomorrow to share it with us—like he's not only sidelong glances and dripping hair anymore, you know? He clears his throat, taking his iPad back and cutting off whatever type of moment we had going on.

"C'mere." He walks over to the other side of the counter and shoves a spoon in my hand. If this is homemade frosting, there's a 97 percent chance that I'm about to combust.

I lick the spoon. Yep, I'm for sure gonna combust. "No way." I take another lick. "Is this buttercream?"

He nods and I groan from the pure unadulterated joy that comes from eating homemade icing in the kitchen of a cute boy. Okay, so maybe that's oddly specific, but still. It's accurate.

"Made it myself," he says, like I didn't already know. Seeley laughs a little from her seat, but then goes back to looking at her phone. "You have a little on your—" he says, gesturing at my face.

My cheeks burn because of course I do, of course. I wipe at my face and look up at him. "Did I get it?"

He shakes his head, and I wipe at the other side, but that just makes him laugh and shake his head even more.

"You're making it worse." He reaches his hand up and rubs at my lips with the pad of his thumb, exactly the way he rubbed grease off my face that night in the rain.

"What's going on?" Jessa's voice cuts across the room, and I twist around, praying I don't look as guilty as I feel.

"Frosting cupcakes." I'm blushing so hard my face is on fire.

"With your lips?" I can tell by the tone of her voice she's not impressed, and I guess I can see why. I mean, she did walk in on her boyfriend's fingers on another girl's face, and that's got to be weird. I look over at Seeley, but she's frowning into her phone, her fingers flying across the glass.

Nick grabs another spoon and dips it into the frosting, crossing the kitchen to stand toe to toe with his girlfriend. She narrows her eyes, somehow engulfed in his shadow even in this, the brightest of rooms. He drags some frosting across her bottom lip with a smirk and then leans down to kiss it off. She purses her lips, fighting the inevitable smile, but I can see her eyes crinkling up even from here.

He smiles. "Better?"

"Better." She sighs, but I don't miss the way she looks at me and at Seeley. I swear I catch her rolling her eyes; not in an obvious way, more like a way that will give her plausible deniability or whatever. Still, coupled with that look she gave me earlier, I don't like it.

Jessa looks down at the cupcakes dotting the counter. "You made these?"

"Yeah." His voice is all shy and tentative now, not excited and loud like he was when we first got here.

She picks one up, turning it around in her hand slowly. "You're really into this, huh?" I can tell by the way his whole body kind of deflates that that wasn't the reaction he was hoping for.

I look back at Seeley, who sticks her tongue out at me before reaching out her hand. I fall back to her, lacing our fingers and bumping her with my shoulder. It's probably good that we sell our relationship, especially with Jessa here looking all suspicious.

"Okay, what's the plan?" Seeley asks.

I wriggle my toes on the cold tile and slip my messenger bag down, opening it up to fish out a pair of fuzzy socks.

"You carry socks in your purse?" Jessa laughs, and it's not a mean laugh really, but my ears burn just the same.

I bend down to slip them on. "Yeah."

"She never travels without them. She has the coldest toes on the planet," Seeley says. "I think it's adorable."

"It's something," Nick says, but in a tone that makes it smart a little less.

"Anywho, how about Jessa and I handle the rest of the baking, and you and *Elle* handle the frosting," Seeley says. "We'll make a few different flavors, and tomorrow we can bring them all in and see which ones get eaten first, kind of like a taste test before the big day."

Jessa looks down at a messy mixing bowl with a frown. "The big day?"

"The day we launch our parking lot cupcake invasion, of course," Seeley says, spinning around all dramatic-like. "Elle and I figured out that we both magically have the weekend after next off, so it's perfect for the bake sale."

I glance over at Nick in his apron. He looks at his calendar and seems a little disappointed. "I have three shows both days," he says.

"We can work around it." Seeley shrugs, and I can tell she's actually given this some real thought. "You go on at twelve thirty, two thirty, and four thirty on Saturdays, right?"

"Yeah." He wrinkles his forehead a little, no doubt wondering how she knew. I mean, I've had that schedule memorized since I could read, and probably so has she by default.

"I'm thinking we'll do cupcakes that morning until like twelve, and then Elle and I can come back here or to my house to grab some more or bake them if we run out. We'll reconvene around five to catch the late crowd leaving. If we don't sell out in the morning, Elle and I will hang around selling off the rest while you dive." Seeley crosses her arms and leans against the counter. "Am I good or what?"

Jessa stirs the mix a little harder. "I work all day every Saturday, not that anyone bothered to include me in the plan."

"I didn't realize you wanted to help with the actual sale," Seeley says, scrunching her eyebrows together. "We can definitely work around your princess stuff."

Jessa sighs. "No, it's fine. It would be too obvious if we all left."

"Yeah, good call." Nick kisses her temple. "All right, enough talking. Let's get to work."

It takes two hours to finish baking all the mix he made up; we have chocolate, vanilla, and something pink that I think is supposed to be strawberry but doesn't taste quite right. Once they're all frosted and packed away, Nick volunteers to be the one to bring them in the morning. The plan is to leave them scattered around the break areas at work and to see which ones go first.

It was as good a night as any, but I'm grateful when Seeley and I are back in my room picking frosting out of each other's hair.

"I think Jessa hates me now," I say.

Seeley checks her phone again. I wish she'd put it down. "I'm not sure she's capable of hate."

"She didn't seem happy that I was partnered up with her boyfriend all night. I don't know what she thinks she has to worry about—I'm a taken woman." I laugh.

"I wouldn't stress about it." Her phone vibrates again, and she stares down at the screen, the divot reappearing in her forehead. "Shit, I'm sorry, Lou. I gotta go." She grabs her backpack and starts shoving her stuff back into it.

"You're not staying over?"

She hesitates, but her phone buzzes again, which gets her moving. "My mom keeps texting me. Grandma Bobby is having a bad night, and she wants me to come home, just in case."

"I'm sorry." I mean it too. "Do you want me to come?"

"No, it's okay. It's probably another false alarm. I'll come back over if I can. In the meantime, think of more bake sale ideas and stuff. I'll leave you the notebook."

"Okay." I bite the inside of my cheek, suddenly feeling like I'm not doing enough. "See you soon, I hope."

"Definitely." Seeley starts to walk out the door but steps back, leaning her head in enough to see me. "But seriously, Lou, can it with the low-self-esteem crap. You're better than that. A lot of people really do prefer hot dogs to princesses, I promise."

"You're such a nerd," I say, and throw my stuffed bear at her. She dodges it easily, crossing her eyes and sticking out her tongue before disappearing back out the door.

I get to work on the plans, just like Seeley told me to. I plaster links to the fund-raising site all over social media and text everybody I can think of to retweet, reblog, like, and share it. Seb messages me right away, telling me it sounds awesome and to let him know how he can help. I offer him a couple cupcake-selling shifts, and we pretty much chat all night about the park and stuff. I even remember to have him tell his mom that my dad says hi. All in all, not bad for a day's work.

I text Seeley a few hours later for a status update, throwing in some cupcake emojis that I hope make her laugh. She texts me back a little while later that she's still at the hospital, but it probably is another false alarm. She's planning to crash at home since it's getting late, but promises she'll see me tomorrow either way. I text her back a bunch of thumbs-ups and silly faces to get her through and crawl under my covers wishing she was here.

It isn't a false alarm, though. Not this time.

Seeley creeps into my bedroom in the middle of the night, well past midnight but nowhere near dawn, shivering hard with tears in her eyes. I know without her having to tell me. She spends the night curled up against me, her head under my chin, our knees slotted together, as she streams old shows on her phone.

She sneaks home around six a.m., afraid that her mom will freak if she goes to check on her and finds her gone. I get it. She calls me around nine a.m. to tell me she's not going to work, and I don't need to bother picking her up. Somehow, she seems better in the light of day and tells me all about how busy she is with funeral stuff, like ordering flowers and helping her mom pick out an urn. I sort of wonder if she's in shock or if her grandma's death really was a relief, but I figure that's not something you really ask—that's something you wait for the other person to tell you.

CHAPTER 23

I'M ON MY THIRD GONDOLA RIDE OF THE DAY WHEN I see it.

I've been riding it on every break today, trying to process everything going on. I still can't believe Grandma Bobby is dead, and I'm not at all convinced that Seeley is as fine with it as she's pretending to be. So yeah, that's why I'm swinging my legs in the warm summer breeze, spending my break pounding Gatorade and just kind of lazily watching the park below me while I clear out my head when, boom, there are Jessa and Ari totally kissing behind the castle.

Of course, because I'm me, I jerk up just enough to send my bottle flying and then watch in horror as it lands with a bounce right beside them. Ari and Jessa both look up, eyes wide and mouths falling open when they realize exactly whose Gatorade just interrupted their little make-out session. We make eye contact, and before I can stop myself, I'm sort of grimacing and waving. Oh my god. What is wrong with me? I jerk back, burying my face in my hands. Shit, shit, shit.

I wasn't spying or anything, I swear, and god I wish I could *unsee* that, but I can't. So here I am, in a little green gondola, being dragged back to the platform. I peek between my fingers long enough to see them racing through the park to intercept me, and I can definitely already make out the bright blue of Jessa's dress on the platform as I come in for a landing. Damn.

Jessa is helpful enough to unlock the safety bar for me, but I wish the ride had kept right on going and swung me away from this inevitable mess. I walk out behind her, my stomach in knots, to where Ari is sitting on the wall with my bottle of Gatorade in his hand.

There's no way to make a clean exit, so I stare at the ground instead, watching the ants race to and from the garbage can. I wonder if the little bit of sweetness is worth the risk of being trampled. Maybe sometimes it is, but I bet usually it isn't.

Jessa takes a deep breath. "Are you going to say anything?"

"Can I have my Gatorade back?"

Jessa huffs and rips it out of Ari's hand, shoving it into mine so hard it hurts. "That's it?"

"What do you want me to say?"

"Were you spying on us?" Her voice modulates somewhere between anger and fear, and I know the feeling. If I could find my voice at all, I'm sure that's what it would sound like.

"Yeah, what the fuck?" Ari sneers.

I stand up a little straighter because, hey, I'm not the one cheating on my perfectly sweet boyfriend over here. "I wasn't spying on you. I was riding the gondola."

"Right, because everybody rides the gondola when they're supposed to be working." He pulls his cell phone out of his pocket, very un–Prince Charming–like. "Jessa, your carriage leaves in five minutes. You have to get over there."

"You'll take care of this?" she asks before bolting, seemingly satisfied by his single nod. I'd sort of think he was going to kill me based on her tone, except he's dressed like Prince Charming and there're about five billion sweaty people milling around us right now. I'm pretty sure I'm safe.

"All right." Ari hops off the wall. "What do you want from us?"

I'm staring at him, sort of dumbstruck, because I don't know. I cross my arms in a kind of pathetic self-hug. "What do you mean?"

"What's it going to take for you to keep this quiet?"

I widen my eyes. "You think you can bribe me? Seriously?"

"I don't know, can I? I barely know anything about you."

I sigh, because come on. "We've literally worked together for two summers, Ari."

"If you open your mouth about this, you're going to ruin everything, for everyone."

"What do you mean?"

"Do you even know what Jessa's mom will do? And how do you think Nick is going to react?" Ari looks down at the ground. "A lot of people will get hurt by this."

I snort. "Well, I guess you guys should have considered that before you decided to have an affair."

"An *affair*? What are we, thirty-five?"

"You know what I mean."

"Please don't do this to us."

"What about what you're doing to Nick?"

"We messed up, it's wrong, okay? I know that. But you don't understand—if this gets back to Jessa's mom . . . Listen, I don't care what you do to me, or what I have to do for you, but please, don't tell anyone about this. We didn't mean for this to happen. You try being Prince Charming and Cinderella and not falling in love."

My lips quirk up all on their own accord. "You're in love with her?"

"I don't know." He looks a little sheepish, but then something crosses over his eyes, a mix of determination and defeat. "Please don't ever tell her I said that."

"Ari . . ." I feel compelled to comfort him, even though I shouldn't. I mean, falling for a girl with a boyfriend is almost as ridiculous as . . .

. . . forcing your BFF to pretend to be your girlfriend to get closer to a guy. Oh. Right. No position to judge over here.

"Are you going to tell Nick? Please, I'm begging here. Don't."

"I don't know." It's not a lie. I really, truly don't. "It's the right thing to do, isn't it? I mean, I should?"

Ari shakes his head. "Are you asking me if telling my girl-friend's boyfriend that she's cheating on him with me is the right thing to do? Because I'm probably not the person to ask."

I tug the elastic band off my wrist, pulling my hair back into a sloppy bun to buy myself more time. "I wasn't actually asking you. I was thinking out loud."

"Well, what did you decide?"

"I didn't yet. What do you mean about her mom?"

"Nothing, forget it." He runs his hands through his hair. "Look, you don't know what to do, right? Don't do anything, then. You don't have to."

I push my shoulders back, trying to scrape up enough confidence to cope with this scenario. "You know she's with Nick! Why would you even try to get with her? It's gross and desperate, and . . . I don't even know, super wrong." Wow, I am terrible at this.

Ari drops his chin to his chest. "You're right, okay? You win. And you can hate me all you want, but please keep this between us."

"Why doesn't she break up with Nick if she wants to be with you so bad?"

"She doesn't want to be with me." And I can tell by the way his hands squeeze into fists that he didn't mean to say that.

"But you're Ari Seimer," I say, like that's important. Be-cause to me it is, or it was, and maybe if I say it enough it'll go back to being true. Finding out these people are no better than me, and actually might even be a little worse, is kind of like expecting a sip of Sprite and finding out you got water instead.

"I don't even know what that means," he says.

I look away, because how do you explain to someone that they're basically top tier when it comes to amusement park hotties without sounding like an asshole? "I just didn't think someone like you would have trouble getting a date."

He puffs out his chest like he's offended. "I don't. Do you want to see my phone? Girls blow it up all day."

"Okay, well, now you just sound like a jerk."

"I'm making this worse, aren't I?" he says all low and bitter, kicking a rock into the bush behind us with a little sidestep. I forgot that he played soccer. I forgot that he was a person outside of a prince. He doesn't even go to my school anyway; he goes to Jessa's on a soccer scholarship, which, hmm.

"How long have you been, you know." I wave my hand between us, hoping he doesn't make me say it.

"I dunno, since seventh grade?"

My eyes go wide. "You've been sleeping with Jessa since seventh grade?"

"What? No! I thought you meant how long have I been into her."

"Okay, first, wow, but second, how long have you guys actually been, you know, acting on it?"

"Does it matter?"

"I don't know? Maybe?"

"Since last fall."

"Is that why she kept dumping Nick?"

Ari shakes his head. "There's more to it than that. You'd have to understand her family to—"

"Okay, I changed my mind. Stop talking now. I have no idea what to do with any of this information." This was so much easier when these people weren't, well, real people.

He runs his hand over his face, and I can already see Jessa's carriage slowing down from here. Sure, she has a few more kids in line for a turn, but it won't be too long before she'll be back, and I definitely, without a doubt, don't want to be here for that. "I'm gonna go."

"What are you going to do?"

"I don't know yet, but I won't say anything until I do."

"Thanks."

"Don't thank me yet."

A bit later, when we're all back in the breakroom getting our stuff out of our lockers, and I've changed the last of the garbage cans, Jessa approaches me. She stands beside me quietly, leaning against the locker next to mine while I grab my bag and stuff all my belongings inside. It's sort of creepy.

"Can we talk?" she asks.

"I'm kind of all talked-out right now." And it's true, I am. I glance over to where Ari is sitting at one of the tables, lacing up his shoes, slowly, obviously trying to drag out the time either to eavesdrop or to catch Jessa before she leaves.

Nick chooses this exact moment to wander in, slinging

his arm around Jessa and leaning in for a kiss. It's quick and chaste, and she looks at me while he does it. I look away, turning back to my locker to grab the last of my belongings.

"You guys aren't talking bake sale without me, are you?" Nick looks mock wounded, and it hurts to watch knowing he's one sentence away from looking like that for real.

Jessa looks down at the floor. "Wouldn't dream of it." Somewhere behind her, a chair slams into the table so hard I jump. I can't believe it didn't break, or maybe it did. I can't tell with "Nissa" currently blocking my view. I almost feel a little bad for Ari; watching this has to suck.

"Ari, man." Nick wrinkles his forehead, craning his neck around to see. "You okay?"

Ari shoves the door open. "Why wouldn't I be?"

Nick watches him go and gives Jessa another kiss on her temple. "Seriously, what are you thinking cupcake-wise, though? It seemed like everybody really dug the flavors we brought in."

"I don't know."

"We don't have much time to figure this out, Elouise," he says.

I push past them, but they both follow. I pick up the pace, but then so do they. Time to change tactics. I turn to face them so quick we almost smack into one another. "Soon, okay? We'll talk soon. But I have to go. Seeley's grandma died last night." And sure, maybe it's not totally right to use other people's dead relatives to get out of awkward situations, but desperate times call for desperate measures and all.

The smile drops off Nick's face. "Oh man, is that why she's not here?"

"Yeah." I shift the strap of my bag up a little higher on my shoulder, the weight of the conversation combining with the weight of my life in uncomfortable ways.

"Sorry, Elouise," Jessa says. Nick looks at her like she's the cutest thing and rubs his hand up and down her arm. I turn my head and look away, because I know what she's really apologizing for, what she really means, and I don't know what to do with that at all.

CHAPTER 24

Me: You were right about Jessa

Seeley: I figured

Me: How's your mom?

Seeley: Hangin in there

Me: . . . 🙁

Seeley: Why is your front door locked?

A grin stretches out across my face. I didn't think I'd be seeing Seeley for a couple days with everything going on. I race down the stairs, smashing into my dad and spilling his soda all over both of us.

"Elouise!" he yelps.

"Sorry," I say as I bolt past him, flipping the lock on the door and whipping it open. I'm just in time to see Seeley smoosh a giant mosquito on her arm, leaving a smattering of blood and wings in its wake. I can relate, Mr. Mosquito—it's been that kind of day for me too.

Seeley leans around me to peek at my very wet, very annoyed father. "What'd I miss?"

I step outside, shutting the door behind us. "He locked the door on you." I smirk. "He can handle a little soda on his shirt. Wanna go for a walk?"

She nods, shoving her hair out of her face. It's a dark brown color now, instead of purple, and I wonder if her mom made her dye it back for the funeral or if she did it all on her own. I touch it without thinking, and she smiles. We hop down off the front porch and out onto the deserted street. It's almost nine o'clock, which means everybody in my neighborhood is either inside for the night or working on it. I glance over at her, our feet falling into step as our sneakers thump the pavement.

"You okay?" I've been wrestling with cleverer, nicer ways to ask her that since we started walking, but none of them seemed right.

"Yes? No? Maybe?" She twists her lips up into a sad little smile.

I nod and go back to studying the ground as we walk. I've never known anybody firsthand who has died before now. When my mom left, her whole side of the family basically disappeared along with her. My dad's an only, and his parents died when I was a baby, so that really didn't leave anybody else.

"I think it's okay not to know." It feels like the right thing to say, and also I know it's true because sometimes I don't know how I feel about my mom. I can get how stuff like loss and love can be really complicated, how it can tie a person up in knots.

We follow the street as it meanders past all the houses, turning into a little cul-de-sac with a park at the end. I climb onto the bright red merry-go-round thing and lie down, staring up at the stars as the cool metal presses into the fabric of my tank top. Seeley grabs one of the handles and runs around, getting a good spin going before jumping on right next to me.

Some of my hair gets stuck under her knee, but I don't say anything. I know she'll move soon enough. And she does, lying down to watch the stars shine above our heads, a sleepy smile fixed on her lips.

"I don't think I'm sad enough." She waits until the world has stopped turning, or maybe until we have, to say this. I can't be positive, distracted as I am by the way the moonlight glints off her eyes as she's trying not to cry.

I inch closer to her. "It's not a contest."

"Shouldn't I feel really bad? Like really, really sad?"

"You're crying now." I don't think she even realizes it. She paws at her cheeks and looks back at the sky.

"I'm only crying because I'm not sad." Her breath hitches, and then the tears start coming in earnest; big, fat, ugly tears rolling down her cheeks, complete with snuffling breaths and boogers.

I let her be until she starts to slip deeper into it, and then I climb over the bar between us and wrap my arms around her, holding her tight until she melts against me. "It's okay, it's okay." I rub my hand over her back as she sobs into my shoulder.

"It's not okay!" she shouts. A tiny stream of snot drips down her lip, and she inhales hard before wiping at it. "It's not okay, Lou. Nothing is okay."

"I know," I say quietly. "I only meant you can feel sad, or not feel sad, or even feel sad about not feeling sad; anything you want. It's all okay, I swear. It's all totally in the realm of like a normal reaction." But she shakes her head, and I know I'm not getting through.

"I just." I take a deep breath. "I don't know either, okay? But I want to help. If you need someone to hug or scream at or, I don't know, punch or something, I want to help." I pause, biting my lip and wishing I didn't suck so bad at this. "But please don't really punch me. I was only trying to be dramatic and you know I bleed easily."

Seeley's lips, once pinched tight against a frown, break into a smile as she starts laughing. I know this is all part of it, probably, this roller coaster of emotions she's on. But I can't help but feel, if she can laugh like that, she's gonna be okay.

She wipes at her nose and takes a shuddering breath. "Does my makeup look okay?"

I rub a finger under her eye, but it's no use. "You look like a raccoon after a three-day bender."

"You be nice to me, Elouise Parker, or I'll tell." And now it's my turn to smile, like I did when we were little and she threatened me with that on the daily.

I grab her hand and pull her up. "Please don't tell."

CHAPTER 25

"HI."

I slam my locker door shut and jump so high I hit my elbow on the lock. "You scared the crap out of me, Jessa."

"I have cake mix." She holds out the grocery bags in her hands like some sort of offering. "I have a lot of cake mix. All the flavors you guys could possibly want for the bake sale and more. I want to help."

I grab them and shove them into my locker, hating the way the plastic sticks to my skin. Who even gets plastic bags anymore, knowing how bad they are for the environment?

"Thanks," I say, "but I think Nick's making them from scratch." I grab my hot dog suit and head into the changing room, but she follows me. I roll my eyes and shimmy into my leggings. It's pretty hard to feel like you have the moral high ground when you're standing in a cami and green tights pulling on a hot dog bun, but I do my best.

"Can we talk?"

"I have to be the hot dog right now, obviously." I gesture to my suit. "So, no."

"I need to explain." She scoots after me, and I hate the way her dress rustles around her. It's annoying, like pencil tapping during a test is annoying, or someone snapping gum in your ear.

"You don't actually," I say, darting past her and heading for the nearest exit. "If you really want to explain it to somebody, you should explain it to Nick."

"Come on." She cuts back between me and the door, trapping me inside, and seriously? Seriously? Because I'm already starting to sweat.

"You know there's a time limit on how long I can be in this suit. Now move."

"No," she says, "not until you listen to me."

I try to elbow her out of the way, but she pushes back and I go flailing into the wall. A princess and a hot dog wrestling in the middle of the park breakroom, and of course I'd be on the losing end. A bunch of people look up, and a group of guys from the ride crew walk in—friggin' perfect.

Jessa looks a little shocked and offers me her hand. "Sorry, I didn't mean to."

I slap it away and push myself upright with what little dignity I can muster. "Just get out of my way."

I can hear her skirt rustling behind me as I shove open the door and break into a jog. This is stupid because a) this suit weighs roughly a thousand pounds and acts as an insulator, b) it's probably ninety degrees out here right now, and c) she's right behind me anyway because of course she can run in heels. I mean, she's Jessa. Perfect Jessa.

Perfect Jessa who has two people in love with her and probably doesn't give a crap about either one of them, and because of what, a complicated family life? Is that what Ari was implying? Hello, I'm the poster child for complicated family life and you don't see me being horrible and . . . oh. Okay, but still, screw this.

I turn around so fast I almost tip over. "What do you want?" I shout, and try to ignore the stunned faces of all the children who have probably never seen a giant hot dog scream at Cinderella before. One bursts into tears, and I immediately feel like the worst. Add it to the list.

Jessa puts her hands on her hips. "I want to explain."

"It's eight thousand degrees outside, and I am dressed like a hot dog." A bead of sweat trails down my face and drips off the tip of my nose before I can wipe it. "Not. The. Time."

"All right, later, then."

I drop my head back as far as it goes in this suit; raising my hands in the air at all the poor life choices that led to this moment and at the universe that put me on this planet in the first place. Because, seriously? I mean, seriously?

"Meet me by the castle at the end of your shift," she says,

"or I'll come find you." I'm sure she means it in a nice way, like if I can't get to her she'll come to me or whatever, but it doesn't *feel* nice.

"Whatever," I say, heading down the path toward the food court. I may be sweaty and miserable now, but the show must go on. Even if it kills me.

CHAPTER 26

I DART INTO THE CHANGING ROOM TO SWAP MY SUIT
for my park uniform, and then head to the bathroom. I want
to wash the sweat off my face and maybe even shore up my
self-esteem with some perfectly applied lip gloss before heading over to Jessa.

There's nothing to be done with my hair—it was a goner
the second I saw the forecast for today. But still, I pull as much
of it as I can under my fingertips, wrapping it three times with
a black elastic. Angie walks in as I finish up, glaring at me in
the mirror as she walks by, and okay, I guess I deserve that.

I scoop my hot dog suit off the floor where I tossed it, and shove it into one of the large garment bags we keep stashed in the back of the breakroom. We're not allowed to carry our characters without one; Mr. P's afraid it will traumatize the children.

Seb is sitting at one of the breakroom tables looking a little sweaty-sick as I walk out and check the time. I should be at the castle already probably, but Cinder-home-wrecker is going to have to wait a few.

"You okay?" I ask.

Seb gestures toward his Gatorade. "Will be," he sighs. "Why is it so hot?"

"Because it's summer?"

"Right," he says, lowering his head to the table. "Oh, my mom says to tell your dad hi back, by the way."

I chuckle. "Awesome. But if they keep this up, we should start charging them for this service."

"You taking that to Marla?" he asks, pointing toward my bag.

"Yep."

"Tell her I'm sorry again."

"Man, I'm everybody's messenger today," I tease, and I hear him laugh as I head out the door.

Marla eyes me as soon as I step inside. "Please tell me you didn't get sick again. I've lost three suits to puke already today."

I set my bag on the counter. "No, gross, but thanks for the visual. I'm just checking it back in. Who went down today?"

"Seb, Megan, and Ari."

"Ari?" That doesn't make sense at all. Seb and Megan are both costume kids like me, so that's not really out of the ordinary. But Ari? He's got no excuse. He's just in a glorified suit.

"Yeah, poor kid. I don't know what happened, but he left early and there's puke all over his shoes. He looked like he was about to cry."

"Weird," I say, and then it hits me. I bet Jessa dumped him or something. I mean, what else would make Prince Charming blow chunks all over his special shiny shoes?

Marla unzips the garment bag and pulls out the hot dog. "I'd take sweat over puke any day, honey."

"Me too. Are you even gonna have time to clean that tonight with everything going on?" I grimace because the idea of having to do another round in that sweat-soaked thing super skeeves me out, but I'm basically at her mercy.

Marla winks and leans over the counter. "For you, I can get it done."

"Thanks, lady." I give her a wave and head out. If I hurry, I'll still have plenty of time to catch Jessa.

My phone beeps as I'm halfway across the park, and I slide my finger across the screen to unlock it.

Seeley: Funeral tomorrow 10 a.m.

Me: K, I'll be there.

Seeley: Thanks. How's work? Miss me yet?

Me: Hardly 😊

Seeley: Brat

Me: Punk

Seeley: You say that like it's a bad thing. 😉

Me: . . .

Seeley: You see Jessa yet today?

Me: On my way now. Ari puked!

Seeley: What? Why? Figures all the good
stuff happens when I'm stuck home.

Me: Heading to the castle now for the dirt.

Seeley: 😕 I want an update ASAP.

Me: Leave your window unlocked then!

Seeley: Always ♡

Jessa flings open the castle door, and I jerk my head up.
"Hey, I was coming to look for you." She smiles. She's still in
her princess dress, and that annoying crinkling-paper sound
of her skirt roars in my ears again.

I stop short of her, glancing down at my phone one last time. "Here I am."

"You want to come inside?" She stretches out her arm like this is her honest-to-god house. It's almost too much to take, the way the world seems to hand her things without making her work for it; like, oh, here you go, you want a castle? Have this one! Oh, you want more? How about a beautiful gown and a handsome prince *and* a diving pirate? Anything else? Anything at all? Gah, I can't stand it.

The shift in temperature as I step inside smacks me in the face. "You have air-conditioning?"

"Yeah." She slips out of her skirt and tosses it in the corner. "You'd be surprised how hot it gets in this costume. Mr. Prendergast put that little portable AC thing in here for whenever we need to cool down for a minute." She fans herself with a piece of paper and tugs at the sweaty leotard she has on underneath.

"I wear a twenty-five-pound hot dog suit—trust me, I would not be surprised." I rub my hands up and down my arms, warming them up as I look around the room. It's not very big, a little larger than the size of an average bathroom, really, but there's enough space for two chairs and a tray. I wonder how much time Jessa and Ari have spent "cooling down" in here together, and shudder.

"Right, sorry." She reaches down and pulls out a couple of small containers, setting them on the tray. "I got some stuff for us. I made the hummus fresh this morning, and there's veggie chips, carrots, celery, and, um, ranch dressing that I stole from the breakroom. I didn't really know what you liked."

"I like fries," I say, to be a jerk.

"I can run over to the Fry Shack. They always hook me up when Nick wants some."

"They do? They always make me pay." Wow, like I really needed one more reason to dislike Jessa.

"Oh, I can get fries for you all the time if you want. I don't mind."

"No, that's okay." I grab a carrot off the tray and flash her a big fake smile. "I don't need you to buy me off with fries, but thanks."

"I'm trying to be nice."

"Okay, well, I want to believe that." I sigh. "Except that it never came up until now, when you're actively trying to convince me to keep a secret for you, so . . . "

She dips a carrot in her homemade-fresh-this-morning hummus with such a frown on her face that I almost feel guilty. Almost.

"I just want you to have the whole story before you do anything. That's all," she says. "If you get to the end and you still want to tell the whole world—"

"Whatever you want to tell me, can we just get to it?" I grab another carrot from her pile and drop into the chair across from her. My seat wobbles on the uneven floor, and I try to look dignified while tilting slightly from side to side.

Jessa bites her lip. "I already broke it off with Ari, just so you know."

"I figured." I flick my eyes to the concrete wall of the little castle. I can't look at her anymore right now.

"You did?"

"Marla told me he puked and left all upset." I shrug. "I figured it was because you dumped him." Jessa laughs, like what I said was the funniest thing in the history of funny things. "Are you all right?"

"No, it's just . . ." She shakes her head, struggling to get the words out. "Do you honestly think Ari threw up because I dumped him?"

"Well, didn't he?"

"No." Her voice comes out all deep and scratchy, like she tore her throat up laughing. "Some kid got sick on him, and it triggered a chain reaction."

"Gross."

"Right?" She takes another deep breath, like she's trying to reset herself or something. "You need to understand, Ari and I were never this big dramatic thing."

"Except he's totally in love with you," I say, because I feel like if Jessa is going to break someone's heart, she should at least have the decency to realize she's doing it.

"Ari Seimer is not in love with me." Jessa's voice gets a little quiet, a little unsure, as the words come out of her mouth.

"Okay." I mean, it is okay. The only reason I told her was to hurt her, not to make her look all excited and confused. "My mistake." I grab my napkin off the table and toss it in the little garbage can beside me.

"Elouise, wait." The fear in her eyes looks real, like she only now realized that I really could take all the toys—hers and mine both—and go home. "Please, you can't go yet."

"Why not?" I stand up, brushing off my pants even though carrots don't make crumbs. I'd like to think it still conveys an air of nonchalance, though—at least that's what I'm going for.

Jessa, however, looks absolutely stricken. "Will you let me explain? Please."

I want to say no, but also I'm a teensy bit curious. Okay, maybe more than a teensy bit. "I guess I have another minute or two."

"The first thing you need to know is that my mom has these . . . rules."

"Rules?" I ask, because what do household rules have to do with anything anyway?

"More like expectations, really. I have to act a certain way and dress a certain way and . . . we didn't used to have money like we do now. My mom was a waitress, for god's sake. We wouldn't have anything without my stepdad, and it's like she's terrified that I'm going to embarrass him or something and he'll leave."

"That's messed up," I say, kind of pity-smiling so she knows I'm not a total asshole.

"Yeah, which is why if my mother ever found out Ari and I were even friends outside of work, she would flip. A townie on scholarship? That's her worst nightmare. The only reason she's okay with me dating Nick is because he's not from here *and* his parents have money."

"Oh, Seeley thought you kept dumping him because your mom made you."

Jessa scoffs. "If you think my mom would ever make me dump a dive team captain from a wealthy family, you've obviously never met her."

"Wait, hang on, do you even like Nick, or are you just

using him to get your parents off your back?" I ask. Okay, maybe I shout it a little, but come on.

"I care about Nick a lot. I would never intentionally do anything to hurt him. But Ari . . . he's my best friend. He's my Seeley, basically. Yes, things got out of hand, it was wrong of us and—"

"If Ari is your Seeley, then you should be with him."

"Like you and her are?" She raises an eyebrow, and I recognize the challenge.

I look down at the floor, wishing I could melt into it. "Yeah, exactly."

"Come on, are you really together?"

"Yeah," I say, a little too quickly. "Why would you even ask that?"

She wipes at her eyes and sniffs. "Because it doesn't make sense. Angie and Seeley went out the night before you told Nick you were together. And you always seem to have an excuse to be near my boyfriend, when you should be with her."

I scratch the back of my neck. "Well, I don't know what to tell you except you're wrong."

Jessa tilts her head, and for all the times I wished someone like her would see me, this isn't at all how I dreamed of it happening. "There's got to be more to it."

"There's not," I say, and did it get hot in here?

Jessa narrows her eyes. "Look at your face, Elouise."

"I can't actually look at my face because it's, you know, on my face." I check the time on my phone and scowl when I see it's five thirty. "I should already be home."

"You're lucky. I'm stuck here until after the six o'clock dive show."

"There is no six o'clock show," I blurt out. "How do you not even know that Nick's last dive is at four thirty?"

Jessa smirks. "You seem to know an awful lot about where my boyfriend is and when for somebody with a girlfriend."

"That doesn't prove anything."

"Listen, Elouise, I won't see Ari like that again, I swear. It was a mistake, and I fixed it. How about we both just agree to keep our noses out of each other's business and forget any of this ever happened?"

I push open the door and keep walking without answering, because what am I supposed to do with all this? What am I even supposed to do?

CHAPTER 27

IT'S LATE BY THE TIME I GET TO SEELEY'S.

She was with her mom shopping for "funeral clothes" all evening, and I had to have dinner with my dad first and let him know I was sleeping over. He's coming to the funeral tomorrow too. I knew he would, but he's letting me sleep over anyway because he's cool like that. Also, he knows if he didn't say yes, I would most likely sneak out anyway.

I climb up the tree, careful to skip the most rotted steps. Her dad already replaced the ones that ripped off after I fell, but I don't trust the rest of them. If I learned anything today, it's that even things that look great on the outside can be total crap underneath.

Seeley's window is closed when I get to it, the air-conditioning probably making the place subarctic as usual, but I can still see her through the curtains. I crouch down to get a better view, watching her sketch away in her pad. Her dark hair is pulled away from her face with four brightly colored clips, and she's in her favorite gray tank top and kitten pajama pants.

She looks up at me and smiles the kind of smile that you could just fall into forever and still never get sick of. I take a breath and smile back, sliding the window open and crawling inside. My foot gets a little tripped up on the sill, and I land on the floor with a less than graceful thump.

"Hi, Elouise," Seeley's dad calls from the other side of the closed door, and I laugh as I dust myself off before going to join Seeley on the bed.

She pulls out one of her earbuds and hands it to me. I pop it in, stretching out next to her and resting my head on my arms. It's a song I've never heard before, quiet and slow; a sad man singing a sad song to the whine of his guitar. She's drawing her two favorite superheroes kissing, and watching it all come together with this man crooning in my ear feels kind of . . . perfect.

I scoot a little closer, loving the way her arm brushes against mine as she sketches, so warm and alive, and I imagine her creativity sparking through her veins like magic. I don't know what I did to deserve her.

Seeley finishes up, dropping her pen onto the pad and

pinning it between the two covers. Her laugh comes out like a quiet huff. "What are you staring at?"

"You," I answer honestly. I roll to my back, which pulls the cord of her headphones tight against my face. Awesome.

She smiles again and pulls it out of my ear, taking hers out too and tossing them up on her nightstand. "How was work?"

"Hot," I say.

"How was your thing with Jessa?"

"Strange." I bite the inside of my cheek, deciding how much to divulge. "Honestly, it was kind of a disaster. One second she was promising me all the free fries I could eat, the next she was accusing me of faking being your girlfriend, and then she was back to begging me not to tell anybody what I saw." I tip my head to see Seeley better. "Did you know her mom used to be a waitress?"

"Wait, what?"

"Yeah, I didn't either. Bananas, right? I can't picture Mrs. Holier-Than-Thou walking into Dylan's Diner, let alone working in it."

"No, back up. Jessa said she knows we're faking?"

"Not really *knows*, more like suspects."

"Shit, this isn't good." Seeley starts messing with the clips in her hair, like she does whenever she gets really worked up.

I watch her for a second, narrowing my eyes. "Why are you freaking out?"

"This is bad. If she tells Nick we're faking and he believes her, it'll blow any shot you have with him."

"I actually still kind of feel weird about the plan anyway."

I flip onto my stomach and prop myself up on my elbows. "But we shouldn't be worrying about this tonight, tomorrow is your—"

"I don't want to talk about my grandma." She huffs. "What do you mean you still feel weird? This isn't more woe is me stuff, is it?"

I sigh. "It feels like I'm being all manipulative and sketch."

Seeley laughs. "That's because you literally *are* being all manipulative and sketch."

"What should I do?"

"We have to break up, I guess." She grabs her sketchbook again and starts frantically drawing another figure. I can't tell yet what it is, but I can tell by the way her pencil digs into the paper she's upset.

"We don't have to," I say.

Her head snaps up. "What do you mean?"

I can't really place the look on her face, but it makes my brain feel kind of itchy and warm. "I don't know. I think breaking up right now is a bit of an overreaction. I don't think we need to, yet. Let's stick a pin in it and see what happens."

Seeley goes back to sketching, creases forming on her forehead. "Stick a pin in it?"

"Yeah, I mean we have your grandma's thing tomorrow, and then we have the fireworks and the bake sale all coming up. I think we should take a minute and think about how everything should play out, you know?"

"Okay." Her hand freezes for a second, and then goes back to shading the curve of what I think is going to be a flying shield. "I mean, if that's what you want."

"Cool," I say, flipping around so my head is on a pillow. I pull out my phone and check on our fund-raiser. "Hey, look, we've been shared sixteen times and got some new donations."

"What are we up to now?"

"Eighty-seven dollars."

"Great, only one million, nine hundred and ninety-nine thousand, nine hundred and thirteen dollars to go." She sighs and sets down her drawing, crawling up the bed to lay beside me. She reaches over and flicks off the light. "Tomorrow is going to be a long day. We should get some sleep."

I don't say anything, but I can feel her still looking at me. I move closer again, making our arms touch.

"Good night," she says. Her voice pitches up at the end like it's a question.

I feel like I should say something deep here, something important and relevant that will carry us through all the weirdness of tomorrow, but when I open my mouth, all that comes out is: "Night."

CHAPTER 28

FUNERALS ARE WEIRD.

First there was the viewing, and what a mind trip that was. Everything smelled strange and a little off, and you have to stand really still while people walk up to you, pretending like they know you. Everyone, and I mean everyone, tries to hug you. I think half the time the hugger was mixing me up with Seeley, and the rest of the time I guess they didn't care. I went along with it either way, because it seemed like the right thing to do. Eventually my dad showed up, and it was such a relief to see him that I pretty much collapsed into him.

Next came the service. I sat with Seeley and her family on one side, and my dad on the other. I tried to remember all the appropriate times to say "and also with you" and stuff like that, and when to kneel and when to stand, and half the time I got it wrong. And Seeley was right next to me, but she might as well have been a million miles away.

After that was the gathering. This basically meant that everyone went back to Seeley's house and ate sandwiches. When they left, Seeley's mom did the dishes alone, even though I offered to help.

I heard her crying twice.

So that's what funerals are like. They hurt.

I used to sometimes think it would be better if my mom was dead, like if she'd been taken away from us instead of leaving by her own choice. But no, I was wrong. After today, I know I was wrong. Leaving is better. Leaving is definitely better.

Which is exactly why I'm sobbing into a pile of postcards when my dad comes upstairs to tuck me in. He scoops me up and carries me into bed, like he did when I was little, and I watch him clean up the mess through heavy-lidded eyes. He shoves one into his pocket as he heads out the door, and I wonder if he's thinking the same thing. The tears come again, but this time, I'm careful and I'm quiet and I don't bother anybody.

CHAPTER 29

"TONIGHT'S GONNA BE THE BEST." I'M STANDING BESIDE the carousel, waiting for Seeley to finish cleaning up her station so we can leave.

She shakes her head as she wipes off the last of the horses. "I don't know why you're getting all excited about a few fireworks and a bunch of fair food that you can literally eat here every day."

I widen my eyes in mock horror. "Don't you dare trash-talk the fireworks at the commons!"

"Who's going tonight anyway?" Her eyes flick back over to the diving area, where Nick is practicing flips on the trampoline. "Just us?"

"Has it ever been just us at the fireworks?"

Seeley rolls her eyes. "Okay, who, then?"

"Everybody, pretty much. Us, Nick, Jessa unfortunately, probably Seb, maybe Craig, Marcus, some girl from housekeeping, and I don't know, like the whole town. Are you new here, See? Everybody goes to Founder's Day fireworks."

It's true, they do. It's our only chance to see fireworks without having to watch them on TV or drive forty-five minutes. See, our town is way too cheap to put on a full Fourth of July fireworks display, especially not one that rivals other towns, so we just let them all have it and combine ours with Founder's Day the weekend before. I mean, nobody truly expects an epic fireworks display in June, right? We're all just willing to take whatever we can get, which more often than not is about two dozen fireworks, fired off one at a time, several minutes apart, from Mr. McClellan's field.

It never occurred to me that it was weird until last year, when Nick was still new and couldn't believe he had moved to a town that didn't put on their fireworks show on the actual holiday. He even made a shirt that said "The Fourth of July is THE FOURTH OF JULY" and wore it in protest.

But, judging by how many times he asked what the plans were for tonight, I think he's ready to fully embrace the practice this year.

Seeley groans, tossing the rag over her shoulder. "I just don't feel like dealing with a ton of people."

"We need this, Seeley," I whine. "*You* need this. Trust me, you'll have a good time. I'll make sure of it."

She sizes me up for a second and then rolls her eyes. "Fine, but you're buying the snacks."

"Deal."

The grass itches and tickles my feet where they hang over the edge of our too-small blanket. I try to keep them still anyway, focusing instead on the sight of Seeley pulling cotton candy by the handful out of a sticky plastic bag. I had meant to bring paper to make a petition for the park, but I forgot. Seeley says her sketchpad is way too expensive to use, so at this point, we've sort of all just resigned ourselves to eating junk food and people-watching. There are worse things, I guess.

Nick and Jessa showed up a half an hour or so ago, and now we're all kind of huddled together on a pile of overlapping blankets, Nick looking relaxed and happy, and Jessa coiled tighter than a rattlesnake. She's being extra nice to me tonight too, which makes me feel all weird and twisty inside.

Seb and Marcus only showed up long enough to drop off their gear, and then took off to find this new girl they met at the park today. I'm tentatively planning to resent them forever for abandoning me in this cesspool of awkwardness, but we'll see how the night goes.

Seeley grabs another chunk of pink fluff and tries to throw it in my direction, but Nick snatches it from the air and makes a big show of eating it. I grin and nudge him with my foot before rolling onto my back to stare at the darkening sky. It's barely dusk, so we have a bit before the fireworks start.

"It's gonna be really weird to not have the park next year," Nick says, because of course he can't just let us stew in this totally uncomfortable silence without putting in his two cents. "Who knows where we'll end up or what's gonna happen."

I sit up, frowning as I look at him. "Next summer is going to be miserable, probably, if we don't do something about it. People aren't even sharing my posts about the GoFundMe anymore. It's like they don't even care! Literally everything I read about making your page go viral says that it has to be successful in your own community first." I tilt my head back and glare at the sky. "Our community sucks."

Seeley bumps her shoulder against mine. "You promised me a good time, remember? No whining." Seeley tugs her backpack onto the blanket beside us and pulls out two bottles of what appears to be very flat Sprite. "And speaking of a good time . . . "

"Warm soda?" I arch my eyebrows. "Wow, you're really living on the edge."

"Ha, drink up." She twists the cap off hers and takes a swig, coughing a little as she swallows.

I grumble and follow suit, doing my best not to choke as the bitter taste of soda mixed with alcohol scorches its way into my belly. "Holy crap." I cough. "What is this?"

"Sprite." She smirks, and I raise my eyebrows. "Plus a healthy serving of vodka."

Nick chuckles and scoots up on his elbows. "Hey, share some with the rest of the class."

"You are such a dork," I say, but then he blushes, so I reach over and mess up his hair. Jessa frowns so hard I can feel it in my bones. Too bad, Jessa, you brought this on yourself. Sort of. I guess. I don't know.

Seeley nudges the bottle back to my lips. "Drink up, girlie."

"I have to drive later," I say. "I shouldn't." I don't even know why I'm fighting it. It's not like I've never had a drink before. Well, okay, only once and just beer, but still. It counts, right?

Seeley tugs on the various necklaces that dot her neckline, running one of the charms up and down the chain. "We can walk this whole town in thirty minutes, Elouise. We'll leave your car here if we have to, and you can crash at my place."

I snort. "If I didn't know any better, I'd think you were trying to get me drunk."

Seeley frowns and starts picking at a dandelion beside us. "I just need to not think tonight, okay? I need a night of . . . nothing."

I scrunch my forehead. "Seeley—" But she just sighs and takes another sip.

Nick takes the bottle from my hand and raises it for a toast. "To friends, fake Fourths, and feeling nothing." He leans forward to tap it against Seeley's, and everybody laughs except Jessa.

Nick offers her the bottle, but she shakes her head, so he passes it back to Seeley. I intercept it, curious to taste the plastic his lips just touched. It doesn't taste like anything, just regular old plastic and a little bit of booze. I sputter as the liquid slides up my nose, sending a bolt of pain shooting through my head. Alcohol plus nostrils does not equal a good time. "You win, vodka." I cough again. "You win."

"Lightweight." Nick laughs, and then Jessa smacks him on the bicep. I stare a beat too long at the rising red mark on his arm, and then I turn toward Seeley and take another swig. She's lying on the blanket with her arms raised over her head, like she's adrift on a little fleece raft in an ocean of grass. She looks at me and rolls her neck from side to side, smiling when there's an audible pop.

"That cannot be healthy," I say, feeling a little warm, a little tingly as the alcohol soaks into my bloodstream.

"You know what's not healthy?" She opens one eye and snatches the bottle from my hand. "How slowly you're drinking that."

I giggle, an actual honest-to-god giggle, and drop onto the blanket beside her. We're close enough that I can feel her body heat, warm and damp on this, the hottest of nights. I flick my eyes to the spot on her shoulder where her freckles match the constellations in the sky, and I smile. I get lost in her skin, sipping my drink and mapping the stars on her arm while everyone else talks and eats and laughs around me. I roll to my back and stare up at the sky. I count three shooting stars, but Seeley insists one of them was a plane.

She smells so good up close, like flowers and sunblock, and I realize that, if I stuck my tongue out right now, I could probably taste her perfume . . .

Which, okay, wow, that's a weird thought. How drunk *am* I? I lift the bottle, my eyes widening to find it significantly emptier than when it was handed to me.

I jolt up, staring into the lights of the food truck barely fifty yards in front of me.

Nick says something to me that sounds a little bit like "Welcome back," but I can't be sure because everything's gone a little fuzzy, a little spinny now. This is not great. Pull it together, Lou. Focus.

There's grease and sugar and fried dough all around me, the unmistakable scent of small town summer. I breathe deep and try to forget about any other smells that I might be smelling, like my best friend's skin or Nick's deodorant or Jessa's scowling face. Wait, you can't smell a face. You know what I mean. God, I hate vodka. I'm never doing this again.

"Are you gonna puke?" Nick asks, scooting back away from me.

"She's not going to puke." Seeley props herself up on her elbows, concern etching lines into her forehead. "Are you?"

I shake my head, but that makes my stomach flip. "Stop talking about puking."

Seeley sits up, leaning forward to take a good look at me. "You need to eat something."

"I like popcorn," I say, because my brain is hazy now and also because it's true. I scrunch up my face and drop back to the blanket. "Oh my god, I don't like this anymore. Someone invent a time machine. I need to go back and stop old me from opening the bottle."

"You're an adorable drunk, Elouise," Nick says, leaning his face over mine. "Do you want me to get you popcorn?"

"No, you are the adorable one," I mumble, and then, because I want to be sure to hate myself in the morning, I stick out my finger and boop him on the nose. Like, I literally even say "Boop." Somewhere, in the tiny last sober corner of my brain, my dignity is screaming.

Nick crinkles his forehead, and a little bit of hair slips into his face, which, being the Good Samaritan that I am, I reach up to push back. Nick looks surprised, and Seeley sort of gasps, and then I shut my eyes, all smirky and snuggly feeling.

"What the hell, Elouise," Jessa shouts. And oh, I forgot she was still there.

"Leave her alone, Jess, she's super drunk," Nick says.

I push myself back up and flick my eyes to Seeley, who looks decidedly unimpressed. Shit.

"Leave her alone? She's practically making out with you in front of me and her supposed girlfriend!"

"She is not," Nick groans.

"Yeah," I say, retreating to where Seeley is sitting. "Am not."

Jessa narrows her eyes and turns back toward Nick. "You don't think it's strange that she's all touchy-feely with you, but *they* never kiss, and *they* never make out? They barely act any different!"

"We're not exactly going to flaunt our relationship all over this backwoods town. We do have some sense of self-preservation, Jessa. Sorry to disappoint," Seeley says, and I've never been more proud. I have the smartest, cleverest best friend.

"Yeah, sorry to disappoint." I scowl and lean my head against Seeley's shoulder, which is sweaty and hot but somehow more comfortable than any shoulder in the history of shoulders ever, and oh my god, I am too drunk for this.

"We kiss all the time—you just don't know it," I say, shutting my eyes, and I'm just sober enough to feel Seeley stiffen beside me.

Jessa snorts. "Then why does Seeley look terrified right now?"

I open my eyes and sit up, studying Jessa's angry, pinched face, and Nick's confused one, before finally settling on Seeley's. "You're not terrified," I mumble. "Are you?" I don't know if she's looking at me like "Yay" or "Shit," but she shakes her head and I instantly feel better.

But everyone is staring, and I am so drunk, and, wow, she's kind of beautiful in the glow of the food truck, with her hair all clipped back and smelling like summer. Her face is only inches from mine and I could do it, you know. Right here, right now. I shut my eyes and lean forward and—

I am

      pressing

           my lips

                to hers

                     before I

                          can catch

                              myself.

She's soft, and warm, and tastes like spun sugar and vodka. Her lips are parted, and I can't tell at first if it's surprise or encouragement—but then she's kissing me back, and holy shit my best friend is a good kisser. I open my eyes long enough to see her, to make sure this is really happening, and then I slam them back shut, overloaded by the sensation. Seeley leans forward a little, losing her balance, and I drop back to the blanket.

"Get a room!" Nick whoops, and when we pull apart, I touch my lips because wow that was amazing. And then I freeze, my whole body tensing up like I've been electrocuted, because um . . . what? Seeley's staring at me with wide eyes and yeah, I wanted to kiss her, wanted to get Jessa off our back, but . . . I don't even know.

I squeeze my eyes shut; this is too much: too much alcohol and cotton candy coursing through my veins, too many people here beside me, staring and wondering and wanting me to do things or not do them, and I can't even think straight anymore with so many sets of eyes on me. My lips taste like the cotton candy Seeley was eating and the crowd is filling up around us, coming to see the spectacle of explosions in the air, and they're stepping and squeezing onto my little fleece oasis like animals charging the gate, and I can't.

I can't.

I have to go. Right now. Immediately. Before my brain flips itself inside out and all the butterflies welling up in my stomach come screaming out of my throat. I open my eyes, frowning at the confusion scrawled on everyone's faces. "I gotta go."

I jump up and start walking, not even caring that my flip-flops are still tucked under the edge of the blanket behind Seeley. I weave through the crowd, feeling so, so lost, and drunk and mixed up beyond belief. I start to run, shoving people out of my way, until my feet can match the speed of the thoughts spiraling through my brain. I shove until I break out, until I'm standing in the gravel beside the road at the very edge of the park, the small stones biting hard into my soft skin.

Seeley's hand wraps around my wrist, an anchor in the storm, and she jerks me around fast before I run into the road. I stare at her with wide eyes as the first firework goes off, spattering against the dark sky in a mess of bright pink and white. A bead of sweat trails down her neck and gets caught in the strap of her tank top, and she's staring at me, and I can't tell if she's mad or not. I can't even tell. We're just standing here, waiting for something to happen, anything. Our eyes flick to the sky, and then back to each other.

"Come on." She tugs my wrist hard after her. "You want to run, let's run."

And so we do, around the edge of the crowd and across the street, with the earth scraping at our feet where it can't quite catch us, her blanket whipping against my legs as I race to the beat of her backpack. She leads this time and I follow, darting into the quiet, dark part of the park where no one goes on nights like this because half the sky is obscured by old willow trees.

We run until her grasp slips from my wrist to my hand, until our fingers tangle together and lock into place, until my breath hitches and my foot slips, and we crash to the ground together, our bodies vibrating from the force of our laughter.

"Are you okay?" she asks, but I'm laughing so hard I can't talk and there are tears in my eyes. Because this is a summer night, and a boozy head, and my best friend in the whole world, and everything else is just clutter to untangle in the morning. It doesn't even matter right now. It doesn't.

Seeley pushes on her thighs with her hands to stand up and walks over to where the blanket fell when we did. She tosses it in my direction and I bunch it under my head, letting the damp earth soak into the back of my clothes while I stare up at the sparkling sky above.

"Oooh, a heart. I love when they do that one." Seeley pulls the bottles out of her backpack again and hands me one. "Drink, before we sober up."

"I don't know," I say, because more booze sounds like both the best and worst idea ever. But I take the bottle and gulp until I feel the burn even in my feet because I kissed Seeley, and it really didn't suck.

"That was kind of an amazing kiss," I say, because I have no filter without alcohol, so I definitely don't have one with.

"Yeah?" she says, and kind of ducks her head and blushes.

"You gotta teach me how to do that."

"Okay," she laughs.

I smile and stare up at the sky, watching the little bit of fireworks I can see through the branches. I have the best, best friend in the world, and everything is roses. "They totally bought it too."

"What?"

I turn my head toward her, a sleepy smile on my face. "Nick and Jessa, I mean."

"Right," she says, gripping her bottle so hard it crinkles. "Yeah."

It's not what she says, but the way she says it, that cuts

through the haze enough to set off an alarm. "Are you mad?"

"No," she huffs, ripping the blanket out from under my head and shoving it into her backpack. "How could I possibly be mad, Lou?"

I sit up slowly, rubbing the back of my head where it hit the ground. "What's your problem?"

"What's my problem? Oh gee, I don't know. Maybe it's that you've been using me all summer, and I'm over it. Am I even on your radar as a person anymore? Or am I just this thing that follows you around and does whatever you want?"

"What are you talking about? Of course you're a person." I rub my hand over my face. "You're my best friend."

"Are you sure about that?" she snaps.

"I'm way too buzzed for this." I rub my eyes and yawn. "Can we talk about it in the morning?"

"Whatever."

"Okay, good," I sigh, hoping we can put this behind us and go back to drunk-watching fireworks.

"You are so dense, Elouise Parker," she says, and there are tears in her eyes . . . and okay, hang on a second. What am I missing?

Another round of fireworks makes me jump as it crackles across the sky. I reach my arm out toward her, but she jerks away.

She hugs her arms tight across her chest. "This is over."

"What's over?" I ask, standing all the way up, because this feels way too important to be lying on the ground for.

"Whatever this was." She waves her arms between us.

"Everything okay here?" Nick asks suddenly, and I jerk

227

my head toward him. He's standing a few feet away, with Jessa trailing behind him. They must have followed us when we ran off.

"Peachy," Seeley sneers as a smiley-face firework explodes into the sky over our heads.

Jessa tilts her head, looking from me to Seeley then back to me again. "What did you do now, Elouise?"

"Oh shut up, Jessa," Seeley groans.

Jessa's eyes go wide. "I'm on your side here!"

"No, you're really not," Seeley says. "And even if you were, you would be the last person I'd want on it."

"What's that supposed to mean?"

Seeley raises her eyebrows. "You know exactly what that means."

"If everybody could stop yelling and talking fast right now, that would be great," I plead.

"Screw this," Seeley yells.

"All right, everybody calm down." Nick drops his arm around Jessa. "We've all been drinking tonight—"

"I didn't have any," Jessa says, like that makes her better somehow.

Nick sighs and pinches the bridge of his nose with his free hand. "Okay, we've all been drinking tonight, except Jessa." He drops his hand. "I think it would be best if everybody went back home and slept it off. We can figure everything out in the morning."

"I'm too drunk to drive," I say. Also, I'm a horrible person, apparently, based on how Seeley is acting.

"We all are, except—" Nick says, looking at his girlfriend.

Seeley hangs her head back as far as she can and straight up growls, "I'm walking." She throws her bag over her shoulder and starts marching away. So, naturally, I march right after her.

"Seeley—"

"Stop following me!" she yells, and it's loud, super loud, the kind of loud that shakes a friendship to its core.

"Can we talk about this?"

"No!" She doesn't even hesitate, doesn't even slow down.

I sprint forward and grab onto the edge of her backpack, yanking her back. "Stop!"

She jerks it away with the most furious face I have ever seen. "Get away from me, Elouise!"

"You're not walking off alone, even if you don't talk to me!" I yell back, because if she's being dumb and loud, then fine, I can be too.

Nick comes jogging up, standing between us and holding up his hands. "Okay, listen, nobody is walking around drunk by themselves. Either we all walk together, or we all ride with Jessa."

"I go where Seeley goes," I say.

Seeley looks at me and shakes her head. "Screw it," she says. "Driving will get this over with faster."

We all sorta turn back to where Jessa is standing. "I hate you guys." She sighs, pulling out her keys, and then stomps back the way she came. We stand there for a minute, not totally sure if she's abandoning us or saving us, but then she turns around and flails her arms. "Well, come on, then!" And wow, she sounds totally pissed.

CHAPTER 30

"WILL YOU TALK TO ME, PLEASE?" I THINK I'M BEING very, very quiet and also very, very convincing, but based on the way Seeley sighs and goes back to staring out the car window, I suspect I am being neither.

We're crammed into the backseat of Jessa's tiny car, squished in beside a pile of princess dresses, which, weird, because nobody else takes their costumes home, but whatever. Nick is sitting up front in the passenger seat, frantically flipping through songs, and if he's looking for something in particular, it doesn't seem like he's finding it.

"Why are you so mad at me?" I whisper.

"Probably because you're a crap girlfriend, *Elle*," Jessa says from the front seat. Which I then kick, because come on, a little privacy, please.

Nick shushes her and starts murmuring something I can't make out, and I go back to staring at Seeley. I reach out and tug her wrist, but she yanks it away and glares at me like I burned her or something.

"Seeley," I say, but then I drop my head back. There's no use in finishing. I don't even know what to say.

Jessa pulls up to my house first, because of course she would want to get rid of me the fastest, but I don't move.

"Elouise. This is *your* house," Jessa says, as if I don't know that. "Get out."

"I'm not getting out of this car until Seeley talks to me." I cross my arms, feeling a little bit proud of myself for coming up with such a clever plan in my current condition.

Seeley stays staring out the window. "Get out of the car, Lou."

"Lou?" Nick turns toward us, scrunching up his face. "You call her Lou?" He kind of chuckles to himself, and I swear Jessa groans, but I can't even worry about them right now, because Seeley being this upset is freaking me out.

"Look at me, at least," I beg. "Please. I don't get why you're so pissed."

Seeley pushes out her lips and nods a few times, like she's

figured something out, and when she turns and looks at me, my stomach sinks right down to my toes. This is bad. This is real bad, the kind of bad that sobers a person up real quick. "I can't do this with you anymore."

"Can't do what?" I choke out, my voice low and quiet.

"Anything. Everything." And the tears are back in her eyes, and maybe mine too, because everything is a whole lot of things, after all. Everything is *everything*. It's too much. My best friend, my Seeley, is looking at me like she hates me right now, and I'm suffocating.

I lean back against the car door, knocked back by the weight of what she said. "I mean, not *everything*-everything, right? Like you're still my best friend and—"

"Just go," she says, turning back to the window.

"No," I say, but the door is opening behind me, and Jessa is sort of half catching me, half pulling me, as I spill out. She drags me back away from the car, and Nick is getting out and telling her to stop, that he's got this, but I keep looking back at Seeley, and she keeps staring out the other window and none of this makes sense at all.

None of this makes sense at all.

CHAPTER 31

MY HEAD HURTS.

My head hurts really bad.

I sit up slowly, untangling my limbs from the blankets and taking inventory of all my sore spots. How did I end up here again?

Oh right.

I reach over to my nightstand and grab my phone. There's a text from Nick asking if I'm okay, but nothing from Seeley. I start to text Nick back, but that feels a little weird, like I'm going behind Seeley's back or something. I lean against my pillow, stare up at my Black Widow poster, and try to tease apart this giant knot in my head. The only thing is, Seeley gave me this poster, and we hung it together, so staring at it kind of gives me this awful feeling all over, because what did I do?

I mean, when she said she was done with everything, she couldn't have really meant *everything*, right? Like she didn't mean being best friends, or hanging out all the time, or whatever. There's no way. What would that even look like?

I kind of want to shoot her a text that says something like "Define everything, please." But I'm scared that would piss her off even more. I need to come up with something clever, something sweet, something that will make her forgive me right on the spot. I pick up my phone again, totally determined to type out something so charming and delightful that it will immediately fix everything, make her happy, and/or create world peace, all at the same time, but instead I write:

Me: Can I come over?

I can see that she read it, and that she started to reply, but the little dots disappear just as quickly as they appeared. I'm left staring at this useless hunk of glass and metal in my hand—and what good is it anyway if it can't get me my best friend back? I stay like this, perfectly still and ridiculously hungover, until my phone vibrates in my hand.

Seeley: I'll stop by this afternoon. I need to get my stuff anyway.

Me: What stuff???

Seeley: Don't make this harder, please.

Me: . . . ???

Seeley: I have to go.

I sit up all numb and dumbstruck because what is she doing? I mean, what stuff is she even talking about? After ten years of hanging out on the daily, we don't really have our own stuff—we just have stuff we share. Where does she think she ends and I begin? How can she even tell?

My walls are literally covered in her drawings, and most of the pens on my desk are those expensive Copic markers she always insists on using, not to mention like half the stuff in my closet is technically hers and half the stuff in hers is technically mine. I wouldn't even begin to know how to separate it all. I wouldn't want to. I don't want to. I won't.

I roll over to my side, burying my face in the pillow she always uses. I pull it into a hug, but it's cold and fake and I liked it better when we were lying shoulder to shoulder with our arms barely touching, and better still when we had the most phenomenal kiss of my life. I mean, wow, thanks for holding out on me, Seeley. If I'd known she could kiss like that, I would have been doing that all along with her.

I mean, wait, no. What am I talking about?

My phone buzzes, and I flip it around to check who it is. Please let it be Seeley, please let it be Seeley, please let it be—

It's not, because of course it isn't. It's Nick. The same Nick I have a crush on, I remind myself. The same Nick that I have been scheming and plotting to win over all summer. The same Nick that I booped on the nose last night—I still can't believe I did that. But that's beside the point.

His text sounds concerned. He wants to know if I'm okay, wants to know if I need to talk, wants to be there for me, it looks like, exactly as planned. Exactly on schedule. Exactly everything I ever wanted.

And there's that word again: *everything.*

I hate it.

I should be jumping for joy right now. I should be over the moon. I should be doing a happy dance on the way to my diving pirate wedding . . . but I'm not. I'm sitting here freaking out because my best friend wants to take her stuff back and keep her lips to herself. What the hell is the matter with me?

I take a deep breath and slide my fingers over the letters on my screen. I swear to god I mean to text Nick, I swear to god I do, but something happens and my finger slips and whoops, look at that, I'm texting Seeley instead.

Me: Please don't bring my stuff back.

Me: Like if you were going to when you get yours, I mean.

Me: And if you didn't think about that yet, then like, don't.

Me: And pretend I didn't say anything.

Me: Don't let this give you any ideas.

Me: Just keep not thinking about it.

Me: Because . . . just because, okay?

Seeley doesn't write back to any of my messages. She doesn't even open them, but I stare at the screen until I can't anymore, until my eyes are burning out of my head. I don't blink and she doesn't write back. She doesn't. And my head is spinning out at a million miles per hour because it just hit me that I might have feelings for my fake girlfriend slash best-friend-forever, who I'm pretty sure dumped me on both accounts last night.

I'm definitely . . . something . . . with her. Something more than friends. Something more than friends that definitely should involve more kissing.

But here's the thing.

Nick is around, and Nick is the easier choice. Even with Jessa still in the picture, Nick would be ten thousand times less complicated than trying to win over Seeley. But even thinking about Nick feels messed up, and strange, and twenty-five kinds of wrong because my brain is inside out over this girl, this girl who's been standing right in front of me for almost my whole entire life, and I feel like I'm finally seeing her right now, for the first time, and she's—

She's done.

She's coming over here to get her stuff.

She dumping me as a girlfriend and a friend-friend, and I don't know if I can stop her and I don't know if I should. Maybe I deserve it. Maybe I'm just the kind of person you leave. Maybe it's better this way, without her knowing how I really feel.

Oh god, I can't. What if I'm just still drunk or something? I mean I'm not, but like what if my judgment is eternally impaired from kissing Seeley while under the influence? What if these aren't real feelings, what if these are vodka feelings that somehow got permanently imprinted in my brain? Is that possible? Oh god, I am never drinking again.

I run to my laptop and google "vodka feelings" because I feel like that's a thing that the internet would know about and talk about with each other, but all that comes up is people talking about whether different types of alcohol cause different types of moods, and dammit, guys, who even cares when I'm trying to figure out if I have real feelings for the girl who is planning to totally gut me by taking back every single shred of my life that she ever touched.

YOU ARE NOT HELPING, PEOPLE OF GOOGLE.

I squeeze my eyes shut and count backward from ten, the way my dad used to make me do when I was all little and irrational and whatnot. So, okay. Calm down, Lou, focus on counting, because we need to stop this line of thinking. It's no good for anybody. I need to be worrying about fixing this friendship, not falling in love.

Okay, deep breath. Let's be logical about this.

I mean, I'm definitely not in love with my best friend. That would be bananas. So no, I am definitely, definitely not.

Definitely not.

Just so we're clear.

CHAPTER 32

I AM DEFINITELY IN LOVE WITH MY BEST FRIEND.

Fuck.

CHAPTER 33

I'VE BEEN CLEANING MY ROOM FOR AN HOUR.

I want it to be perfect.

I shouldn't care, probably. This afternoon, for all intents and purposes, Seeley will carve out my heart and feed it to me, while having basically zero idea that she's doing it. I mean, she's going to know she's gutting me as a friend, but she won't know that she's also gutting me as a girl I'd like to spend a lot more time kissing and snuggling and generally staring at with goo-goo eyes.

Anyway, deep breath and all.

I flick my eyes to the mirror, staring at the five billion or so pictures of us shoved between the frame and the shiny glass beneath it. And because I'm a total glutton for punishment, I sorta wonder when exactly I fell in love with her. Because the whole thing feels so inevitable and eternal or something, now that I've gone ahead and wrecked it before it even got off the ground.

To be honest, it sorta feels like maybe I was born loving her, like "property of Seeley Jendron" was stamped across the bottom of my heart this whole time—in a tiny hidden place where I couldn't read it without the right perspective. I wonder what name's written on hers. Probably not mine, at least not anymore.

I mean, thinking back, I broke up with Malia last year because she wanted me to hang out with Seeley less. And I was always jealous when Seeley was with Sara and was all distracted and wrapped up in that. And I don't really think there's been like a single day since we met that we haven't at least talked or texted. So, I mean—

No, I have to stop. I can't think about this anymore. Because like five minutes after I realized that I was absolutely, totally in love with Seeley, it hit me that telling her that would probably be the worst thing I could ever do to her. And I've done some pretty terrible stuff to her already this summer.

I've sort of been obsessing over that all afternoon, running through everything that's happened. And wow, okay, I don't think I'm a terrible person, but I've definitely been acting like it. I've been selfish, the most selfish person in the world probably, I've been a liar, and I've been an all-around shitty friend. Which means, as much as I want to run up and tell her I'm in love with her, I know I shouldn't. There's no way she feels the same way, so telling the truth would just be one more selfish thing. It would ruin everything even more.

There's that word again: *everything*. I hate that word.

I wipe at my eyes—I'm not crying, you're crying, or whatever—and go back to cleaning my room. When she shows up here this afternoon, I'm going to apologize until her ears bleed, and I'm gonna find a way to make it up to her. Like, sure, I fell in love, but that's on me. I didn't think it would ever happen, I didn't at all.

I Just Didn't Think: An Autobiography by Elouise May Parker, and all that.

No, what Seeley deserves—what I hope she still wants—is a real best friend, someone that puts her first and doesn't drag her into schemes all the time. And I think I can be that. God, I *want* to be that.

So I sit in my chair, and I twist it from side to side, and I think of all the very perfect and not at all weird or revealing things that I am going to say to get our friendship back on track. And, maybe once or twice, I think about what it would be like to look at her and say, "I love you," and imagine what it would feel like if she said it back. But mostly the other stuff, the friendship stuff, because that's what matters the most, and I almost sort of have it figured out, the perfect thing to say . . .

. . . when I realize that it's getting dark, and she's not coming.

CHAPTER 34

IT'S BEEN FOUR DAYS SINCE SEELEY TEXTED.

Four days since she didn't show.

And I've felt every second of them without her.

I faked sick for the first two, spent them lying in bed rehearsing speeches and typing out texts to her and not sending them. But by day three my dad started to catch on—especially when I refused to even come downstairs and watch the Fourth of July fireworks on TV. The only thing worse than going through this is going through this with my father anxiously pacing outside my door. I couldn't take it anymore. So here I am today, standing in a hot dog suit with my heart in my throat, staring at the breakroom door and hoping Seeley will walk in.

"You never texted me back," Nick says, shoving his face into my line of vision. "I was worried. Did you guys really break up?"

I blink slow, and take a deep breath. There hasn't been enough time yet for me to learn how to answer that question without feeling like I'm being swallowed up by the sun. I look at him, squinting, like if I try hard enough I could feel something for him again. If I could, maybe all the hurting would stop. Maybe everything would be okay. Maybe all the people I love wouldn't leave. I don't know.

The breakroom is filling up with people on lunch, and he's dripping all over the floor, his skin prickling under the air-conditioning, like it doesn't even matter. I wonder where his towel is, and why he's standing here soaked, as if he rushed right over when he saw me walk by in my suit. I squeeze my hands into fists at my sides, fighting the urge to yell in Nick's face about how this is all his fault somehow. I know it's not, but still.

Why did he have to be cute? Why did I have to be stupid? Why did I have to crush on a sweet boy with a secret lisp who jumps into pools and bakes cupcakes and is *just* insecure enough to be endearing? And how come his girlfriend is the one who's cheating, but I'm the one whose heart is broken? I glance down at the floor, nodding twice and keeping my lips pressed in a hard line, too scared of what will escape if I don't.

Nick runs his hands through his hair, sending rivulets of water streaming down his face. "Sucks." His eyes are so full of pity when I look at him that I almost hate him. I swear to god, in this moment, I really could. The words are right there, on the tip of my tongue. It would be so easy to open my mouth and let them fall out, to tell him the truth about Jessa, if only to wipe that look off his face.

It's not fair that I'm the only one hurting here.

Angie walks in with a couple of the girls from housekeeping, rolling her eyes when we make eye contact. Sorry, I want to shout. Sorry for everything and to everyone, but mostly to Seeley, who won't even pick up her damn phone.

I bite my lip and scrunch my eyes shut, because I can't do this right now. I can't. I'm trying to be a better person. For real. At least that would make this whole situation mean something—like if I grew and embraced the life lesson here or whatever. At least that would make it count.

"Elouise." Nick reaches for my hand. "Lou." And I hate the way that sounds coming from his mouth. It's all wrong.

I think for a second that he's going to say something deep, something meaningful and sweet, some attempt at trying to cheer me up, at making me feel better. I hold my breath, waiting, because I want something like that to exist, for something, anything, to be the Band-Aid over this gaping wound. And I get it now, I know that's all he could ever be, that's all anyone else could ever be: a Band-Aid, a butterfly strip, a temporary measure, because this is the after, and all of the good stuff got left behind in the before.

"Yeah?" I ask, and my voice is just . . . it's just aching.

"Are we still getting together tomorrow night to get things ready for the bake sale? We're still on for Saturday, right?"

I pull my hand back, because even I have my limits. What does it really matter anyway? Why am I trying to be a better human being if it means I'll still be without the one person in the whole world that matters the most to me? I guess if I'm going to be a shit person to Seeley, then I might as well be a shit person all around, right?

I flick my eyes up to his. "Jessa's been cheating on you with Ari."

It's like the whole breakroom goes still. Nick is gaping like a fish, opening and closing his mouth with no words coming out, and I wonder if that's what I looked like after Seeley and I got into our big fight. I bet I did. And man, this whole room smells too much like chlorine and heartbreak and other people's food. My stomach flips, and I can't be here anymore. I can't.

"Sorry," I whisper, and then I bolt. I make it all the way to the second bathroom before I completely lose it. I duck inside, locking the stall door and peeling off my costume, letting the sobs wrack my body while all around me toilets flush and nervous mothers dart in and out, keeping their children safe.

CHAPTER 35

I BLINK SLOW AND STEADY, LONG ENOUGH AND SLOW enough that the whole world disappears and reappears between my lashes every single time. Now I'm here, I blink, now I'm not. I don't feel particularly inclined to get out of bed, let alone face the outside world, where I have successfully destroyed not one but like a thousand relationships, effectively tearing apart almost my entire circle of friends during what was supposed to be the most magical, best, perfect summer of my life. The impossible summer has been impossible all right.

I pull the blankets up to my chin and let my eyes drift closed. Is it possible to sleep until I leave for college next year? Probably not. Not on my dad's watch, anyway.

"Hon?" My dad cracks open the door. "You up yet? Don't you have to be at work at ten?" His words are soft, like I might still be sleeping, but he knows me well enough to know that I'm definitely not. I know he's noticed that Seeley hasn't been around for nearly a week, and I'm sure the curiosity and concern is eating him up. I wonder if he's called her parents yet. I don't think I want to know.

"I'm awake," I say. "Sort of."

"Are we going to talk about whatever's going on with you?" He pushes the door all the way open, leaning against the frame and tucking his hands into his pockets the way he does whenever he needs to look all small and nonthreatening. He used to do that around my mom a lot, especially when she was yelling at him. I haven't seen him do it in a while.

I pull the blanket back over my head with a groan. "No."

The bed dips under his weight as he sits beside me. "You know you can always talk to me, Elouise."

I frown. I know he really believes that, but I also know that may not include me telling him that I am definitely in love with Seeley. Because he'd probably freak, right? I mean, that's what parents do about that sort of thing.

"I can't tell you this." It hurts to say that. He pulls the blanket down, and I can tell it hurts him too by the way his forehead crinkles.

"Lou, I know it might feel like that, but I promise you, you can. Whatever it is, let me help you."

"I think I'm in love with Seeley." I blurt it out, just like that, and I don't know if it's because I'm brave or overtired or because I want to test this theory of his out right now. If anything is going to make him run screaming from my room, it would probably be that. He met Malia, sure, but even if I didn't exactly hide it, I never came out and said she was my girlfriend either. And even if I had, this is a whole different ball game since Seeley's practically a second daughter to him.

He freezes for a second and then tucks my blankets around my arms the same way he did when I was little. "And?"

I raise my eyebrows. "And? That's all you have to say?"

My dad leans back to look at me. "And what's the problem with that? She doesn't treat you well? Did she do something awful and now we have to hate her forever?"

"We don't hate her." Even the idea of hating her hurts too much.

"Oh, good, because that would have made it very awkward when her parents come for dinner next week." He chuckles, clearly enjoying his own little joke. "But if we don't hate her, if she doesn't treat you bad, and if you love her, then why isn't she here? I haven't seen her for days, which has got to be a record for you guys."

"How are you being so cool about this?"

"Cool about what?"

"Cool about the fact that I told you I was in love with Seeley, who is a girl. And I'm a girl. So I'm a girl that likes girls. Sort of."

"Sort of?" He crinkles his eyebrows. "What does 'sort of' mean?"

"I mean that I don't only like girls, like I'm not, you know."

"A lesbian?"

I turn about a thousand shades of red and wish the earth would swallow me whole, because my dad said the word *lesbian* and it's the weirdest thing ever.

He lets out a nervous laugh and shrugs. "What?"

"It's weird that you're not freaking out."

The smile slips off his face a little, and he squeezes my arm. "I think I'm freaked out by the fact that you felt you had to keep this a secret from me. I know there're things you don't want to talk about with your dad. You're allowed privacy, same as I am, but, Lou, don't ever feel like you *can't*. This is a big thing to feel like you had to hide."

I find a particularly interesting spot on the wall to stare at, afraid that if I look at his face, I'll completely fall apart. "I wasn't hiding it. I was just . . . not telling you." I look up at him and he tilts his head. "Sorry."

"You don't have to be sorry."

"I bet you're totally freaked out right now and trying to cover it up."

"Lou, this isn't news to me, even without you putting it in so many words before. If you think I didn't know what you and Malia were up to last year . . . " He trails off. "And no, I'm not 'totally freaked out' right now. Are you 'totally freaked' that *I* like women?"

"Why would it bother me that you like women?"

"Oh, it doesn't?" He grins. "Huh, weird, because it doesn't bother me that you like them either." He laughs, and everything about his body language says *I told you so*.

I huff and turn away. "I guess I expected it because *I'm* freaked out that I like girls." I reconsider. "Okay, no, that's not true, girls are pretty great."

"All right," he chuckles. "But you're going to have to fill me in here. If we aren't freaking out about liking girls, then what are we freaking out about?"

"It's more that I like *this* girl in particular."

"Is that why Seeley hasn't been around? You're taking some space to work out your feelings for her?"

"Sort of," I say.

"Do you want to tell me the rest?"

"No." I try to hide under the blanket, but he stops me, pulling it back down from my face.

"Fair enough. I'm not going to pry, but I'm here if you need me." He looks at his watch, the corners of his lips twisting up as he thinks. "Pancakes or waffles? You should have enough time to eat before work." Only, when he starts to get up, I sit up fast and grab his wrist to make him stay.

"I used to like this boy Nick," I say.

Dad wrinkles his forehead and sits back down. "I thought you said you liked Seeley?"

"I do, but I didn't then. Or I did, but I didn't realize it." I shake my head. "Just, let me say this before I lose my nerve, okay?"

"Okay, shoot."

"So, I liked Nick, but Nick was dating Jessa. I kind of made Seeley pretend to be my girlfriend so that I could get closer to him, in the hope that we'd end up together before he left for college and I missed my chance."

"How would dating Seeley make you and this Nick boy get together?"

"I don't know, I thought it would for some reason, like maybe we could be better friends and it wouldn't be a big deal because I had a girlfriend too. And then, I don't know, maybe he would break up with Jessa or something, and then I would fake a breakup with Seeley, and Nick and I would live happily ever after."

My dad sighs. "Until he leaves for college next month, you mean."

"I guess. Yeah. But people have long-distance relationships all the time."

"They do." He frowns. "But usually not ones built around the fact that one of them lied and schemed to get the other one to like them."

"Okay, true," I say, "but anyway, none of that really matters because then something happened."

"You realized how ridiculous this all was?"

"No. Well yeah, kind of. Mostly I realized that I didn't want to break up with Seeley anymore, at the same time I also realized that Seeley never actually wanted to date me in the first place. She just sees me as a friend, same as always. But none of that matters anyway, because we got into a giant fight and now she doesn't even want to be that." I exhale, and it sounds all shaky and pathetic. "Whatever happens, I don't want to lose her forever, I can't."

"I don't think it's possible for you two to lose each other forever," he says, and I want to believe that so bad, I really do, but I know there's no way he knows that for sure.

"People lose each other all the time," I say. "We lost Mom."

Dad swallows hard; we both know there's nothing he can say to that.

"I want everything to be okay, and it's not."

"I know, baby, I know." He pulls me in, wrapping me up tight in his arms. I don't know when exactly I started to cry, but I don't think I'm ever going to stop. And the worst part is that my dad really does know. He lost the love of his life, and he never got her back; he just got stuck with me and a bunch of postcards that I steal from him and hide underneath my mattress.

"Waffles?" He leans back and wipes at his own eyes. "If we hurry, you'll still make it to work on time."

I rest my cheek on my knee, wishing I was five years old again. "Do I have to go?"

"Yes." He smiles. "You have to."

I slump back in my bed with a sigh. "Okay, but Death Star waffles today, because that's just how it's gonna be."

"Fair enough," he says, heading to the door.

"Hey, Dad?" I mean to thank him for being cool, for this conversation, for life, but the words get all stuck in my throat.

"Yeah, honey?"

"Um, Seb's mom says hi back." I don't know where that came from. It's worlds apart from *Thanks for being a good dad*, but still.

He looks confused, and then sorta happy.

"You should call her," I say, deciding to run with it.

"Why would I call Sharon?"

"She obviously likes you. She said hi back."

"Oh, well, if she said hi back." He laughs, and his voice goes all soft. "I love you, Lou."

"Love you too." I flash him a watery smile. "Now scram so I can get dressed for work."

He shakes his head, grinning. "One Death Star waffle coming up!"

CHAPTER 36

I SLIDE MY CAR INTO THE SPOT AND PUT IT IN PARK, MY spine temporarily propped up by officially licensed waffles and another pep talk from my dad. I deflate the second I see Nick walk by, studiously avoiding eye contact with me as he books it through the gates. I don't blame him. In fact I'm kind of grateful for the reprieve. If everybody would go ahead and avoid me today that would pretty much be the best.

"What is the matter with you?" Jessa screeches.

I knew I jinxed myself as soon as I had that last thought, but I didn't think it would immediately conjure Jessa to my car window. Her hard, angry hands knock against my driver's side window like she wants to smash right through. She just might too. Hell hath no fury like a princess scorned or whatever.

I contemplate sitting here, staring straight ahead until she leaves or gets tired, but neither of those options seems super possible considering the intensity with which she is currently knocking. I sigh and flick the keys to turn off the ignition, pulling them out slowly and shoving them into my bag. Jessa seems to calm down a little, but she makes no move to leave. She's leaning against the car now, her arms crossed in front of her, her lips turned down in a tight angry frown.

I pop my door open, perching my butt on the edge of my seat and biting my lip as I slide to face her. She opens her mouth to yell, and I can tell by the way she straightens up and squares her shoulders that it's going to be a doozy.

I drop my head, letting my ridiculous hair fall around my face like a protective shield. "I deserve it," I say, which must catch her off guard because her breath hitches in her throat a little, and her hands fall to her sides.

"What?"

I tilt my head up to see her better. "I said I deserve it, whatever it is you're about to yell at me. I absolutely deserve it. Telling him the way I did was a crappy thing to do. I've been acting like an absolute monster, and I'm sorry." I know this now because my dad pointed it out to me twice over waffles this morning, but I'm not going to tell her that.

Jessa looks up at where the roller coaster slowly cranks up the incline on its morning test run. I can already imagine the mechanic standing there with his clipboard, shaking his head. I wonder if there's any hope for it.

"It's a lot less fun to scream at you when you're apologizing."

"Sorry." I fiddle with my finger, biting the skin at the side of my nail. "It seemed like you were gearing up for something pretty impressive too."

She smirks a little, like she can't help it, but then frowns, turning back to me with hard eyes. "You ruined everything, you know. Nick won't talk to me, and now neither will Ari. If it gets back to my mom, I'll probably be grounded for life. I can't believe you. I thought we were friends." I hear the pain in her voice, and it makes my head hurt in places it shouldn't.

I rub my hands over my face. "If you want to rip into me, if you think that will help, then we can do that. Like I said, I probably deserve it. But I don't think we were ever really friends, do you? I mean, we never hung out one-on-one or anything. I don't even have your number. We were like acquaintances or whatever at most, right?"

Her eyes widen as her hands make her way to her hips. "You are so screwed up, Elouise. I don't even know why I'm wasting my time."

"No, seriously, you can yell at me."

Please yell at me. I deserve it. I need it. Anything to unload a little of this guilt I'm carrying around. But Jessa shakes her head and walks away.

I sit in my car, hide in it really, until I'm positive that everyone else has spread out into their various positions around the park. I swear my feet weigh ten thousand pounds as I finally trudge across the parking lot to the entrance. The large iron gates loom ahead of me, more like a warning than a welcome. It's never been like this before, and I hate it.

The girls at the ticket booth giggle when I walk by, and it could be a coincidence, sure, I don't ever even talk to them, but also it could be the more likely thing, which is that the whole park knows what I did during my meltdown.

"Elouise," Mr. Prendergast says.

I'm attempting to slink past his office unnoticed on my way to the breakroom, but obviously the universe can't even give me that. "Hey, Mr. P."

"Is everything all right?"

"Not really, no." There's no use lying. If the girls up front heard about what happened, I'm sure he did too.

"Would you mind coming in here?" His voice is stern enough to suggest trouble and I start running through all the things I've done in my head. I mean, you can't get fired for being a bad friend, right? Or can you? Shit. I never actually read that HR guidebook thing he gave me when I first started here, but that seems like an oddly specific rule. Unless there's like a morality clause. Do part-time amusement park jobs *have* morality clauses? Is that a thing?

"Relax, Elouise, you're not in trouble. Have a seat."

So, okay, I guess I'm not doing a great job covering up how much I'm panicking. "What's up, Mr. P?"

"I wanted to check in with you before the day got busy. I spoke with your father this morning and he told me what happened and that you were still very upset."

"He did?" And I'm sure my father meant well or whatever,

but like it's a little weird for your dad to call your boss to tell him you're really upset about being in love with your best friend that won't even talk to you because you made her fake date you. I mean, I know this is only my first real job and boss or whatever, but that's weird, right?

Mr. P leans back in his chair. "We were going over some tax documents that seemed to be out of place in my file for some reason."

I slink a little lower in my seat. So my dad did know I took the files, which makes him being nice to me this morning all the more incredible.

"He mentioned to me that you were struggling with the idea of the park closing. He also expressed some concern that you might actually be plotting something, which apparently is something you're quite well known for." His voice is serious, but there's a slight hitch in it when he says this last part.

I don't know what to say here, so I don't say anything.

"I don't make a habit of explaining my personal life to my employees, but I'll make an exception since I've known you and your father for so long. Elouise, I'm not closing this place because I can't afford it. I am closing it because I have a grand-daughter in Boca who was recently diagnosed with leukemia, and whom I'd like to see more of."

"Adelyn has cancer? Is that why you've been making so many withdrawals?" I blurt out.

Mr. P leans forward over his desk. "For your father's sake, I'm going to pretend you didn't ask that. But hypothetically, if I had been making a lot of withdrawals, then yes, it would have been to take care of some expenses related to Adelyn's treatment." He leans back again, resting his hands in his lap. "But to get things back on track here, I want you to understand that this is not me walking away because I don't care—this is me making the decision that's right for my family, for myself, and, believe it or not, for this entire town."

I frown a little. "The town?"

"I have a good offer from a microchip plant that's been looking to move into the area for a while now. A business like that would do more for this town than this little amusement park could ever do. It could put this town back on the map."

And okay, I don't love the idea of a factory or whatever, but I can see for the first time that he's right. I'd heard people talking about that chip plant maybe moving in over the last couple years, and all the adults seemed super excited about it. Which maybe explains why my GoFundMe has been dead in the water.

I look down at the floor, toeing at the closest scuff mark. "What's going to happen to Butters?"

"Butters?"

"The carousel horse." I blush because I'm definitely too old to care, but I do.

"Oh." He smiles. "Butters will be moving to the town park with the rest of the horses. I'm donating the carousel; they belong here. The rest of the rides are being distributed around the state. Some will probably be sold for scrap, but no, Elouise, the carousel isn't going anywhere."

Tears prick my eyes, and for once, they are happy. "It isn't?"

"The only place it's going is five minutes down the road."

Mr. P stands up to open his door. "Now, if I'm not mistaken, there's a hot dog due in the food court in twenty minutes. Oh, but before you go, I have something for you."

I raise my eyebrows, because what could it possibly be? He pulls a tiny cardboard box out of the mini fridge he keeps filled with water beside his desk. It's wrapped with beautiful red and white string, and I'd recognize it anywhere.

"Is that what I think it is?"

He smiles and sets the box in front of me. "If I remember correctly, I owe you a cannoli, my dear." And if I come around the desk and give him a big hug before I walk out the door, well, nobody has to know.

I pull my phone out to text Seeley while I devour the cannoli on my way to the breakroom. I forgot for a second how screwed up everything is between us, and when I remember, it feels like I've been punched in the stomach. I guess sometimes your heart can feel light for a second, even when you don't deserve it.

I keep my head down as I cross the room, pulling the hot dog down from the rack and unzipping the black garment bag surrounding it. A piece of paper skitters to the floor, and I scrunch up my forehead. For a second, I think it's from Seeley and my heart starts to pound, but when I pick it up, I see that it's just a cleaning tag from Marla. *Hot Dog Girl*, it says, followed by the date.

And suddenly I feel more lost than I ever have in my whole life. I shove myself inside the hot dog suit, wishing I could disappear inside it completely, wishing I could be anything but me. I've always been loud when I should have been quiet, soft where I should be hard, frizzy instead of sleek, self-centered and selfish and self-absorbed. Maybe Seeley was right to blow me off. Maybe I'm no good for her or anybody else. I zip up the bun and adjust my ketchup-bottle shoes. Maybe I'm a crappy person, but at least I'm a good hot dog.

Seeley walks by with Seb and Marcus as I stand in the shadow of the Fry Shack. I tell myself I would have talked to her if she were alone, or if I were less sweaty, or if one of us wasn't dressed like a hot dog.

I think that's true, I hope that's true, but either way, I stay in the food court, dancing and smiling and taking pictures until I'm totally light-headed, until I can't take it for another second, until I've given it all I've got. I trip once as I stagger back to the breakroom, skinning my knee and tearing a hole right through my leggings. I don't even care.

I'll patch it up, and I'll have some water, and maybe . . . maybe I'll find a way to make everything as good as new.

CHAPTER 37

NICK IS PERCHED ON ONE OF THE TABLES, HIS HEAD hanging down, arms limp between his knees, as I walk into the breakroom.

"Shouldn't you be finishing up a show right now?" I blurt out.

He tilts his head, and I gasp when I see he's sporting a very swollen eye.

"Nick!" I rush closer, my hand over my mouth. "What happened?" A few of the other employees look up at me, and yeah, I guess it is kind of hard to ignore a giant shouty hot dog, but still, mind your own business, people.

"Ari happened."

"Ari punched you? But he was the one—" The look Nick gives me cuts that sentence off real quick.

"Nah, it was Ari's brother, Kurt."

"What?"

"Yeah, according to him, I'm an asshole for dating my own girlfriend."

"Wow," I snort. "Wait, isn't Kurt only in ninth grade?"

"Thanks for reminding me."

I reach for his chin, forgetting all about my skinned knee. "What'd he do?" Nick flinches, but then settles into the touch, shutting his eyes while I tilt his head to the side.

"Well, he took his hand, and made a fist, and then—" Nick starts, and I give his chin a little shove backward.

"You're such an ass."

"Yep." His tone is playful, but his eyes are wary, like he doesn't quite trust me. I wouldn't either if I were him.

"About yesterday . . ." I shift my weight from foot to foot. "I'm sorry. I shouldn't have blurted it out like that. If you hate me for it, I totally get it."

He crinkles his nose. "I can't have this conversation with you while you're still in that hot dog suit."

My ears burn. "Right. Give me one sec."

I grab my clothes out of my locker and dart into the changing room. I get dressed as quickly as I can, tugging my Magic Castle T-shirt over my head and pulling on the bright orange shorts I came in with. Yeah, I know they're hideous, but they're comfortable, okay?

I have a half-second flash of fear about looking totally ridiculous in front of Nick, but then I remember, at this point, he's already seen me sweaty and pukey and everything in between, so the bloom is off the rose or whatever. Nobody looks up when I walk over to the first aid box, and I'm pleasantly surprised. I grab a wipe and a Band-Aid and perch next to Nick on the table.

"What happened to you?" He nods toward my leg.

"Skinned my knee." I smirk. "Obviously."

"How?"

"I fell."

He leans over for a closer look. "We're the regular walking wounded around here."

"Pretty much."

"Anyway, I don't hate you."

"I would hate me," I say. "I do hate me, actually."

He shakes his head. "Don't say that. It was a dick thing to blurt it out like that, but I get it. Honestly, how long did you know? Like, how embarrassed should I feel right now?"

"Only a couple days."

He takes the Band-Aid out of my hand, unwraps it, and puts it on my knee himself.

Naturally, Jessa chooses that exact moment to walk in, along with about eighty billion other park employees because, shit, one shift just ended and I didn't even realize it.

"What the hell?" Jessa shrieks. "Are you guys hooking up now?"

And of course that's when Seeley trails in, just in time to catch the end of what Jessa said. She lets out this kind of grunt-sigh thing, and shakes her head before disappearing into the bathroom.

"Seeley." I jump up but Jessa blocks my way.

"Haven't you done enough already? Who knew you were such a snake, Elouise."

"It's not like that, Jessa," Nick huffs.

"Right, Elouise is sitting here like the cat that got the cream, while you kiss her knee or whatever you were doing, and it's totally platonic. I'm sure the fact that she told you about me and Ari right after Seeley 'dumped her' is a total coincidence, right? Come on, Nick, she planned this!"

I look up in time to see his face fall. The wariness is back, the distrust, and god I fucking deserve it, I do, but I can't handle it, not right now. Not with Seeley on the other side of that wall and me still stuck out here.

"Is that true?" Nick looks at me, his eyes hard, like he's trying to see right inside my brain.

I squeeze my eyes shut and take a deep breath. "Is what true?"

"Is everybody I know lying to me?" He chews the inside of his lip, hurt and anger radiating off him in waves.

And yeah, I suspected this would all unravel eventually, but not right here, right now, when a thousand million other park employees are filtering in to clock out.

"No." Okay, so maybe some of it was a lie, but . . .

"Is that why you told me about Jessa? Because you wanted me to go out with *you*?" It's the way he says it, the way he says "you," as if liking me would be some big impossible thing, that twists me hard. I know it shouldn't, I know my heart's really on the other side of that concrete wall, tucked away in the bathroom, but I guess Seeley left me with just enough of it to break a little more.

"No." I roll my eyes back to keep from crying. "I didn't tell you because of that. I don't have some big ulterior motive here."

"Sure." Jessa sneers. "Like I believe that."

"Do you ever shut up?" I whirl around, pointing my finger right in her face. "You act like you're the victim, but you're the one cheating! The only reason you're not with Nick anymore is because of *you*, not me. And I'm sorry if people finding that out messes with your perfect image or whatever, but that's on you. Nick is a great guy, a really great guy, and you cheated on him like it didn't even matter. You did that. Own it." The room goes all quiet then, no more shuffling or lockers shutting or random laughs. Just dead silence as everybody waits to see what happens next.

Jessa scowls and crosses her arms. "Not until you admit you've had a thing for Nick all along."

I bury my face in my hands and groan so loud it hurts my ears. "Will. You. Just. Stop." I drag a shaky hand through my hair. "You win. I admit it, okay? I used to like Nick. But who cares? And yeah, you got me, Seeley and I weren't really together in the beginning."

"See?" Jessa waves her arm, staring at Nick. "I told you it's all fake."

"No," I say, cutting her off. "It's not, or it wasn't, at least not at the end. At least not to me. So yeah, you don't have to worry about me and Nick. Because the only person I want to be with is Seeley. But I probably fucking blew it, so—" But the rest of my rant dies in my throat because Seeley is back again, standing right behind Jessa, staring at me. And if I wasn't wishing for the floor to open up and swallow me whole before, I definitely, definitely am now.

"Lou?" Seeley steps forward, trying to get around the crowd.

"Sorry," I whisper, and I bolt, the hot burn of tears pricking at my eyes. I don't look back to see if they're all still watching. I'm sure they are . . . but Seeley doesn't come after me and that's all that really matters.

CHAPTER 38

"LOU, HONEY." MY DAD CALLS UP FROM DOWNSTAIRS, but I'm buried under three miles of blankets, sobbing into my mattress, and I don't intend to move. "Elouise." This time it's a bit louder, a bit closer to the door. His knock feels inevitable now.

I burrow down, wiping at my eyes and tugging the blankets tighter around me. It's hot, and I'm sweaty, but this is the closest I can get to disappearing, and oh god I want to disappear. My phone has been buzzing nonstop since I left work, but I'm not about to answer it. I can't right now, simple as that.

My door clicks open, the sound quickly followed by my dad's heavy sigh. Pillows and blankets are lifted away, and the air feels cool on my clammy skin when he pulls back the last one. "Lou, you have a visitor."

My heart pounds in double time, and all the air goes whooshing out of my lungs. I don't know how to do this. I'm not ready. There is no manual for how to navigate this big of a cluster, no matter how bad I wish there was. Maybe I should write one later, when there's time, when it doesn't feel like my heart is leaking straight out of my eyes.

"I can't see her right now." I wipe away some of the snot dripping from my nose and pull the blanket back up. "I can't do this."

And his face is kind, and his face is sad, and I know the words that are about to come out of his mouth before he even says them. "It's not Seeley, honey." He puts his hand on my arm, and I didn't know anything could hurt this bad, but it does.

"Oh." I look down at my blankets and will myself to not start crying all over again. "Who is it, then?"

"It's a boy. A very blond, very tan boy. And—" He hesitates for a moment. "He has a lot of cake mix with him for some reason."

"Are you serious?" I take a shaky breath.

"Do you want me to send him up?" Dad glances at my mess of a room before leveling his gaze back at me. "Or are you coming down?"

"I'll come down." I sniffle. "Just, just give me a minute, okay?"

"Take two," he says, pulling my ponytail holder from where it's tangled up on the side of my head. "Should I give him access to the kitchen or keep him corralled in the living room?"

I take the hair tie back and set to work smoothing it down. "Living room."

My dad smiles and then heads out the door, his footsteps disappearing back downstairs. I take a deep breath and push off my bed, frowning at my puffy red eyes in the mirror. I think about putting on some makeup, some concealer to hide the fact that my heart is broken in a million places, but Nick can probably relate anyway, and besides, who cares? I run my finger over one of the pictures of Seeley and me that's up on my mirror; we are sunburned, with smiles that take up our whole faces. Her arm is slung around my shoulder, and mine is around her waist, two interlocking pieces, always . . . and I shatter all over again.

"Hey." I step off the bottom stair, having spent the last ten minutes trying to piece myself back together.

Nick's eyes widen at the sight of me, and I guess my swollen eyes and raw runny nose have definitely registered. My dad glances between us and excuses himself, telling us he'll be right upstairs if we need him. I don't know if that's a threat or a promise, but the way he squeezes my shoulder when he walks by makes me think it's the latter.

Nick rubs his hands up and down the legs of his jeans. He is a jumble of tight energy perched on the edge of a couch cushion. "Hi."

"What are you doing here?"

"Bake sale's tomorrow." He nods his head toward the piles of boxes and pans he's brought with him. "We gotta get baking."

"There's not going to be a bake sale." I drop into the chair across from him, kicking my legs up over the side.

"Why not?"

"Because there's no point." I sigh and dangle my head off the other end. "Because Mr. P is selling the place so he can go live with his granddaughter who has cancer, and that's actually a really good reason. Because our GoFundMe is a joke. And because it was messed up of me to try to scheme my way into keeping the park open. It was messed up to try to scheme anything."

"That's a lot of becauses," he says.

I flick my eyes to his, puzzled. "Why are you really here?"

"I've got nowhere else to go." Oddly, even though the words are sad, his voice isn't. It's more like open, resigned, accepting.

"Doubtful."

"Really," Nick says. "I can't go to Jessa's, obviously, and most of the pirate squad are now desperately scheming to *get* with Jessa, which also rules them out." He flops back on the couch and looks at me. "And I didn't want to be around anybody tonight, you know?"

"So you came here?"

"I figured you didn't want to be around anybody either." He shrugs. "I figured we might as well not be around anybody together."

"I can get that." I search his face, settling on the blotchy purple welt roaring up from his cheekbone. "How's your eye?"

"It feels strangely like it got punched. Why do you ask?" he says, dropping his head over the back of the couch. "I should probably be furious with you, you know?"

"Yeah." I watch him sit there, and I feel—nothing really. A week ago, I would have died to have him sitting on my couch, but now it's hard to imagine ever feeling like that. I wonder if someday, I'll think the same thing about Seeley. If she'll just be a blip on the radar.

Doubtful.

If there's one thing I learned from watching my dad pine over my mom, it's that there are some people you don't get over, ever. Some people get in so deep, they just stay with you, holding part of your heart hostage long after they're gone. You can move on, sure, I'd love it if my dad did, but they'll still have that little piece of you, and there's nothing you can do about it. I think Seeley is that for me.

Nick lifts his head up enough to look me in the eye. "Did you really only date Seeley to get with me?"

"Yeah," I say, low and resigned because there's no sense in hiding it anymore. "At first."

"How was that supposed to work? I don't get the mechanics of it."

"I didn't really either." I sigh.

"But why me?" He chuckles, and I can tell he thinks it's totally ridiculous that anyone would go through all the trouble.

"Have you seen you?" I ask, because now that the urgent,

desperate need to have him is gone, it's easier to talk honestly.

"Yeah, I'm a dumb blond who jumps off stuff for a living."

"Or," I say, "you're a hot, sweet, diving pirate–slash–future college boy with a knack for cupcake baking."

"You give me too much credit."

"You're a good guy, Nick. I could tell the moment I met you."

He tilts his head. "Then how come you spent all last year avoiding me?"

"I did not!"

"Yeah, you did. I practically had to chase you down in the hallway at school just to say hi."

"Oh, give me a break." I laugh. "Why would you want to hang out with me when you had Jessa, anyway?"

"I did want to, you know," he says, and his cheeks get all pink. "I was trying to ask you out or whatever, that time with my car."

"No way."

"Yeah, but after that day you pretty much avoided me the whole rest of the summer, so I figured you weren't interested."

"You are not serious."

"I am, sorry. I feel like I'm letting you down over here." He snorts. "But yeah, I was trying to ask you out with that whole 'We should hang' thing. I'm not really as cool as you seem to think I am."

We both get all quiet for a minute, and I try to wrap my head around the fact that I built up an entire idea of a person in my head based on a pile of misunderstandings.

"I'm sorry." My words come out slow and heavy, like they're burning up on the way out. "For whatever it's worth."

"What are you sorry for?"

I stare down at the threads of the chair. "For trying to manipulate you and stuff, for trying to make you into something you weren't."

"S'okay," he says. "You weren't very good at it anyway."

"That doesn't make it okay."

"No, it doesn't." He bites his lip a little, like he needs to chew on whatever's coming next. I watch him, content to wait.

He shoves his hair back off his forehead and sighs. "If we're coming clean, I guess I should tell you that things with me and Jessa were already falling apart anyway."

I kick my feet and let them bounce back up from the side of the chair. "You guys seemed pretty happy from the outside."

Nick shrugs and stares down at his feet. "I'm not how people think."

"Nobody is, apparently."

"No, but I'm *really* not." Nick scratches the back of his neck and exhales for what seems like an eternity. "I was a massive loser before I moved here." He looks up at me, and I hope I don't look as confused as I feel.

He kind of crinkles his forehead and looks down at the floor. "I have this thing that makes it hard to read, so I would get extra time on tests and extra help with my homework. Plus, I used to have a really bad lisp, and I spent pretty much all of elementary school doing intense speech therapy. It still comes up when I get nervous, but I can mostly deal, and when I can't, I play it off like I'm joking or doing it on purpose. But yeah, I was a nobody at my old school, and I was treated like it every day."

"That doesn't make you a loser," I blurt out before I catch myself. "I, for one, love your lisp!"

"Fuck," he groans. "I knew it was coming out more, but I'd hoped no one noticed."

"I don't think anybody really has; I was just kind of creepily tuned in for a minute there."

Nick smirks and shakes his head. "Anyway, we came here because the bullying was so bad at my old school that my mom got scared."

"Seriously?"

"Yeah, that's why I've taken judo since I was a kid. My mom wanted me to be able to defend myself." Nick gives me a sad little smile and tucks his arms behind his head. "But yeah, I spent the whole time before we moved hitting the gym, buying new clothes, and doing everything I could think of to fit in."

"At least it all kind of worked out," I say, and instantly regret it.

"Do you know how strange it is to wake up every day and know that the kids I hang out with now are the same kind of kids who made my life hell at my old school?"

"Then why do you?"

"Wouldn't you? Honestly? It feels good to be liked."

I drop my head back and shut my eyes because, yeah, I guess we all do weird things to get what we want sometimes.

"Then Jessa came along last year, and it got even more complicated." He swallows hard and looks up at me. It's a little bit surreal to have him confiding in me like this, but a good surreal, like it turns out that Nick-the-friend is better than Nick-the-crush that I've been imagining in my head all year.

"I don't know," he says, running his hand through his hair. "I'm rambling. I'll shut up. Your turn: Are you really in love with Seeley? No games?"

His question stabs me straight in the belly. Yes, I want to say. Always have been probably. And now it's ruined. But I just shrug and tip my head to face him.

"I'm going to go ahead and take that as a yes," he says, and then we get all quiet again. "All right, enough whining for both of us."

I eye the various boxes of cake mix peeking out from the plastic bags surrounding him. "What happened to home-made?"

"Time crunch." He laughs. "Plus, I didn't know if you were going to go for it, so I opted for something transportable and returnable—which I guess was the right call since there's no point in making cupcakes now."

I nod, lost in thought, and then sit upright in my chair. "But what if there was?"

"I think we've had enough of your scheming for one summer," he says, frowning.

"Wait." I hold up my hands. "What if we still do the bake sale, and give him all the money? Not to keep the park open, but—"

"But to give to his granddaughter," Nick says.

I smile, a tiny flicker of hope unfurling in my chest. "I think we should do it."

"Yeah?"

I nod my head, grinning when he jumps up and gives me a high five.

It is 11:54 p.m., and my dad is being unusually cool about the fact that I am still up banging pots and pans all over our kitchen with Nick at my side. He's come down twice to check on us, but abandoned ship quickly both times after being forced to act as our unofficial taste tester. Nick started combining the store-bought stuff with ingredients we had in our own kitchen a few hours back, and it got a little wild. I think we lost Dad for good sometime after the maple bacon flavor, but I can't be sure. It could have also been the lemon churro twist.

At any rate, it's late and we're covered in dry mix and batter and powdered sugar, and I know that tomorrow the world will go back to falling apart—that tomorrow everything will be wrong again and Seeley will still hate me—but, right now, we've managed to carve out a tiny little spot where we're both somehow okay.

There's a dab of frosting stuck to the left of Nick's lip, and without thinking, I reach out and I wipe it with my thumb. He leans into the touch, just enough to let me know that I could kiss him if I wanted, two lonely desperate people wishing they were other places with other people. It would be so easy to scoot up on my tiptoes and press my lips to his, to let my whole life melt away in this haze of confectioner's sugar and flour and cute boy, to finally know what his skin would taste like under the tip of my tongue.

Salty, I bet—salty with a hint of chlorine.

It sounds fascinating in a super detached sort of way, and that reaffirms everything I already know. This isn't my person. I look at the floor and take a step back. Nick lets out a shaky sigh, and I wonder if it's from relief or disappointment, or maybe even somewhere in the middle. We're the walking wounded all right, from start to finish.

"Yeah." He drops his chin to his chest and runs his hands through his hair a couple times. "I should—"

"Yeah." I nod, puffing out my cheeks as I exhale. "I should too." And I don't know exactly what I should be doing—cleaning the kitchen, maybe, going to bed, calling Seeley over and over again until she picks up and then declaring my love for her— but I know that whatever it is, it doesn't involve Nick.

"Do you need help cleaning up?"

I scan the kitchen. There are dishes piled up in the sink, and every available surface is dotted with flour and frosting. It will take hours to clean, but I have plenty of time. "I got this. It'll give me something to do."

Nick raises his eyebrows. "It's already midnight."

"Exactly," I say, and he nods again, like he gets it, like he knows that the nights are the worst parts.

Nick asks me again if I'm sure, and I am. God knows I won't be sleeping tonight anyway. I follow him to the door, fully intending to lock it behind him. It fact, he makes it all the way to the end of the sidewalk, all the way to his car before I grab my bag and go flying out after him, flagging him down and shouting his name.

He looks at me, tilting his head. He's still got his hand on the car door, ready to make a quick exit. "What's up?"

"Can you drop me at Seeley's?" I don't know if it's the running or the adrenaline, but I'm out of breath, and I feel like I'm never going to catch it again if I don't see her tonight.

"It's the middle of the night," he says, like that matters.

"I don't care."

"Are you sure you won't regret this in the morning?"

"Please," I beg, because yes, I will walk there if I have to, but this would be so, so much faster.

"Get in," he says, and a grin breaks out wide across his cheeks.

CHAPTER 39

I AM STANDING UNDERNEATH OUR TREE.

Half sitting, really, leaning against the trunk, and counting and recounting the steps in an effort to calm down. It's one thing to show up and try to win back your girl shoeless and in pajamas, but it's another to try to win back your girl shoeless and in pajamas and in the middle of a self-induced panic attack.

Nick left a while ago, and I'm sure it's well past one a.m. now, but I don't care, I don't. I crawl up the steps, the rough wood and nails biting into the underside of my naked feet as I scale the tree, and then step onto the roof and to her window.

I reach my hands out, muscle memory expecting it to slide easily, but it doesn't. I try again—it must be stuck, a simple trick of humidity and wood conspiring to give me a heart attack—but it doesn't move an inch. I slide my gaze up to the latch. I have to be sure.

Locked.

This is all wrong. I had a plan, not a scheme this time, an actual plan. The window was supposed to slide up easily, her curtains whipping out in the gentle night breeze. I would creep inside, expecting her to call me out, or throw something, or scream at me, but she'd be curled up, asleep. I would say sorry and she would give me a sleepy smile, lifting her blanket so I could come in from the cold of her room.

That's what we do. That's how we are. A million nights like this, nights where we crept into each other's rooms and each other's beds, mornings when we woke up tangled together, unable to tell where one ends and the other begins. Tonight should have been a million and one, but it's locked.

I hate this.

I hate that I've ruined it all in so many ways.

There's a notebook in my bag, the same one she sketched cupcakes and smiley faces in while we planned the fundraiser. I flip to a blank page and search for a pen way down in the bottom, beneath the pile of crumbs and stray tampons. My fingers finally find one, and it's teal of course, like her hair when she's happy. I want to cry, but I've done enough of that and know it'll get me nowhere.

I lean back against her window and bleed my words onto the page. I don't know if it matters, I don't know if there's a way back from locked windows and broken hearts, but I have to try. I have to. I fold the note and set it on her sill beneath a pack of gum and some quarters. I hope it doesn't blow away. I hope it helps somehow.

I hope.

CHAPTER 40

Seeley,

 I'm in love with you.

 I wanted to say that first in case you stop reading because you ~~probably should hate me now~~ *might not want to hear it. But if nothing else, I wanted you to know that. I love you, and I'm in love with you. Both things. Every second. And I've made so many mistakes. If you don't want to ever see me again, I understand completely.*

I don't know how we got here. No, that's a lie. I do. We got here because I brought us here, dragged you, kicking and screaming the whole way. I have been selfish, I have been terrible, and you deserve better. I'm so, so, so friggin' sorry for what I put you through.

And I'm also sorry that I wasted so much time looking at him, when I should have been looking at you. ~~Because you deserve to be looked at all the time. I want to look at you right now.~~

~~Wait. That sounds creepy. Let try this again.~~

~~I'm sitting on your roof right now while you sleep, thinking about how I wish I could look at you right now. Wait, that's also creepy, actually that's creepier than what I had before. Shit.~~

I am so bad at this.

I know you heard what I said about you in the breakroom, but just in case there was any doubt in your head, I wanted to say it again. To your face. Well, to your face in a letter, I guess.

And I know you probably don't feel the same way. That's okay, you shouldn't, because you are good and kind and EVERYTHING that is right in this stupid town, and maybe in this whole stupid world (but I'll have to let you know, since I've never been farther than the Target two towns over BUT I HAVE SUSPICIONS, OKAY?).

But Seeley, honestly, all the good things left in me are the things that you put there, you know? Because even when I was scheming and angry and wrong, you were there. I am a mess. I am a hurricane of frizzy hair and bad ideas, but for someone like you to love me my whole life, even if you weren't/aren't/will never be IN love with me, I don't know. It's kind of amazing. And I ruined that because I got too lost in my own life to remember yours.

And you were right about Mr. P having a good reason to close the park down too. He does. You were right. And I want to scream that out forever because you always are, and I never say it enough.

I could have kissed Nick tonight, that's the other thing I wanted to tell you.

It was late, and we were both so sad, and it was like all those movies of mine you roll your eyes at, where the music swells and the actors kiss, and then it fades to black and you know it was MEANT TO BE. And I felt like I could do it too. I could have closed my eyes and pushed all my rough edges into his wounds, and it would be just wrong enough to be right maybe. Except I didn't do it.

Because all I could think about was the way your lips felt that night under the fireworks, and the weight of your bones on mine. And it took me a long time, but I figured it out. The difference between liking and loving, the difference between make-believe and what's real, the difference between right now and please, please, let this last forever.

So this is me telling you that I would rather have my heart broken by you than anybody else. And if you don't want me, that's fine too. Well, it's not, but I'll deal. I hope *we can find a way to still be friends, though, because I'm yours, and I always have been, even if I was too foolish to realize it.*

What I'm trying to say is that I love you. I love you, Seeley.

~~And I'm sorry for taking so long to tell you. And also I'm sorry for telling you, depending on which way you feel.~~ I'm a shitty person, but I'm working on it.

Yours,

Lou

CHAPTER 41

MY PHONE IS OFF, AND IT'S DELIBERATE. IT'S MORNING already and Seeley isn't here climbing in my window or running up my stairs. And even though I know what that means, I *know*, as long as I don't turn on my phone, I can still pretend I don't.

I can't pretend forever, though.

I flick on my phone and stare at the background, a selfie of Seeley and me at junior prom. She's sticking her tongue out and I'm kissing her cheek like we have a thousand times before. Except now it's different and I would give anything to go back to that moment. But I can't, and the worst thing is, that's it. That's all there is to see. No texts, no missed calls, no desperate voicemails, no reprieve at all waiting for me on the other side of the off button.

She doesn't love me back. She doesn't.

I hurl my phone across the room. It doesn't break, but I wish it did. I grab a pen off my desk and pull the notebook out from my bag, not for any real reason other than to take up space in a room I want to disappear in.

I doodle a dot that turns into a sun, which turns into an explosion, which seems fitting somehow, par for the course. I'm still tiptoeing through the minefield in my head when my dad knocks on my door, popping it open without waiting for me to invite him in.

"Elouise?" he says, and I look up. I can tell by the way he instantly furrows his brows that I must look like hell.

I spin in my chair, slipping back and forth a little, waiting for him to say something. I wonder for half a second if he's going to tell me that Seeley's downstairs, my stupid hoping heart, but I can tell by the frown set on his lips that she isn't.

"The boy is back." Dad pushes my door open wider. "Something about frosting and banners, I don't know. You're going to have to handle this. He's talking incredibly fast, and I haven't had any coffee yet."

"Same." I yawn. "Did you put some on?"

"You're not drinking coffee. You're sixteen years old." He looks scandalized, like I just asked if he could hook me up with some meth on his way out or something.

I laugh. "Seventeen next month!"

"Don't remind me. But right now: Boy. Downstairs. Take care of it."

Nick is standing in the foyer, rocking on his feet with his hands in his pockets.

"How much coffee have you had?" I hop off the bottom step. "And why is there none for me?"

"Coffee is for losers. Here." He shoves an energy drink in my hand and darts into the kitchen, pausing when he sees the mess from the night before. "You didn't clean up." He turns around. He looks all happy and expectant, but it slips off his face when he takes a good look at me. "Oh."

Nick grabs his phone, crinkling his eyebrows and firing off a text. "Sorry, I'll help you clean up."

"Why are you here again?"

"We have two hours before we have to be there, right?"

"And?"

"And that's just enough time to make some flyers and a banner and stuff, update the GoFundMe, and post that shit everywhere. And come on, Elouise! Think, think, think!"

"Do we really need all that?"

"Do you want to raise a lot of money for Mr. P, or do you want to make five bucks and call it a day?"

"A lot of money."

He whirls around the kitchen, grabbing pans and bowls off the counters and tossing them in the sink. "Okay, you can draw, right? I mean I've seen all the drawings on your shoes and stuff."

"A little." I shrug. "Seeley did my shoes. She's the one that's good at drawing." And wow, just thinking about my shoes hurts.

"Shit. I was hoping you would say 'A lot,'" Nick says, yanking me out of my head. "Okay. New plan. No, wait! Maybe old plan still." He laughs and pounds the rest of his energy drink. "If you really suck, maybe they'll think his granddaughter drew it." He looks down at his phone again, as his lips curl up. I wonder if it's Jessa; I wonder if they'll find their way back to each other. I watch him punch in a response with his twitchy, over-caffeinated fingers. I don't know if that makes me happy or sad.

"Okay." I'm trying to snap out of it, trying to keep up with the words that pour out of his mouth even as he texts. "I'm definitely good at sucking at drawing. Seeley used to—" But I catch myself, because I can't go there right now, not if I want to stay standing.

"All right." He flips on the water, squirting in a ton of soap and staring at it until the bubbles are up to his elbows. "Let's see what you can do, okay? Grab the markers and stuff out of my backpack, will ya? I left it by the door." He jerks his hand out of the water. "I would get them myself, but I'm totally, undeniably soaked."

I roll my eyes and hop off the stool next to the counter, walking back out into the foyer, where he left his bag. I crouch down next to it, messing with the zippers and the ten thousand compartments, trying to find the markers and other supplies he was babbling on about.

A noise from outside makes me pause: a scuffling sound, a tentative footstep, a hand on a knob it doesn't twist. I look up, hopeful and desperate. Seeley's there, standing awkwardly on the other side of the storm door, one arm wrapped around herself as she looks down at me.

"Seeley?" I blink hard, my voice soft like I'll scare her away if I'm too loud, too fast, too me. Maybe I will, maybe I already have. I stand up slowly and go still, afraid to touch the handle in case she won't come inside. I want to memorize every second of this, just in case. She raises her other hand slowly, biting on her nail as she looks at me, and I wonder if she's thinking the same thing. I yank the door open, because if this is my last moment with her, I want to at least be breathing the same air.

"See—"

Her lips are pressed against mine before I can finish and I freeze, my whole body rigid and my eyes squeezed tight. She steps back, takes a deep breath, and then lets out a sigh. "Open your eyes, Lou."

I blink hard against the sunlight. Did it get brighter out, or is it her? Nick bangs some pans around the kitchen, and I turn my head toward him, just for a second, but long enough for the smile to slip a bit on Seeley's face. And now it's my turn to take the lead, to bring a clumsy kiss back to her, because Seeley kissed me and that's got to mean something, it's got to, and I will spend the rest of my life doing whatever I can to bring her smile back, swear to god.

I press my forehead to hers, smiling so hard it hurts. "Hi."

My cheeks heat furiously because that was dumb, but I didn't know what else to say.

"Hi," she says back, and I wait to see if she's going to say anything else, but she doesn't.

"I guess you got my note?"

She nods, lacing her fingers into mine and leading me over to the chairs on the side of the porch. "Lou," she says.

My heart pounds so hard I can feel it in my ears because it feels so good to hear her say my name again. It feels like my whole brain is burning down and she's the only one that can stop it.

She sighs. "I'm not having this conversation with Nick and your dad watching us."

Okay. So, if I made a list of all the possible things that could've come out of her mouth next, that . . . would probably still not have been on it. I dart my eyes up to the two people standing sheepishly in the window. They wave, the curtains trailing after them as they beat a hasty retreat. I groan and drop back into my seat, staring at the ceiling and trying to swallow the tears and the laughter that are bubbling up inside me.

Her chair creaks as she leans forward, scratching at my knee gently with her nails until I look up. My eyes are glassy and I feel like I've lived twenty lives in the span of the last thirty seconds. "You kissed me."

Seeley laughs and wipes at her nose. "I did. And then you kissed me."

There's a clunk behind the door and the curtains shift

again. I roll my eyes because seriously, guys, seriously? I stand up and pull Seeley to her feet, bolting into the house and up the stairs to my bedroom before anyone can stop us, careful to never let our fingers disconnect. Seeley wraps our hands tighter, laughing as she kicks the door shut and falls onto the bed on top of me. She sits up, and she's practically kneeling in my lap, her legs pressed hard and warm against the outside of my thighs, her fingers wound around mine, holding them tight.

I stare up at her. "You liked the note?"

"I liked the note." Her words come out sort of breathless, sort of quiet, and her eyes get all watery to match mine. "But I love you, Elouise May Parker, and I'm in love with you too. Both things."

"But . . . "

"But what?"

"How long—" But the knock on my door effectively shuts downs that line of questioning.

Nick peeks his head inside, and I fight the urge to throw my pillow at his face. Seriously, guy?

He glances down at our hands and grins. "Glad you got my text, Seeley."

My eyes dart back between him and the girl on my bed. "You told her to come?"

"I may have texted her that I had a sad sack on my hands, and that she had better get her ass inside because I was sick of you guys both moping around when we have cupcakes to sell."

Seeley rolls her eyes. "I was already in the driveway when I got it, which you know because I pulled in right behind you."

"Wait, what?" I ask, but they just talk over me.

"I'd like to think I at least helped get you to the door faster." He drops down into my desk chair with a satisfied smirk. "Listen, I'm sure you guys have hours of angsty conversations and kissing ahead of you, but if we don't get this stuff done, our sale is going to be a total bust."

"Five minutes." Seeley gestures toward the door. "Give us five minutes, and we'll be down."

"Fine," he grumbles, and pushes up off the chair. "But I'm setting the timer on my phone."

"Fair enough." Seeley follows him to the door and flicks the lock, crossing back over and pushing me back down. Her lips turn up against my cheek when she settles in beside me. Her arm winds over my stomach, and she finds my hand and laces our fingers together again.

I turn, leaning my head back to look at her even if it makes me go a little bit cross-eyed. "You love me?"

Seeley nods with a sleepy smile.

"You're in love with me?" I clarify, because I don't think this can be really happening, can it? But she smiles and nods again, leaning forward to kiss the tip of my nose.

"Both things?" I ask. Even though she said it once, I have to be certain before I can dare to believe it.

She nods again. "Both things."

This time when she leans in, her lips meet mine, gentle

at first, but then more urgent. It feels like lightning striking right in my chest as she rolls over on top of me. We barely stop for air before her lips are back on my skin, teasing and tasting, and when the tears come this time, they are happy, so happy.

CHAPTER 42

SHE TELLS ME AS WE DRIVE THAT I CAN KISS HER WHEN-
ever I want.

So I do.

Twice at a red light, and a third time when we park. Kisses four through seven take place as we unload the cupcakes from the back of her mom's car and onto the little folding table that Nick found in his basement. Kiss eight is after we sell the first cupcake of the day.

I didn't realize I was such a tactile person, but I can't

stop touching her: my hand on the small of her back as we walk from the car, my fingers tucking her hair behind her ear when it falls in her face. I even drag her chair so close to mine our legs are touching. I didn't realize how much my skin needed her skin until I had to face the idea of living without it.

I am impossibly distracted during the bake sale, which is fine, I guess, because so is Seeley, but somehow we're still managing to sell a ton of cupcakes.

Or rather, they're selling themselves.

We strategically placed our table just inside the parking lot, right where you have to walk to get to the park entrance. Seeley made a big banner filled with pictures of happy cupcakes on amusement park rides, so it's all very hard to miss. We priced everything at one dollar each, a price point that even the stingiest parent seems to be able to rationalize. I mean, even the kids who come to smoke pot on the Ferris wheel and the gondolas start buying three each.

"Holy shit," Nick shouts, jumping up and down.

I hand some change back to a very harried-looking mom, and glance back at him. "What?"

"I just got an email from that guy on the news. The good news guy. He saw the update to our GoFundMe about Mr. P's granddaughter and he wants to do a story on it!"

"The good news guy? That doesn't sound like a real thing."

Nick flips his phone around, and sure enough there it is, an email from the news station asking if we can do an interview tomorrow. I read it, raising my eyebrows. "This says he heard about it when our fund-raising page picked up steam? What's he talking about? There's like a hundred dollars in there—since when did it pick up steam?"

Nick grins. "I may have shared it a bunch of times last night after you told me the real reason the park was closing, and then my mom and a lot of other people started sharing it this morning, and it kind of blew up."

My eyes get huge. "Are you saying we went viral?"

"Well, viral for around here anyway."

"Awesome, so how much is in there now?"

"About two thousand last time I checked, and that's not even twenty-four hours. People really love Mr. P, you know."

"That is the best news I've heard all day," I say. Seeley kicks my foot and raises her eyebrows. "Second best, I meant, obviously."

Nick slides his phone into his pocket and laughs, turning back to talk to a customer.

"Relax, you're the best news of my life." I drop back into the chair next to her. "Not just the day."

"Yeah, yeah." She smiles.

My dad walks up to the table with some money in his hand, and I don't think I could look any more surprised. He glances at Seeley, and then at me, and then he looks at where our hands meet under the table. The biggest grin stretches across his face, and he holds up a hundred-dollar bill. "Hello, girls, I would like as many cupcakes as this will get me."

"That would get you all the ones we have left and change, Mr. Parker," Seeley says.

"Hmm," he says. "Then I would like two cupcakes and to donate the rest of the money."

"Coming right up," Seeley says as I scoot around the table.

"What are you doing here?" I ask. "How did you even know where we were?"

"First of all, you made the posters in my kitchen, and I was there. Second of all, the whole town knows where you are! It's all over Facebook, and the news station called our house a little while ago," he says. "If your plan was to keep things quiet, you screwed up big-time."

I look around behind him and notice that most of the crowd isn't actually going inside—they're just hanging out, eating cupcakes. Pretty much everyone and their parent is milling around the parking lot buying cupcakes and donating money, and wow, that's kind of cool.

"Touché." I smirk.

"Here you go, Mr. Parker," Seeley says. I didn't think I could love her any more than I already did, but when I realize that she definitely picked out the best two cupcakes we have left for my dad, I sort of do.

"Thank you, Seeley," he says, taking the cupcakes. "And I'm glad to see you girls made up."

"Me too," she says.

"You saving one for later?" I ask, gesturing to the two cupcakes in his hands.

"Nope." Dad looks back behind him, and I notice that Seb is standing there, and then it hits me who he's standing with.

"Seb's mom?"

"Hey, you told me it meant something that she said hi back." He raises his eyebrows. "Let's test the theory."

"Go get 'em, tiger," I say, and then dissolve into giggles.

"Thanks, kid," he says. And when he walks up and holds out the cupcake, she takes it with a smile.

Seb wanders over a little bit later, shoving his money in the donation box and swiping a cupcake out of my hand that wasn't even meant for him. "I think your dad just asked out my mom with a cupcake. Adults are so friggin' doofy." He takes a bite out of his cupcake, and his eyes go wide. "Shit, is this bacon-flavored frosting?"

"Yeah, Nick got a little mad scientist on the flavors," I explain.

Seb raises his cupcake toward Nick and gives him a nod. "Compliments to the chef, dude." Nick rolls his eyes, but I can tell he's totally beaming inside. Good, he deserves it. Seb takes another bite, chewing thoughtfully. "Your dad seems all right, but if you end up my sister, that's gonna be weird as shit."

"Okay, slow down," I say. "Let the kids have their date before you go planning a wedding."

Seeley shakes her head, pulling me back down into my chair, and this is when it hits me: this is one of those forever moments. One of those impossible "I can't believe it when" moments that I've been chasing all summer. It's real, and it's better than I ever imagined. Mark it down, today's the day the impossible came true. I lean my head against her shoulder, not even caring that it kind of bounces around as she makes change for everyone.

Barely a minute goes by before she pokes me in the ribs, because here comes Mr. P marching down the pavement looking like he wants to throttle us. I sit up, bracing for impact. Either someone spilled the beans, or Mr. P realized there's an unusually high number of patrons wandering around with homemade cupcakes; either way, he doesn't look happy.

He stomps up to the table and blots his forehead with his rag. "What are you up to, Ms. Parker?" He scans the banner, but it only says BUY CUPCAKES FOR A GOOD CAUSE. He looks so disappointed that I have to look away. "We discussed this in my office. I thought we came to an under-standing."

"We did." I stand up and hold out a cupcake for him. "This isn't about the park."

He takes it with a confused frown. "Then what is it about?"

Marcus comes up behind him then, along with Angie and Jessa and a few other people, which, awkward, plus like who's running the park? But whatever, they stand next to us, just sort of waiting for the big reveal. I clear my throat because having everybody here makes the moment feel bigger and more important than it otherwise probably would, and I don't want to screw this up.

"Well, like I said, you've always been there for us." I stand up a little bit straighter and try to sound confident. "Like when you let me work here a year early so I could start with Seeley, and that time you let Marcus borrow your car, and I don't specifically know what you did for Seb, but I'm sure you did something."

"He gave me free rounds of laser tag when my cat died," Seb helpfully supplies.

I look at him like he has two heads, and then turn back to Mr. P. "There you go, apparently you gave him free rounds of laser tag when his cat died, which is probably not the way that I would choose to mourn a beloved pet, but this is a judgment-free zone."

"Get on with it, Ms. Parker," Mr. P says, and I can tell by his face that he means it.

"Anyway, my point is that you've always been there for us, and now it's our turn to be there for you."

"I appreciate the sentiment, I do, but I need you to understand that I cannot, and will not, keep this park open. My mind is made up."

"This isn't about Magic Castle," I say. "This is about helping your granddaughter get better."

"This is for Adelyn?" Mr. P asks, his voice all quiet.

"I mean, it's not much or anything." I look over at Seeley, who's still counting the money.

"There's four hundred and forty-one dollars here so far," she says. "But the whole town is basically donating to the website, Nick said it's at around two thousand dollars, and they want to cover it on the local news, which will hopefully mean even more."

Mr. P covers his mouth with his hand.

"Yeah, Mr. P," Nick says. He steps around our little table

and drops his hand onto Mr. P's shoulder. "We figured it was the least we could do after everything you've done for us. We wanted to help however we could."

"I don't know what to say." He sniffs and wipes at his eyes; they've gone all bloodshot and runny and yeah, mine too.

"Group hug!" Seeley shouts and then sort of dives against Mr. P, who looks totally confused for a moment, but then we all scurry around the table to hug him too, and pretty soon everybody is tearing up and hugging and saying thank you to each other. I tell Mr. P I hope we can raise more, and he says it doesn't matter how much we raise—it only matters that we cared enough to do it.

Later, when the crowd starts to die down, Seeley and I grab some popcorn and go watch Nick's dive show, right out on the bleachers like a couple of non-stalkers, and he points at us before he does the high dive.

It's pretty damn perfect.

Oh, and it turns out that Nick's whole looking-at-the-sky-before-he-jumps thing isn't all mysterious and spiritual like I imagined it was. Apparently, there's a bunch of pigeons that roost up at the very top where the flag is, and he's just pleading with them not to crap on his head before he jumps—which I feel like is kind of fitting in light of the sort of summer we've all survived so far.

After Nick's show, Seeley and I say our goodbyes to everybody and head to the car. I tell Seeley it's my turn to drive, and she tosses me her keys with a smile. And if we happen to notice Jessa and Ari holding hands as they walk to the parking lot, neither of us mentions it. We leave the radio off as we drive, content with the music from the wind whipping past our windows and the pavement buzzing beneath our tires.

I put my hand on her leg and squeeze, because it's been five minutes since we touched, and I'm already scared that none of this is real. Seeley puts her hand out the window, her palm making waves as it coasts through the wind.

We park so close to the sidewalk that the wheels scrape the curb. Her mom will probably yell at us about it later, but I don't even care. Seeley pulls the blankets out of the backseat. I shut the door but then open it again to pull out some water bottles. And then shut it and reopen it to grab a box of leftover cupcakes. And then do it again once more for bug spray. Seeley shakes her head, and I blush down to my feet. I don't care that she's making me nervous, because at least she's making me something.

"Where are we going?" It's nice to hear her voice again; it's the first thing that she's said in a while.

"Over here." I trudge up the side of the hill and find a spot half hidden by trees and shrubs. It's as much privacy as we are liable to get, especially with my dad, Nick, and probably half the town all desperate to know what's happening with us.

I shake the blanket out and spread it wide, dropping the cupcakes and water bottles down on the edge. Seeley kicks off her flip-flops and sits in the middle, pulling her knees up to her chin. It feels so perfect, being here with her, and I whip out my phone to take a picture.

"What?" She blushes, messing with her hair.

I bridge the gap between us, kissing her quick and then sitting back.

"Hi," I say, because I still can't believe she's here.

"Hi yourself." She slides her foot forward and jabs me with her toe.

I rock backward a little, savoring the moment. "This is where Butters and Racer are going." I point to the wide grassy area beneath us. "We'll be able to come here whenever we want to take them for a ride."

"Really?" Seeley stares at the empty expanse of land like she's sizing up every blade of grass to see if it's worthy. "That's kind of amazing." She smiles a real smile then, wide and perfect, and it hits me square in the chest. I'm dead, knocked off my feet, pinned beneath the weight of it. I flop backward onto the blanket with a groan.

"You okay?"

"I'm better than okay."

"Well, good," she says and lies down next to me, tilting her head enough to see me out of the corner of her eye.

"I'm so glad you're here."

"I've always been here, Lou." She props herself up on one elbow to look at me. "I mean, I cared about Sara too. And I tried to give Angie a chance because she's great, and I didn't think you would ever see me the way I saw you."

"Oh," I say, because it hits me again, what we've gone through to get here, what I've *put* her through to get here.

"I just told you I've been in love with you forever. Don't look so depressed."

I trace my fingers over the freckles on her arm. "I'm sorry I make everything so messy."

Seeley rolls her eyes but smiles, and I'll take it.

"That kiss on Founder's Day was kind of amazing, though, wasn't it? You don't know how bad I've been wishing it was real."

Seeley raises her eyebrows. "It *was* real."

I snort. "We were wasted and I made you."

"That's not how you kiss someone you don't want to kiss."

I tug her closer until she settles across me, her head on my chest, her arm over my shoulder. This is heaven, and the afterlife, and eternity, and reincarnation with a cherry on top, all in one fell swoop.

She nuzzles against me. "Your heart is pounding."

"I don't want to screw this up."

"You won't." She rolls back to look at me, propping her head up with her hand but leaving her leg draped over mine. I hope she never moves.

I rub my finger over her eyebrow, feeling the soft hair there. "I always do, Seeley. I screw everything up."

"We'll figure it out."

I frown and think of my mother. "What if that's not in my DNA?"

"Then fuck your DNA," she says. I'd be lying if I said that hearing that word fall from her lips, with her body all tangled up with mine, wasn't at least a little thrilling.

Seeley pushes herself up and straddles my legs, grabbing my face with both hands. "You are more than the sum total of your bullshit background and your scheming. You're everything I could possibly want." I try to look away but she leans closer, holding my face in place. "Not to mention the best damn hot dog I've ever met."

I roll my eyes, willing away the tears even though they're the good kind. But there's something still gnawing at me, and I can't help it. "You locked your window," I say, and her face falls.

"I unlocked it this morning."

"You did?"

"I wouldn't be here if I didn't." She huffs. "But you really hurt me, Lou. And it kind of spun me when I heard you say all that stuff in the breakroom. I thought maybe it was another part of your scheme and I was so mad at you. But then I got your letter, and Nick was texting me about how messed up you were when he went inside. I was already sitting in your driveway—"

"Why didn't you come inside?"

"I didn't want to regret my decision, whatever it ended up being."

I search her eyes, swallowing hard. "Are you still scared you'll regret it?"

"No," she says, shaking her head.

"Good." I wrap my arms around her waist and flip us over. My hands slide up to hers, and I press our foreheads together. "I wish you could feel how absolutely, totally head over heels I am for you."

When we finally break apart, breathless and grinning, I hear her whisper, "How could I not?"

I look down at her, biting my lip, because wow this girl is amazing, and somehow, through it all, she even loves me back.

Maybe the impossible summer isn't so impossible after all.

ACKNOWLEDGMENTS

FIRST AND FOREMOST, A HUGE THANK-YOU TO MY agent, Brooks Sherman, who somehow knows exactly when I need a cheerleader and when I need a coach. Thank you for believing in me and this book. To Stephanie Pitts, who made this whole experience ridiculously fun, even when it was work. I could not imagine a better home for Lou, thank you. And to everyone at Putnam for believing in this book and turning my dream into a reality. I am proud to be a part of such an amazing team.

Many thanks to:

Beth Phelan for creating #DVPit and helping me find my people. DVSquad for being so welcoming and supportive. Meredith for always being the voice of reason; you are an excellent CP and an even better friend. Roselle for being the best cheerleader on the planet.

Becky for loving my book from the very first pitch. I promise I will find my OTC one day, but until then, thank you for not judging me too harshly. (But Pop Rocks *do* make Oreos better, sorry.) Kelsey for being the nanny to my plant, the true alpha, and the one who reminds me to sleep—even if you are totally wrong about Peter. Sonia, whose kind words kept hope alive in the query trenches. PCC, my first writer friends ever. Lucy/Kate, Sarah, Lilly, Kelly, Karen, and Isabel for always, always being there.

Erin for being the Scott to my Stiles *and* the Stiles to my Derek; there is literally no one better to be on this wild ride with. Shannon, my found family, who loved me even at my most unlovable. One sentence could never be enough to express how much you mean to me, and I wouldn't be here without you. Lacy, who has been there from day one of this writing adventure, equal parts friend, therapist, and beta reader.

My mom, who believed me when I said I was going to be a writer at five years old and did everything she could to foster that. Dennis, the best big brother in the world, who single-handedly got all of Kohl's excited for this book. Bonkers, for not killing me in my sleep, even though I suspect he wants to. Joe, Brody, and Olivia, for being my true north and making even the hardest days brighter. I love you.

And last but certainly not least, to my readers, thank you from the bottom of my heart for being here.

ABOUT THE AUTHOR

JENNIFER DUGAN IS A WRITER, A GEEK, AND A ROMANTIC who writes the kinds of stories she wishes she had growing up. In addition to being a young-adult novelist, she is also the writer/creator of two indie comics. She lives in upstate New York with her family, dogs, and an evil cat that is no doubt planning to take over the world. *Hot Dog Girl* is her first novel.

Learn more at JLDugan.com and on Twitter @JL_Dugan.